SHADOWS AND SUN

Also by Dominique Sylvain in English translation

The Dark Angel

Dirty War

SHADOWS AND SUN

Dominique Sylvain

Translated from the French by Nick Caistor

MACLEHOSE PRESS
QUERCUS · LONDON

First published in the French language as *Ombres et Soleil*
by Éditions Viviane Hamy, Paris, in 2014
First published in Great Britain in 2016 by MacLehose Press

This paperback edition published in 2017 by

MacLehose Press
an imprint of Quercus Publishing Ltd
Carmelite House
50 Victoria Embankment
London EC4Y 0DZ

An Hachette UK Company

ISBN (TPB) 978 1 78087 608 5
ISBN (Ebook) 978 1 78087 607 8

2 4 6 8 10 9 7 5 3

Designed and typeset in 11/16pt Columbus by Patty Rennie
Printed and bound in Great Britain by Clays Ltd, St Ives plc

THE PUREST TREASURE MORTAL TIMES AFFORD
IS SPOTLESS REPUTATION.

Richard II, Act 2, Scene 1

FRIDAY, NOVEMBER 27, 1998

The rain blurs their faces. All Géraldine can make out are silhouettes lining the route. Large numbers of friends and strangers have gathered beneath the angry sky. Defying the cold, they wave as the cortège of black minibuses passes slowly by.

Maman and Camille are silent, clinging to one another, bone weary. The other passengers in the minibus sit staring at nothing. Géraldine feels as if she's the only survivor of a zombie attack. She'll be fourteen in a week, her coat is too short and too tight, she has grown eight centimetres in recent months. That would have interested Papa.

She cannot bring herself to cry. Not from the first moments, when she heard about the catastrophe on the radio, not when the officials came to their home. With a bit of effort she'll be able to cast off this frailty like her old coat.

She catches in the rearview a glimpse of the eyes of the employee acting as their driver mirror. She can read his thoughts. *I work for Aerolix as well. I was lucky not to be in the wrong place at the wrong time. My family was spared.*

Aerolix. The company that brings life to the region.

And death as well. On this occasion at least.

The police open a way for them. How do they manage to stay upright on their motorbikes at such a slow speed? And on this road turned by the rain into a river.

They reach the aerodrome. The police dismount. The drivers park the minibuses. The families open their umbrellas, form a line.

"It's freezing," Géraldine says to her sister.

Camille is still clutching her mother, and does not reply. They both look distraught; vapour is rising from their half-open mouths. Géraldine glances at the cargo plane streaming wet in the rain. Is this the plane the bodies were brought back in from Damascus?

Journalists are pushing and shoving behind a metal barrier. Their microphone poles are ridiculously long. They want to grab the sound of cries, of sobs. Géraldine and the others rush into the hangar.

When they see the coffins, the families look stunned.

Laid out in a row. The French flag draped over each one of them. A herd of people stamping in the cold. Aerolix personnel. Paramedics. Military men. The officials.

A widow's sobs unleash the torrent. The other relatives burst into tears. So do Maman and Camille. Géraldine bites her thumb until it bleeds, trying to finally open the floodgates. Impossible. Stupid coat.

Surely someone will leave the herd and act as guide? But no, the families are going to have to do it for themselves. Géraldine is the first to step forward. Brass plates have been screwed onto the coffin lids. She knows all the names. It takes her some time to find the right one.

There is Papa, stretched out on four trestles, beneath the *tricolore*. She has to get used to the idea now, immediately. Otherwise it will be too late. And she will live her entire life in a parallel world. An in-between world, a zombie life.

Blue, pain. White, nothingness. Red, blood. How poetic, simple and crappy. Since he's there at last, she speaks to Papa. She knows he can't hear her anymore, she's known that from the outset, yet she is even more aware that talking to him is the only thing that can keep her from slipping into the world of no return.

You brought us up to respect other people's beliefs, but also in the certainty that death was the final door. "Certainty", yes, that was the word you used. Where are you? Come on, tell me. I can't believe it's all over. Can you hear me?

A soldier begins a trumpet solo. It's so dreadful Géraldine is surprised to find she wants to laugh out loud. The crowd turns into a single-cell organism; a quiver runs through it. It turns as one towards a person with lined cheeks and noble aspect. Paul Borel. The president of the Republic.

I've only ever seen him on T.V. Was that the same for you, Papa?

A nerdy-looking little man with round spectacles, face buried in a long green scarf, taps the microphone with the palm of his hand. His scarf looks more like a rug: he's not stupid, the small guy, he knows how to stay warm without having to wear a coat. He hands the president a document, then slips back into the shadows. Borel takes a deep breath as if at the start of a hundred-metre sprint, then launches into his speech. His voice drowns out the drumming rain. Borel is like Jupiter. Géraldine imagines him wielding two lightning bolts in his right hand. The white flashes clang.

Borel, the father of the nation.

But you were, you are, my father and Camille's father. And Sandra's husband. I'd like to hear your voice one last time. Hey, can you hear me?

"This was one of the most vicious attacks on our fellow citizens in recent years. This odious crime will not go unpunished. Standing before you today, I solemnly swear that all those responsible will be arrested, brought to justice and punished as they deserve. Terrorism is a plague that must be combated tenaciously and relentlessly. The government and I are as one in our determination to win this battle. We will never allow your dead, *our* dead, to be forgotten . . ."

A soothing lullaby. His voice is that of a god. Of the commander of the gods. No wonder Borel is the big boss. Géraldine thinks of the great men she has seen parading through the pages of her history books. They are born with a magic charm, why deny it?

After the speech, a military man helps the president with the distribution. On this occasion, posthumous *Légion d'honneur* medals. The aide has a large envelope containing small pieces of paper, Post-its so there are no embarrassing mistakes over the victims' names. Eighteen engineers and technicians, eighteen heroes who died in the name of France.

You're the most modest man I know, Papa. Is this Légion d'honneur *something you would have wanted? Really and truly?*

Ten seconds for each family. The president is coming towards her. Elegant as a prince, a smile that says, "We're all in this together," hand outstretched. The aide plunges into the envelope, draws Papa's name out.

Now is the moment.

The moment to be seized or to regret for the rest of your life. Throw the coat of frailty into the dustbin. Now.

"No thank you, Monsieur le Président . . ."

"I beg your pardon, miss?"

"MY FATHER WANTS NOTHING TO DO WITH YOUR MEDAL!"

Maman and Camille turn towards her. Her shout has dezombified them. Géraldine rests her hand on her mother's shoulder. Something stirs in the corner of her field of vision. Probably Jupiter and his aide making themselves scarce. Géraldine smiles. And weeps at the same time. Maman and Camille do the same.

DOMINIQUE SYLVAIN – 4

They talk to each other, but can't hear properly because the angry, never-ending rain keeps pounding on the corrugated iron roof. The din is good news. It means the rain is on their side and will be until the end. That gives you courage.

Look at me, Papa, you'll be surprised.

1 MONDAY, JANUARY 14, 2013

The day was more like night. Pale grey from early morning, slimy grey until bedtime. She should have switched on the light, taken an interest in the world's problems, eaten something other than pasta with ham. She preferred to listen to the rain and drink port. Unbelievable, these floods of rain.

The intercom. She got up from her wing-chair, grumbling all the way.

"Lola Jost?"

"That depends."

"Captain Philippe Hardy, Inspectorate of Police. I'd like to talk to you."

The General Inspectorate of Police. All through her career, she had kept well away from *les boeuf-carottes* – the "beefeaters". Why had this specimen pitched up at her place? Beneath her weariness there was still a sliver of curiosity, so she opened the front door for him.

Energetic footsteps shook the lift cage out of its slumber. Out stepped someone with the interesting look of an Irishman. Light-blue eyes, reddish hair: the unexpected good looks of the police's policeman.

He left his umbrella on the landing; came in, caught sight of the puzzle on the table. Christ the Redeemer spreading his arms above Rio de Janeiro.

"The Corcovado."

"Well spotted."

"How many pieces?"

"Far too many. It's a present from my son."

"You can guess why I'm here."

"I won't even try."

"Haven't you been listening to the news?"

"I haven't been listening to anything. For the moment I'm lying fallow."

"I beg your pardon?"

"Tell me what's brought you here, or this is going to take longer than that damn puzzle."

"Armand Mars' body has been found."

Her heart plunged, as if some idiot had pushed her off an Olympic high-diving board. Hardy brought her a glass of water, opened the window. He told her the divisionnaire had been found with a bullet in the head in Côte d'Ivoire. A building-site on the outskirts of Abidjan. The Serious Crime Squad's number one reduced to a skeleton on the flat roof of an uninhabited house. His body had been identified thanks to the serial number on his watch and collaboration between the local police and the French embassy. D.N.A. tests had confirmed the identity.

"What's your role in all this?"

"When Mars went missing, I was put in charge of the investigation. Now that his body has been found, I'm still at the controls."

"If you'd really been at the controls you'd have picked him up before he was murdered."

He took the insult without flinching. Our flexible friendly cop.

"You and Armand Mars were close. You met him through your friend, Commandant Sacha Duguin, didn't you?"

Mars. Seductive but twisted. Yes, she had become part of the small circle the divisionnaire confided in. And yet he had taken her for a ride just like all the others; just like his most devoted officer Sacha Duguin, just like all his team. The divisionnaire had wreaked his revenge before flying the coop: to Abidjan, apparently.

Mars. A great officer. A sick one too.

"Richard Gratien had the last word, Hardy. What more can I say?"

"Gratien has been in prison for months."

"Prison bars have never stopped anyone taking out a contract on a victim. Last summer that same Gratien paid two bastards to shoot my best friend, in the heart of Paris. Just because Sacha Duguin was her lover. And Gratien was already inside . . ."

The attack that day on boulevard Saint-Michel cost the life of Lieutenant Sébastien Ménard, the youngest member of the Duguin team. A dreadful mess.

"How old was Ménard? Do you remember, Hardy?"

"Twenty-four."

"Well, if you'd done your job properly, he would be twenty-five now."

"Calm down, will you?"

"I am calm. Being at the controls means you anticipate things."

"Listen—"

"Mars fine-tuned his revenge. It took years of preparation. You should have sniffed out that he was a disaster waiting to happen. That's what the G.I.P. is for, isn't it? To identify highly volatile characters."

"Arresting people before they've done anything is science fiction, Madame Jost. A former commissaire should know that."

"Before and after are relative notions. You didn't come and see me 'after' the Saint-Michel incident, Captain, and yet the killer shouted the name of Richard Gratien's wife. It's a calling card that's hard to ignore."

"I've spoken to all the witnesses and investigators dealing with the Saint-Michel murder."

"Am I supposed to be impressed?"

"Mars' death means you are a vital witness, Madame Jost. You were there during his last hours in Paris. He confided in you."

"Mars was a good liar."

"You were close to his team. Especially Sacha Duguin. I'm starting from scratch, and questioning everyone involved."

"Too late. What use would I be?"

"You could help build up a solid case. Against Gratien if he's the one who had Mars shot. Against someone else if it's not Gratien."

"In other words, you don't have a clue."

Hardy's face stiffened. The torpedo had struck home. His smugness well and truly holed.

"O.K. You're to accompany me to the G.I.P."

"No way."

"I've got something to show you. Concerning Saint-Michel."

She studied him, ready to launch another drone against his malice, then changed her mind. Paris, last summer, a café terrace. All of a sudden, a nightmare. Two motorcyclists. The passenger fires at Ingrid Diesel and Sébastien Ménard.

She herself had not witnessed the scene, but had seen it a thousand times in her mind's eye.

Sacha had told her the weapon had previously been used in another murder. An old case, a drug dealer shot by a rival. The 9 mm bullet that had killed Ménard was from the same gun. The owner, who was still in prison, had no links to Gratien or the arms trade. The gun must have been passed from person to person on the black market, but had not resurfaced until the attack on her American friend.

I've got something to show you. Hardy was not bluffing.

Ever since Ingrid's lucky escape, Lola had felt not only exhausted and exasperated but utterly powerless. Now the tiny flame had been ignited once more.

She headed for the shower. Farewell to the dressing gown she had been mouldering in for days. The bathroom mirror presented her with a grotesque reflection: a Gorgon's hair, chalk-white, puffy face. The scales showed she had put on three kilos.

I couldn't give a damn. Nor could Paris.

She opened the window, stuck her arm out to judge the temperature. Warm, foul and wet. A topsy-turvy winter.

The radio in the Audi spewed out evil news. Half the workers at a car assembly plant laid off; a teenager putting his caseworker in hospital; a French pilot killed in Mali.

Lola imagined a helicopter crashing into a sand-dune and exploding in a fireball. That crook Gratien had been the middleman for arms dealers, specialising in African contracts. Journalists liked to call him "Mister Africa". And Mars had gone to Abidjan to die. Africa: for ever and ever that damned continent.

Hardy had put the blue beacon on the roof and was driving too fast. The streets sped by, blurred in the rain. Gusts of wind made the car shake and rattle. They came to a halt at a traffic light. Lola saw the face of an American actress on the back of a bus. Short, very blonde hair. A sawn-off shotgun. The lights turned green. The bus veered off to the right. The rain had played a cruel trick – for a moment, the young actress looked just like Ingrid.

Hardy accelerated down boulevard Beaumarchais.

A short journey for a long address. Rue Antoine-Julien-Hénard, in the 12th arrondissement. A modern glass-and-stone building, as smooth as the captain's manner.

She was put into an almost empty office. A young woman who looked as plastic as her boss brought her a coffee and a glass of water. If they thought they could marinate her to soften her hide, they were making a big mistake.

2

Boulevard Saint-Michel under a cloudless sky. Notre Dame in the distance. Traffic flowing freely along the quai de Montebello. A few people browsing at the second-hand booksellers' stalls. A man taking two greyhounds and a cigar for a walk.

The man and the dogs leave the frame. Passers-by scatter out of the way of a young woman. Tall, athletic, in a pink fluorescent tank-top.

Ingrid.

Her arms chopping the air. She's running like someone possessed. Her blonde hair looks almost white in the sunlight.

Close-up of her face. She's terrified.

An explosion.

The image wobbles. A voice, close to the microphone: "Shit, that was a gunshot!" People running; others hit the ground.

A motorbike. The driver, Pale Helmet, is riding against the traffic. The passenger, Black Helmet, holds up a weapon.

Stunned voice into the microphone: "Did you see those idiots?"

Pale Helmet zigzags between the cars, gets in front of Ingrid, blocks her path. No way out. Behind her, the parapet wall, the River Seine flowing indifferently by.

Heavy breathing in the microphone.

Black Helmet takes aim. Arm outstretched, body braced. A professional. Ingrid begs him to spare her.

The image and the voice in the microphone quaver: "It's not possible, he's not going to shoot, is he?"

Pale Helmet glances nervously around him. Ingrid confronts Black Helmet. Courageous, fragile. No point begging for her life now.

"Oh fuck it, no!"

Black Helmet shouts: "THIS IS FOR ANTONIA GRATIEN, YOU BITCH!" He raises his arm. Adjusts his aim. Fires. Ingrid collapses. A grunt in the microphone. The two motorcyclists seem to be arguing. Black Helmet climbs back on the pillion. Pale Helmet accelerates away in the direction of Notre Dame.

Ingrid on her knees. The empty space around her body flooded with light.

The image wavers along with the trembling hands of the man filming the scene on his iPhone.

"A glass of water, Madame Jost?"

"You've got to stop this habit of making me drink every five minutes, Hardy."

The video taken by a passer-by on his smartphone confirmed what Lola had thought from the outset. And added a piece of information. She was sure of it – now that she had watched the scene several times.

"The gunman could have killed your friend if he had wanted to. At that distance, he couldn't miss."

Instead of that, Black Helmet had fired over her head.

"He aims at her," Lola said. "Then he lifts his arm, only slightly, just enough to modify the trajectory. He changes the angle because he's changed his mind. He's been paid to kill Ingrid, but he spares her at the very last moment."

"Yes, I agree. But without this video, we would have thought he only wanted to scare the daylights out of her rather than kill her."

"But the video shows he changed his mind at the vital moment."

"Correct."

Yes, because it was obvious from the film that the motorcyclist doesn't understand why the gunman has spared Ingrid. His body language questions the other man. Then they have that short argument. There's tension. But Black Helmet is the boss. He orders Pale Helmet to get them out of there as fast as possible.

"Have your boys found the number?"

"The motorbike didn't have a licence plate."

"One of your informers must have heard something about the contract . . ."

"Not so far."

"What about the gun? Still not found it? But it had been used before, had it not?"

"Who told you that?"

"One of my former colleagues in the 10th station," Lola lied. (No point bringing Sacha into this.)

"No, nothing on the Beretta."

"So you know it's a Beretta?"

"Yes, the lab blew up the video images."

They studied each other for a few seconds.

"I told you I had something interesting to show you."

"Out of the goodness of your heart?"

"I'm not working against you. Quite the opposite."

"I don't know a thing, Captain. How often do I have to repeat it?"

"People think they don't know anything, but they do. You don't need me to tell you that. I want what you remember."

Hardy placed a mini-recorder on the table. Lola crushed the plastic cup in one hand, sat back on her chair, and resolutely folded her arms. The day was only just coming to an end. The night promised to be interminable. Behind her, the storm lashed at the windowpanes.

3   TUESDAY, JANUARY 15

The day had not yet dawned. Sacha Duguin consulted his watch. Half an hour late. Hardy had arranged to meet him at seven, but had only just arrived in the office. The G.I.P. captain came in and sat behind the desk the Serious Crime Squad had put at his disposal.

They sat for a moment, glaring at one another across a mini-recorder and a roomful of bad vibes.

"My first visit was a courtesy call, Commandant Duguin. After Mars' death . . . No more courtesy."

"Suit yourself."

"The Serious Crime Squad headed for years by a psychopath. The media salivating. And the soap opera continues in Abidjan. At a time when France is getting involved in Mali, it's embarrassing . . ."

"I don't have time to read the newspapers."

Hardy started the recorder, stated the date, time, his name and Duguin's.

"Commandant Duguin, tell me how you succeeded in finding your superior Arnaud Mars in Côte d'Ivoire at the end of last summer."

"I didn't find him."

"A slip of the tongue. How you tried to find him."

Sacha repeated what he had said on his return from Africa. That he had used the expertise of a female colleague in *la Financière* who had figured out how the commissionaire had financed his escape. The first stop had been an obliging French broker who had opened an account in the Bahamas. From there, Sacha had followed the money trail, which showed that Mars and his family were probably somewhere in Africa. Arnaud Mars had served in Kinshasa during his diplomatic career. So Sacha had caught a plane to the Democratic Republic of Congo.

"Who told you about his career?"

"Mars used to discuss these things."

Hardy made as if he were rereading his notes, then nodded, as though appreciating a good joke.

"So far, your two statements coincide."

He took off his watch, rubbed it on his sleeve, placed it next to his ballpoint pen.

"Remind me how you ended up in Abidjan."

"By questioning Mars' former contacts in Africa."

"A test of your patience, no doubt. But one which paid off in the end."

"Perhaps, but I didn't discover his hideaway."

"That's surprising, when you were so close to your goal."

"My leave had a limit. And I wanted to keep my job."

"I've reread the transcription of our last interview, and still have the same doubt. Why did you want to find Mars?"

This was said evenly enough, but there was a gleam of pleasure in the captain's eye. He had been with the G.I.P. for years, but the asshole still enjoyed it as much as ever. Sacha imagined they were in the ring at his Thai boxing club. A jab to the throat, left kick to the stomach, a quick knee to the groin, and the beefeater would crumble, arms outstretched, balls at half-mast.

"I've already told you."

"Answer my question."

"For an explanation."

"An explanation, man to man. Yes, that's what I wrote down. Tell me, were you armed?"

It was the first time Hardy had asked that question. Sacha sensed he had to tell the truth, at least on this score.

"Correct."

"Your service revolver?"

"No."

"What then?"

"It's not hard to lay your hands on a gun in Africa."

"What make?"

"A S.I.G. Sauer."

"Were you planning to shoot Mars?"

"I wasn't. Possibly he was planning to shoot me."

Hardy paused the recording.

"He made a fool of you, Duguin. Your career is in ruins. In your place, buddy, I wouldn't have hesitated."

The old trick: disdain and mock camaraderie. Too easy.

"What are you trying to insinuate?"

"I'm not saying you were determined to kill him. But the idea must have gone through your mind, otherwise what the fuck were you doing in Africa?"

Sacha tried to restart the recording, but Hardy shot out a hand to stop him doing so.

"Try to pull a fast one on me, and I'll be your Vietnam, Duguin."

The beefeater sat back in his chair and fiddled with his watch.

"You push off all on your own without warning, simply for a man-to-man explanation? And you return empty-handed, but all smiles. Perhaps it was self-defence. Given what he'd done to you, I could understand that."

Silence. Sacha was thinking about the investigation his team was currently working on, how precious the first hours were. This asshole was wasting valuable time.

"Better get it off your chest now, otherwise you're going to find yourself more and more isolated."

"If you say so."

"Mars and you arrest Richard Gratien. Then, oops, his beloved wife Antonia dies in police custody. On your watch. Killed by Mars in fact, although you won't discover that until later. Mars disappears. You gather information, slip off to Africa. Shortly after you leave, a murder on boulevard Saint-Michel. The target is Ingrid Diesel, one of your exes. Lieutenant Ménard is unlucky enough to be with her. He ends up as collateral damage, chewing on a bullet. Before firing at your little friend, the shooter makes it plain: *'This is for Antonia Gratien, you bitch!'* He's fulfilling a contract on behalf of Mister Africa, who has two sworn enemies for all eternity: Mars and you."

"Are you carrying out an investigation or telling a shaggy dog story, Hardy?"

"You're a key figure in that story."

"Gratien is the key figure, not me."

"He denies contracting the motorcyclists. But you already know that."

"That's your problem."

"He also denies killing Mars."

"Were you expecting a full and frank confession?"

"You're wrong to play the strong, silent type. I know more about you than your mother does. I've spent a lot of time on it. What's most striking is the effect you have on women. They think you're far grander than you really are. You go around feeling inordinately proud of yourself. In fact, you and women both tend to overplay your virtues. What do you reckon?"

"Nothing."

"I'm offering you the path to redemption. That's worth a great deal, you know."

Hardy switched the recorder back on.

"Tell me, Duguin, how did you get on with Karen Mars?"

"What's that got to do with anything?"

"You were a friend of the family, were you not?"

"Yes."

"Mars was older than his wife. He'd forced her to go on a senseless adventure. To Karen Mars you must have seemed like her saviour."

"Pardon?"

"Dragged off against her will to the heart of Africa by a half-crazy husband . . . She must have been ever so grateful when you showed up. Perhaps more than just grateful?"

Hardy paused the recording again.

"We can be even more imaginative. Maybe you and Karen Mars had an affair in Paris. When Mars took her away with him, you went charging to the rescue. To her rescue. And that involved getting rid of her old man."

"If you're expecting me to swallow that sort of line, you can think again."

"Look at things the other way round, Duguin. You're the one who will have to think again. By the time you've finally understood what my line is, it'll be too late."

4

A few seconds of bewilderment before Lola realised she was in her own bed. Before the refuse truck woke her, she had been stewing in the G.I.P, in the same office as the previous evening. Philippe Hardy and her, face to face, only this time the wall was filled by a giant screen. Sacha filmed in the street, branded with a cross burned into the middle of his forehead.

I wouldn't make a good subject for my psychoanalyst friend. My dreams are transparent.

She was groggy. Hardy had put a lot of pressure on her: he was obsessed by Sacha Duguin.

As Arnaud Mars' closest colleague, Commandant Duguin had been the one who suffered most from his manipulations. So much so that he had devoted his leave to pursuing him when he disappeared. He wanted an explanation. He came back without one. Weary, but calmer all the same. At least until he learned that while he had been away, Richard Gratien had paid two thugs to carry out an attack on boulevard Saint-Michel. Ménard was Sacha's assistant; as for Ingrid, she had been the love of his life until some grit got in the works.

She could guess what Hardy was thinking: that Sacha was lying when he said he hadn't found Mars. From there it was only one more short step to imagining that he had killed his boss. A really stupid theory. Sacha might have been badly hurt, but he wasn't crazy. Why on earth didn't Hardy focus his attention on Gratien?

With two rotten officers for the price of one, the beefeater had a media sensation on his hands, and would make a meal of it. For the moment he was sizing up where to sink his teeth. Sacha was making him salivate.

The previous evening's port-based remedy had left Lola with a splitting headache, and so she took several paracetamol. She inspected a refrigerator almost as devoid of life as the Alaskan tundra. Eventually she had a fried egg with a piece of stale toast and a strong coffee. She urgently needed to go shopping. But she had better things to do.

Photographs from the Côte d'Ivoire police on Sacha's desk.

Abidjan. A building-site where work was suspended because of the monsoon. The sky a deep violet-blue, the yellow ochre of the buildings standing out against an intense green background. The flat roof of an empty house. The crime scene.

Mars is a sorry thing. A pile of bones on dirty concrete; clothes reduced to rags, his watch tarnished. The only witness to his glorious past were his shoes: good leather, hand-tooled for a gentleman.

The gentleman had been devoured by the continent he loved so much. Rains and vermin had feasted on him. Worm fodder.

She turned to Sacha. The melancholy look suited him: he was waiting to judge her reaction. Mars had played a dirty trick on them both, but he didn't deserve to go like that. What would they have done in his place? Your son is killed: do you seek retaliation, or let "justice take its course"? The Big Chief had not hesitated. He had turned his back on his colleagues and the justice system. He had declared: "Your Republic won't do a thing. So I'll be the executioner. I'll kill the people Gratien loves, but spare him. And my enemy's life will become a living nightmare."

"I wanted to warn you about Mars, Lola. But your phone . . ."

"Yes, I switched it off. It happens."

Sacha nodded, waiting for her to continue. She didn't know anyone whom silence suited more. And yet beneath the calm surface, the embers were glowing.

"I thought Mars had fled with his family."

"He must have sent Karen and his daughter Aurélie somewhere safe before he was murdered."

The little girl was no more than twelve. Hopefully she and her mother were still alive, in Africa or elsewhere.

"It's Gratien, isn't it?"

"I don't know, Lola."

"Who else?"

"Mars had got his hands on a copy of Gratien's notebooks. There was enough in them to incriminate a whole raft of people. Obviously, there's been no trace of the books."

Those damned notebooks. T.N.T. at its most unstable. Everyone keeps their own kind of diary. Gratien's was very special. The lawyer noted down every last detail of the transactions he had "facilitated". Not to mention spicy anecdotes about the politicians, wheeler-dealers and other officials involved in the murky relations between France and its former African colonies. More than thirty years of contracts and deals. Any journalist would have killed his father and mother just to read extracts from them.

"You knew him best, Sacha. And yet despite all the information you had, and despite your stubbornness, you didn't manage to find him. Gratien, on the other hand, knows all the mercenaries lurking in the shadows between the Rock of Gibraltar and the Cape."

Turning away from her, Sacha walked over to the half-open window. Mars had been his mentor, the person who had welcomed him with open arms when he got his dream job: a commandant in the most prestigious police squad in France. But then the divisionnaire had betrayed him.

I can almost touch your pain, Sacha. You loved the old bastard as much as you hate him now.

"Apart from that, how's life?"

"We have plenty of work, and that's exactly what I need."

Lola fished a small metal box out of her pocket. The endless wet weather was affecting her throat. Sacha accepted a mentholated sweet.

"What news of Ingrid?"

Ingrid and Sacha. Those two should have come together again after the storm. Despite their differences, to Lola they seemed like the perfect couple. Yet another precious object Mars had shattered.

"She's been hired by a famous dance troupe in Las Vegas. No more striptease, now it's all glitter and French cancan."

"Do they dance the cancan in Las Vegas?"

"I've no idea."

She told him about Philippe Hardy's visit, and ended with the iPhone video.

"That bastard interrogated me this morning. And he didn't say a word about it," Sacha said.

"*Machiavelli for Dummies* must be his bedside reading."

He offered her a coffee made in a real pot. Things were improving at headquarters: someone had finally admitted that the machine at the end of the corridor was the king of dishwater.

"Lola . . . I blame myself for Ménard, and . . ."

"And?"

"Ingrid . . . that's my fault too. I wasn't there to defend her."

Lola rubbed her back. The rain was rekindling her arthritis, and Sacha's regrets were doing the same for her depression. It was her birthday in a few weeks. She'd be a hundred and fifty.

"The only advice I can give you, Sacha, is to beware of Hardy. You're too much of a temptation for him."

"I realise that."

"I know what he thinks. That you found Mars and shot him. He's searching for witnesses. When somebody wants at all costs for the facts to support their theory . . ."

". . . Anything is possible, especially the worst."

"Quite so."

Sacha explained that, for the moment, Hardy was the least of his worries. The Duguin team had inherited a triple homicide. The staff of a Japanese restaurant in the 9th arrondissement.

Lola could sense that despite his personal troubles, he was very focused on the work at hand. She had always admired his obsessiveness. Together with the ability to reason, that was what made the difference between a good detective and an outstanding one.

Lola crossed the quay, drawn to the Seine and its green smell. The rain had gone off to pester people in other latitudes. A *bateau-mouche* drifted by, crammed with tourists discovering Paris to the sound of

"Firework" interpreted by Katy Perry. Coincidence could harpoon you at any moment: Ingrid had almost based a show on that song. *I've always dreamt of a costume like a firework. You'll have to come and see me dance, Lola.*

Mars and Ménard were dead. Gratien was rotting in jail, Sacha was still in charge of a team, the Serious Crime Squad had a new divisionnaire. And Ingrid had a new life in the States. Her American friend, who had once been head over heels about Paris and Sacha, had pulled out and decided it was time to rediscover her own culture and her roots.

Beyond the Seine lay the Left Bank and Saint-Michel. Lola hadn't set foot there since the previous summer. But Mars' death changed everything.

Lola crossed the bridge. On this unexpectedly mild winter's day, the café terraces were crowded. She found the spot where Ménard had been killed. Ingrid had wanted to see him to get information. He worked on Sacha's team, so perhaps he knew where he was? But the young lieutenant didn't know anything. Nobody knew anything. Sacha had taken off to Africa without telling a soul.

The motorcyclists had come from the Right Bank. Black Helmet had first of all shot and killed Ménard, then they had chased Ingrid along the quai de Montebello.

Lola entered the café, saw the door Ingrid had run out of. She followed in her footsteps, crossed the road, walked past the secondhand stalls trying to imagine her friend running towards Notre Dame. An excellent idea, but Pale Helmet had not hesitated to pursue her against the oncoming cars. That had been risky, given the volume of traffic. Obviously the two of them were determined.

Lola walked to the spot where they had caught up with Ingrid. Her American friend had told her what she felt. That she was sure she was going to die. Her last thought was for Sacha.

Beside the Seine, the bullet had whizzed just over her head. Ingrid had thought she was dead; her body had received an imaginary blow; she had collapsed to the ground. Her eyes had dimmed, time had slowed down, and Death gave her a sour smile before turning on its heel. She couldn't tell which direction the motorcyclists had gone, but remembered Black Helmet shouting: "That's for Antonia Gratien, you bitch!"

After the attack, Ingrid had been through a hard time. She couldn't find Sacha, who was unreachable. He was concentrating on his manhunt and had cut all links with civilisation. She kept having nightmares about the two hitmen and Sébastien's bloody corpse. Killed because of her.

Some time later, Ingrid had decided to make a clean break. Since Sacha was still absent, apparently indifferent to the death of his young lieutenant and all that had ensued, Ingrid saw no reason to stay on in France. If she had escaped death, it wasn't to hang around waiting for a guy who wasn't worth it.

So she took a plane to San Francisco, where she met a friend of her former boss Timothy Harlen's. He suggested Las Vegas. Her talent had done the rest. Only a few weeks after her return to the nest, she had found herself a job in a famous dance troupe. Lola received emails and photos from her more or less regularly. Ingrid in rhinestones and feathers, dazzling in the midst of a line of tall, muscular young women as gorgeous as hearts and always full of joy.

I miss your brightness and generosity, young Yankeedoodle, but I guess you're happy among your giraffe friends. That's the main thing.

She conjured a mental image of the metro map in her mind, and headed for Châtelet station. As she was coming out onto the quai de la Rapée, a raindrop burst on her shoulder. The sky was at it again. It wasn't long before the strangely pleasing smell of wet tarmac rose from the ground.

5

The disinfectants could not entirely disguise the smell of putrefaction. Lola swallowed a mentholated sweet, walked airily past the front desk but was called back by a security guard she did not know. Had the usual old fellow been pensioned off too? The kid asked to see her credentials.

"Your police I.D. is out-of-date."

"Possibly, but everyone here knows me."

"Is it for someone who has passed over in your family?"

Someone who has passed over. Heavens, a poet in the Forensic Institute.

"No. I want to see Dr Franklin. Thomas is a friend."

"Do you have an appointment?"

"Of course."

"I can't see your name on the list."

She had to argue for a while before the guard agreed to contact the veteran pathologist. The old grouch replied that he was in the middle of an autopsy and was unavailable at present.

"I'll wait," Lola said, looking even more determined than the young man in front of her.

"Make an appointment and come back."

"No."

"Yes."

"Do you want an old lady like me to catch pneumonia out in the rain?"

The young whippersnapper capitulated. Lola won the right to wait in the corridor. It wasn't just a ploy: she was shivering, and her body was aching all over.

An hour and forty-seven minutes later, Franklin emerged, wearing a plexiglass visor, plastic apron and doctor's clogs.

"Oh no, not you! I don't believe it!"

"You know what the Chinese say? 'Be patient! In time, grass turns into milk.'"

"I couldn't give a damn about cows or the Chinese. I've got a quarter of an hour to snaffle my lunch before I'm back at the grindstone. Give me a break, Lola."

"In your dreams. Tell me about Mars."

"Not here. A wasted journey."

"Hardy himself told me his body was within these four walls. The file is top priority."

"Why don't you go and take up bridge or wine-tasting, or plumbing? Live the life you've got left! As you can see, it always ends badly."

"And I have a bad feeling about it."

She mentioned the insistent way Hardy was pursuing Sacha Duguin. The G.I.P. captain was more interested in his own career than in the triumph of justice.

"Yes, I know Hardy," Franklin admitted.

"And?"

"He's not an easy man. Beneath the calm exterior, there's something slimy bubbling away."

"So we agree."

"No. Leave me in peace."

Lola insisted: she needed something she could use against Hardy if anything went wrong.

"You're a real laugh. You're going to take on the G.I.P. single-handed?"

"You don't know how much of a nuisance I can be."

"You don't look well. You'd do better to go and have a lie-down."

"Thanks, but I've been doing nothing but that recently."

Ever since Ingrid had gone, all Lola had been doing was spending her life in a stupor. Lola Jost, or the Sleeping Pensioner. Despite her aches and pains, it was time to stand up straight again.

As usual, she wore the pathologist down: Mars' remains had been brought in two days earlier.

"And?"

"To cut a long story short, he was killed last September."

"When in September?"

"Impossible to say, but let me finish. That's still the monsoon season in West Africa . . ."

"And so it wasn't long before his body was reduced to a skeleton."

"Yeah, and that's what is odd, Lola."

"How do you mean?"

"Think for a minute."

"I do nothing else."

"Mars was killed by a pro. One bullet to the head, quick and easy . . ."

"Tell me about it."

"And yet the killer leaves the body on the flat roof of an unfinished house. As I understand it, work on the site was suspended for the rainy season. You can't render buildings when it's pouring with rain. At least not when it's that kind of torrential downpour."

"Obviously."

"After that, you have to wait for things to dry out."

"Yes."

"But equally obviously, they found the body when they started work again. After that, they had to identify him. No identity papers on him, just an expensive watch. And on top of that, he was in the country clandestinely. A foreigner."

"In other words, you can't understand why his killer didn't bury him in the forest, where no-one would ever find him."

"In rich earth, where the maggots are built like Jason Statham."

"I see. Tell me something . . ."

"What now, Lola?"

"A bullet casing?"

"None was found."

"So the killer had a revolver . . ."

"Or a pistol and he picked the cartridge up. The bullet is being tested as we speak. Hardy asked for the results as quickly as possible. The beefeaters usually get what they want."

"Odd the results aren't already here."

"Odd or not, that's how it is."

"Tell me about the angle of fire."

"It wasn't what you might call a real execution style, two slugs to the back of the neck and goodnight everybody. In fact, Mars was lying on his back. He had possibly been beaten up."

"Unless his killer threw him to the ground or ordered him to lie still . . ."

"What we do know is that the killer stood above him. Looked him in the eye. Fired at point-blank range. The bullet passed through the skull and became embedded in the concrete."

"Was there a caretaker on the site?"

"I've no idea, Lola. I cut up stiffs, I don't chat with them."

"You talk as if he were a complete stranger."

"Don't get me wrong. I liked Mars in spite of the absurd choices he made. He had balls and didn't mince words. That was part of his charm. The fact is, we'll never hear from him again. And there's nothing anyone can do about that. In other words, let the workers work and stop pestering me."

"Is it me, or are you even more grumpy than usual?"

"Take up bridge, believe me. Or if I were you, I'd try plumbing."

"Thanks for all the info, old man."

Franklin shook his head wearily and wandered off down the corridor. Lola heard him muttering as he went:

"Plumbing, Lola, plumbing. That'll be your salvation."

She left the building under the security guard's watchful eye. At the café on the corner she ordered a large glass of white to get rid of the mortuary smell.

The killer was standing above him. Looked him in the eye. Why not shoot him in the back when he was trying to run away, and finish him off with a bullet to the back of the head? And on boulevard Saint-Michel, the motorbike riders chased Ingrid and gave her the fright of her life, then spared her. *Looking her in the eye.*

The killer in Africa, the motorcyclist in Paris: were they both working for Richard Gratien?

She offered herself a walk before catching the metro again. The sky was wrought silver. There was a break in the clouds, and a whitish beam of light poured through, brightening the house fronts and forming a miniature rainbow. Lola imagined Ingrid beside her. She would have liked the atmosphere. *I'm so in love with this fucking city, Lola.*

As she was reaching Bastille station, a loud engine noise made her whirl round.

Black leathers, tinted visor. Lola was rooted to the spot, terror rising in her gorge. She made a huge effort to overcome her paralysis.

She plunged down into the station. Even on the platform she didn't feel any safer. This wasn't her first panic attack. She couldn't bear motorcyclists, or motorbikes. She rummaged in her bag, swallowed a pill. An African woman with ritual scars on her face was staring at her. Lola's anguish was plain for all to see: the woman's look was one of pity rather than curiosity.

The screech of train wheels. Lola clambered on board. Her legs buckled, and her stomach was protesting at the glass of wine. She studied the other passengers' faces, gradually relaxed. The motorcyclist was just one more unremarkable guy among thousands.

6

Lexomil Bromazepam, the magic molecule. If a cobra appeared in her living room, she would laugh in its face. She took off her coat and rubber boots and considered the Corcovado. She chose a piece, completed a wave, sat in her wing-chair and folded her hands across her lap. Elsewhere in the building someone was vacuuming.

She took stock.

Mars had been killed by a stranger who had botched the job. Hardy didn't think Gratien was responsible – but was focusing on Sacha. Ingrid had been spared at the very last moment. Richard Gratien's radioactive notebooks were still nowhere to be found. And that must be worrying a cavalcade of top civil servants and arms dealers.

Mars, you old soldier, even though you're dead, you're still hot stuff.

Originally, it had been a vendetta between two men. But when by chance the divisionnaire had got hold of a copy of the notebooks, he had realised the scandal they could cause and had developed a political conscience. Locked in his duel with the shady lawyer Gratien, Arnaud Mars had taken it upon himself to send an extract from the notebooks to the satirical magazine *Le Canard Enchaîné*. The publication of this extract had led to the death of Louis Candichard, ex-foreign affairs minister, who had used his shotgun to commit suicide at his Paris residence the previous summer.

Mars, the god of carnage.

Lola went online. On the *Politika* site she read an article from August:

Some interesting pages from Richard Gratien's sulphurous notebooks have been sent anonymously to our colleagues at *Le Canard Enchaîné*. A copy has reached the prosecuting judges in the EuroSecurities affair, so-called from the name of the bank based in Liechtenstein that specialised in guaranteeing international money transfers. According to these documents, the bosses at EuroSecurities took part in money-laundering operations and allowed hidden commissions and kickbacks to be paid.

The affair goes back to the 1990s, when Gratien was the main intermediary for arms sales between the French state and foreign powers. As was his habit, the lawyer had carefully noted all the details and consequences of these operations. In particular, the comings and goings of a EuroSecurities employee whose job it was to deliver large sums of cash to the Candichard committee headquarters. During the 1994 presidential election campaign, this committee backed the former foreign minister against the incumbent, Paul Borel. The alleged sum involved is 15 million euros. Eurosecurities' bagman is currently being questioned by Judge . . .

Had Gratien, implicated in the affair by the notebooks, decided to eliminate Mars and contract a hitman while languishing in jail? Did that explain why the divisionnaire had not been despatched cleanly? Had his killer wanted to know where Mars was hiding his copy of the notebooks before he finished him off?

The problem was that Sacha Duguin's words and deeds fascinated the G.I.P. More worrying still was the fact that it was impossible to date Mars' death precisely. The details were sufficiently hazy to excite any beefeater.

Bad timing.

The rain was caressing the windowpanes like a jazz brush on cymbals. The best thing to do would be to stay at home, finish the Corcovado, get into a T.V. series. Or to clean the place up a bit. Balls of fluff were rolling under the table at the slightest draught.

Her old address book was stuck between a map of Paris and a telephone directory that was as dog-eared as it was obsolete. The book had been her bible when she was in charge of the local commissariat, and was full of the names of informers and useful contacts.

Armand Bianco.

He must be pensioned off as well.

She listened to the rain.

Bianco had been married a considerable number of times, but never to Lola.

She found his home number, dialled it, recognised his deep voice. He could easily have done radio.

7

He had lost hair but gained eyebrows. His eyes were still an electric blue, and his smile led you to believe something sparkling and exciting was bound to follow.

Lola would have loved to lose thirty kilos and as many years.

"I thought we'd never see each other again in our lifetimes, Lola."

A smell of roasting meat was floating in the air of the kitchen, where she met Sophie, the latest spouse. She was a pretty brunette aged barely forty, with more than one offspring. Their home made Lola's place in rue de l'Echiquier seem uninhabited. She followed Armand to his study, told him what she had learned about Mars' death, brought up Sacha Duguin.

"One minute, Lola, I'm trying to understand."

"Understand what?"

"Why you're getting involved."

"The G.I.P. are after Sacha. I intend to head them off."

"What's the problem? Your friend has only one thing to reproach himself for: believing in Mars' honesty. That man was a genius at manipulation."

"I've heard scraps of gossip from my former colleagues. Hardy isn't the first to imagine Sacha shot Mars."

"If your commandant is innocent . . ."

"He is."

"Then he has nothing to worry about. Our judicial system may make mistakes, but Duguin has a key argument in his favour."

"Which is?"

"A cop would never have left a body and a bullet behind."

"That doesn't matter. I can sense a worrying smell coming from Hardy. And if there's one part of me which is talented, it's my nose."

"Personally, I always rather liked your legs."

They exchanged a knowing smile. Incorrigible Armand: he still knew how to flatter a woman.

"O.K., so what exactly is it you want, sweetheart?"

"I want to understand the link between Gratien and Candichard."

"I'd prefer to talk about the link between Gratien and President Borel. That takes us back to 1994."

As a political journalist on *Le Point* magazine, Bianco had covered the presidential election. Louis Candichard was standing against Paul Borel. The five-year presidential term had not yet been instigated, and France had experienced seven long years under Borel. A stormy economic climate, rising unemployment, an anxious population: the opinion polls showed the head of state was running out of steam. Candichard was the favourite. His relative youth – he was ten years younger than Borel – his past as a captain of industry, his energetic bearing and his successes at the Foreign Ministry were seen as reassuring, and as evidence of a forward-looking outlook compared to the ageing, outmoded Borel. The leader of his party, Candichard had been able to build up a solid electoral base. Yet to everyone's astonishment, he had pulled out before even the first round. As a result, Borel, who had undergone a complete image makeover, had won the election and embarked on a second term in office.

"Some of my colleagues thought Candichard couldn't face the stresses of the campaign."

"Some kind of depression?"

"I never believed it. My contacts explained that Borel possessed information that could sink Candichard. And that this was thanks to Richard Gratien . . ."

Mister Africa, the ambassador who specialised in arms deals, was close to power, and therefore to the president.

"If I've understood correctly, all Borel's team had to do was threaten Candichard by waving Richard Gratien's notebooks under his nose."

"Gratien never denounced anyone to the press, Lola. We even wondered sometimes whether or not those notebooks really existed."

"Mars proved to the world that they did."

"And even though he'd been out of politics for such a long time, Candichard found he couldn't live with it."

The rumours had in fact never completely died out among a small circle. And the previous summer, Mars had launched his nuclear warhead, which had transformed the rumour into a certainty: during the 1994 campaign, Candichard had dipped into a pot of gold consisting of kickbacks from several weapons contracts.

"It took almost twenty years for Mars to strip Candichard of what little honour he had left," said Bianco. "Proof that the past never dies."

"The Chinese prefer to say that 'old sins have long shadows'."

"Nice."

There might still be a few witnesses to the fight for supremacy in 1994, but the main characters had both taken their bow. Paul Borel had preceded Candichard by a long chalk, dying of cancer a few months after the end of his second presidency, in 2001.

"Do you know what would be logical, Lola?"

"Tell me."

"For Gratien to use his notebooks to get out of jail by putting pressure on the right people."

"I thought they'd been confiscated when he was arrested."

"I no longer have a direct line to the gods."

"O.K., so we know Mars had a copy of them that he used against Candichard. Mars has been murdered. We can suppose that his killer was after those notebooks. If Gratien was behind it, he's got them back now, hasn't he?"

"That makes sense, Lola."

"Do you really think Gratien can wriggle his way out of this?"

"It's difficult, but not impossible. As always, it depends on exactly what the notebooks contain."

"A single extract was enough to do for Candichard."

"When it comes to financing, no parties and very few individuals are above suspicion. So Gratien has a bargaining chip. Especially as these are very different times from when Borel was in power."

"Why's that?"

"Things were simpler back then. A politician could drag around all kinds of baggage without it hampering him. Information didn't fly around like meteorites. The internet hadn't invaded our lives. Politicians had time to cook up a counter-attack."

"The gift of resurrection."

"Yes: they'd be thrown out of the door, and climb back in through the window. They could take very dubious decisions behind the scenes, but the main thing was to maintain a spotless façade."

"And all that's gone?"

"Nowadays our politicians are less robust. It's no longer enough to go all confessional in a T.V. interview deliberately set up to unburden you of your sins, make people weep in their country cottages, and win absolution all in one evening. If a politician stumbles, you can see his slip-up thousands of times on the net."

"So seeing the same catastrophe repeated so many times amplifies its effect . . ."

"I think so."

Bianco lit a cigarette and blew out the smoke with obvious pleasure. The former journalist missed the atmosphere of newsrooms and political headquarters. And Lola was stirring his nostalgia.

"Set fire to his reputation, and a politician dies like a butterfly," he said, screwing up his eyes in a cloud of smoke.

"And you find that moving."

"Almost."

"No; you find it *really* moving."

"That's probably because I'm growing old. Are you having lunch with us, Lola?"

Lola was as hungry as a horse, but felt like an intruder in this close-knit family.

"Thanks Armand, but let's make it some other time."

"Don't disappear for another twenty years, O.K.?"

8

David Bowie was singing "Life on Mars?" Back in her own neighbourhood, Lola was struggling to make it through the traffic to her garage. She spotted two familiar shapes on the pavement: Antoine Léger and Sigmund. The best shrink in Faubourg Saint-Denis liked taking his Dalmatian for a walk in the rain. She could have flashed her lights at them, but decided against it. Ever since Ingrid had left, Lola had found it hard to re-establish contact with the human race.

She finally managed to park in her space. She waited in the darkness for Bowie to finish, clambered out of her Twingo, took a detour via a frozen-food store and bought enough provisions to last a week. She was struggling with herself: forget everything and wait for spring to arrive, or leap into the eye of the storm before it caused havoc. She couldn't put her finger on it, but it felt as if something were not quite right.

Back in her apartment, she imagined herself in Sophie Bianco's shoes. A house with green shutters, the inviting aroma of Sunday lunch, loving, well brought-up children. No, that sort of life wasn't for her – no regrets.

She heated some food in the microwave, listened to the messages on her answering machine. Barthélemy, her former assistant, had called three times. "Boss, I'm getting worried. Ring me." Maxime, the owner of the Belles restaurant, inviting her to an evening tasting session of *terroir* wines. And Antoine wanted to get back in touch.

Going unnoticed was becoming an extreme sport.

Friends. She knew she would go back to them one day, but she needed a little while longer.

She lay on her bed with a biography of Winston Churchill. *It's good to be honest, but it's important to be right.* The famous Englishman had smoked tons of cigars, swigged gallons of whisky, lived a thousand lives and put more than one geopolitical theory to the test. She thought of Bianco and his view of politicians. Giants with feet of clay.

Churchill's attraction was his acute sense of self-mockery. An essential quality to avoid crumbling from the ground up.

Sacha had spent the afternoon interrogating a Japanese man who had slit the throats of a waitress, a cashier and a sous-chef who was an expert in the art of sushi. The suspect spoke only halting French, and refused to admit he had swung into action after many years of being a regular and peaceful customer at the Matsuri restaurant.

It not me. I not that person. It not me.

Things had become clearer when Sacha had called in an interpreter. The chance to express himself in his own language had blown the Japanese fellow up like a big balloon, and he started to confess to everything.

The food of words. The essence of childhood.

The interpreter was a beautiful woman with gentle eyes and thick, perfumed hair. When the statement was finished and the murderer was in his cell, she and Sacha stayed on for a while, their backs to the Seine. Her French was perfect, with just a hint of foreignness that made it charming.

"I've heard that police headquarters is moving."

"Yes, no more 36 quai des Orfèvres. We're off to Batignolles. Rue du Bastion."

"Does that make you sad?"

"No."

"That's good. Too much nostalgia is a bad idea."

"Are you hungry?"

He was running a risk. The young interpreter had spent hours listening to the confession of a man who had turned an agreeable restaurant into a waiting room of hell.

"Yes, a little."

They ate some snacks, drank quantities of Côtes-du-Rhône, chatted about their professions, their plans, and ended up back at his apartment on rue du Petit-Musc.

They made love rhythmically, their bodies sweating, finding satisfaction in one another and smiling between embraces. Maya had small breasts but erotic ideas as vast as the galaxy. Sacha even forgot the ghost of Mars standing beside the bed. He was clasping another human being, and could feel life warming him again. He had been cold in Africa.

9

She had dreamt that Churchill was asking her hand in marriage. They were both in military uniform, and were part of the army entertainment corps, like Jean Gabin and Marlene Dietrich. On this occasion, their job was to entertain the French troops stationed in Mali. Lola did a tap dance number, but Winston had rehearsed something far more audacious. He managed to shave off Hitler's moustache in a single sweep of a razor, singing all the while. All the spectators resembled Arnaud Mars.

Lola had fallen asleep still wearing her glasses, and with Churchill's biography on her chest. Somewhere in her apartment a window was banging. The wind was howling through the building's pipes.

She would have liked to be as nimble as the breeze so that she could sneak into every corner and see what people were up to. What was Hardy plotting? And the ballistic experts? Did they already have the results for the Abidjan bullet? What about Gratien? What was going through his mind as he sat buried in his cell? And Sacha, why had he gone off to play the hero in Africa? And what on earth was Ingrid doing in that cardboard city in Yankeeland?

Lola got up. A window in the living room was wide open. Had she opened it for some fresh air and forgotten to shut it again when she went to bed? She couldn't remember. The rain had wet her jigsaw puzzle, so she wiped it with a cloth. A few dozen more pieces and the Corcovado would be complete. She finished the hull of a yacht, leaned out of the window. It was still dark, but a few pedestrians were already walking up and down rue du Faubourg Saint-Denis. The metro was running.

Some stale bits of toast, a shrivelled apple, a cup of coffee, and she settled into her wing-chair. The nagging worry that had bothered her the night before had not gone away. The missing detail. She thought of a technique she had often used on suspects in her days as commissaire. She would ask them to repeat their story, but backwards this time. A simple way to detect any weakness in their alibis.

She closed her eyes, and went through the previous day's events in reverse. She left the garage, out of the car park, learned that Candichard had been sidelined from politics by Borel with Gratien's help, rang Bianco's doorbell . . .

No, she was going too fast. She slowed the film down, trying to remember everything in greater detail. The words, the circumstances, the sensation of the wind and rain on her skin, the sounds of the city, her uncontrolled, fleeting thoughts. Now she was on the quai de Montebello.

She rewound further back, crossed the Saint-Michel bridge, went into police headquarters, climbed the old linoleum-covered staircase, found Sacha in his office. He had the habit of pinning the photographs of the cases he was involved in on a corkboard. *We have plenty of work, and that's exactly what I need.*

The cardboard file was on his desk. He had only opened it when she asked to see the photographs from the crime scene in Abidjan. There was a sharp contrast between the board covered in images and the closed file with a cloth ribbon round it. She saw him slowly undoing the knot, laying out the photographs.

Death on a roof. Abidjan after the monsoon. A shipwrecked life.

She stopped the reel on Sacha's face. It wasn't sadness she had seen there.

It was something else.

When she had mentioned how stubborn he was, he had turned his head and gone over to the open window. *You knew Mars best, Sacha. And yet despite all the information you had and despite your stubbornness, you didn't manage to find him.*

At the time she had thought he was being discreet, that he didn't want her to see how upset he was. But now she thought otherwise. What if he hadn't wanted her to see the expression on his face? She had finally pinpointed the detail that had troubled her so much. That light-as-a-feather moment. A simple gesture. He had avoided her.

He had escaped.

It was a quarter to six in the morning. She dressed in a hurry. If she could question Sacha at home rather than at police headquarters, she would stand more chance of getting answers.

*

He was listening to Maya's breathing. Soft and regular. And was Maya soft? *Don't confuse manners with the woman underneath*, he told himself. He had glimpsed her hard edge. She had a plan. She would marry a Frenchman, someone with a good upbringing and a healthy bank balance, and there would be no children. She had a vocation: there was no question of her being an interpreter forever. She wanted to write, and her literary talent wouldn't be held back by everyday commitments. She had confided some of this to him (nothing serious, he didn't possess the required social status) and he had guessed the rest.

He raised himself on one elbow and watched her sleeping. She was pretty, but she was already calculating like a wily businessman.

He stretched out again, listening to the city. The wind had died down, there was not much traffic. At a guess it must be six o'clock. He thought of the mornings he had woken up next to Ingrid. She was softness itself, from head to toe. Her desire to give, her imperfect French. Her incredible way of dressing. And that even more incredible way she had of undressing in the Pigalle cabaret, in front of her raving fans. He missed her when he was on his own. And even more when he wasn't.

He started up. The doorbell ringing incessantly. He pulled on a pair of jeans.

"The G.I.P.! OPEN UP!"

He did as he was told. A bearded young guy and a massive forty-something with a squashed nose threw him to the floor. They handcuffed him. A pair of loafers appeared level with his face.

"Search the place."

Hardy's voice. Sacha was hauled back to his feet.

"What are you playing at?"

"Shut it."

Maya appeared, already dressed. The giant with the bulbous nose stopped his search to give her the once-over. She didn't lose her cool.

"What has he done?"

"And you are?" asked Hardy.

"Maya Murata. Japanese interpreter. Are you the police?"

"So it seems."

"But so is he."

"We're the police's police," said Big Nose. "So we win."

"I've done nothing wrong, and my papers are in order, your honour. I barely know this man. We've only spent the night together."

"I believe you," said Hardy. "Now clear out."

Maya left, casting a furtive glance back at Sacha. He smiled at her; she remained as cold as marble. He heard the door slam behind her. The end of another great love story.

"Found it, boss," said the bearded cop.

He was waving a plastic bag.

And my Smith & Wesson is in it, Sacha could tell. He turned towards Hardy. His eyes were glinting with triumph.

"Remember that little ass that's just left here," sniggered Big Nose. "Because you're not likely to get your hands on another one any time soon."

Lola was listening to her car radio, waiting for a more respectable time. Marc Bolan and the impeccable "Hot Love". Ingrid had danced a wild number to that music. The customers at the Calypso had all sung the refrain in unison, at the tops of their voices.

She saw four men leave the building.

Sacha. Hardy. Sacha's arms were behind his back.

She got out of her car.

"Captain . . ."

"Madame Jost. What are you doing here?"

She thought it best to play it cool, as it seemed Sacha was doing.

"Nothing special. Commandant Duguin is a friend."

"I don't often turn up at my friends' houses at first light," laughed a big ugly guy whose nose seemed to have been through a mangle.

Lola took Hardy by the arm.

"I think I'm owed an explanation. You interrogated me for hours, and I laid all my cards on the table."

Hardy signalled to his men to put Sacha in the patrol car.

"He's not the man you think he is, Madame Jost. He manipulated his team. You included. He did find Mars in Africa."

"He swears he didn't. And I believe him."

"The bullet that killed Mars was fired from Sacha Duguin's service revolver."

Impossible. Hardy was bluffing. He had nothing. He escorted Lola over to a public bench, made her sit down.

"Would you like some water?"

Would he ever stop trying to get her to drink? She studied his face. He was enjoying a little private celebration. As for her, the truth hit her like a rock. As hard as flint.

"You knew about the ballistics, Hardy."

"Excuse me?"

"When you questioned me you already had the results . . ."

She recalled her conversation with Thomas Franklin at the mortuary. *Odd the results aren't already here.* In fact, Hardy had got them from the lab before he had visited her. He had known it was Sacha's weapon. And wanted to confirm the evidence as quickly as possible.

So that Sacha wouldn't have time to ask me for help. Because I'm the only one he has left.

His colleagues would never have risked their positions for him, not with all the rumours flying around about him. And now my statement is there in black-and-white for the G.I.P. There's nothing I can do to get him out.

"Bravo, madame, I see your reputation is justified. But you're wrong to get so worked up about it. Especially for someone who isn't worth the trouble."

A tinted windscreen. She couldn't see Sacha. She couldn't see anything anymore.

Mars, you're making us dance in a hurricane.

"Don't get any further involved: is that clear?"

He left her on the bench. The car disappeared, beacon flashing, at the end of the street.

She found her Twingo, and automatically switched on the ignition. The car radio came on. She cut the engine with a trembling hand. She had no idea where to go.

Hardy was a nasty piece of work who used underhand methods, but he couldn't reinvent reality.

The revolver was Sacha's.

She remembered his simmering anger before he left for Africa. He was mortified, his honour red-raw.

Gratien's wife, under arrest and in his charge, had been shot. Mars was responsible, but it was Sacha who had taken the blame. A silent blame. His colleagues thought he had worked for months on the orders of a dangerous madman and had not seen any of it coming. An unforgivable mistake for a commandant in the Criminal Investigation Bureau.

She felt angry because she could see it from Hardy's point of view.

Being a cop was like riding a bike: you never forget. It all added up. Sacha's possible presence in Abidjan when the crime had been committed. His weapon. And his stubbornness. The tenacity that was the source of his talent, that had now pushed him onto the roller-coaster of disaster.

And his rage. I'm not chasing after you to shoot you in the back. On the contrary, we're face to face. You're on the ground, I'm standing over you, dominating you, enjoying your terror. The notebooks mean nothing, it's you I want.

Looking him in the eye.

Sacha, one of the most brilliant cops she had ever known, one of the most unpredictable.

What have you done, my friend?

Tears began to course down her cheeks. She wiped them away with her sleeve.

Ingrid is going to stay in America. And now Sacha's been taken from me.

The sound of something bouncing off the car roof. Hailstones. It sounded like the end of the world.

From rain to hail. The sky gave her an idea. When everything goes wrong, there are only two ways out. Shut up shop, or go for broke.

Her mobile was on the passenger seat. There was one person who appreciated her so much he would do anything for her. She called Captain Jérôme Barthélemy.

10 THURSDAY, 17 JANUARY

Five in the morning. Bad dreams, a feverish night. The paracetamol box was empty, her body was screaming that there was a crisis she couldn't understand. She called the same number a fourth time.

He picked up at last. His voice was a murmur.

"Hello? Lola?"

"You owe me an explanation, Sacha."

Silence, and the sound of his breathing. What was he waiting for? There was no time . . .

"I lied."

Lola clenched her fist.

"I did find Mars in Abidjan. He was planning to use Gratien's notebooks."

"Against whom?"

"He didn't want to tell me."

"That doesn't make sense."

"Yes it does. To protect me. But I didn't kill him, Lola. And I left my Smith & Wesson in Paris."

"Was your apartment door forced?"

"No."

"You were followed as far as Africa."

"I must have been."

If anyone could have found him, it was you, Sacha. Lola heard voices. Her heart sank to her knees.

"Joseph Berlin, Lola. You have to—"

The call was cut off. Lola buried her head in her hands. After a few moments, she forced herself to control her emotions. The conversation had been too brief, but it was better than nothing. Barthélemy had done a good job. He had managed to get into the G.I.P. building and slip Sacha a mobile.

Her own phone rang. Barthélemy.

"Hello, boss? Did you get through?"

"Sacha swears it's not him."

"I've never doubted it. You choose your friends well."

"He thinks he was followed. Mars wanted to use Gratien's note-books again."

"Is that why he was killed?"

"Possibly. How did Sacha seem to you?"

"Tired, but combative. I only saw him for a couple of seconds before I cleared off. He's counting on you to get him out."

A heavy responsibility. She could hear Franklin the pathologist in his butcher's apron: *You're a real laugh. You're going to take on the G.I.P. single-handed?*

"But I think he's being selfish, boss."

"How's that?"

"The guys who despatched Mars are rats, but they're efficient rats. And you are the age you are, boss. Sorry, but it's true."

"I've no intention of joining Mars in cop paradise for the time being, Jérôme. I'll make sure I take my gun whenever I go out."

"It'd be better if you didn't go out at all."

"Old doesn't mean obsolete, you hear me?"

"True enough, but . . ."

Does the name Joseph Berlin mean anything to you?"

"No . . ."

"Could you search for any possible link between him and Mars?"

"I'll get on to it straightaway."

"Thanks."

"You're all worked up, but basically you have no idea what to do, do you, boss?"

"You're right . . . apart from getting him a good lawyer . . ."

This gun business stank to high heaven. Sacha swore his Smith & Wesson hadn't left Paris, and yet that was the revolver used to shoot Mars. Sacha had found Mars in Africa. If he carried on lying about that to the G.I.P., he would only make things worse for himself. Hardy could find witnesses, and prove Sacha was committing perjury.

"I need to think, Jérôme. Let's stay in touch."

"If you need anything, I'll be here."

He had taken a huge risk for her. Barthélemy had his whole career ahead of him; she mustn't let Sacha's problems drag him down too.

She hung up and made herself a strong coffee. Sacha had reached the same conclusion as she had. Somebody was trying to pin Mars' murder on him – and very cleverly so far. Sacha was on his own. With only a battered ex-commissaire to count on. *You are the age you are, boss.*

Yes, she really did need to think.

Joseph Berlin.

She could wait for Barthélemy to get back to her. Yes, but no. Waiting was counterproductive. She had to keep going.

Searching on the net, she found a thousand articles about someone called Josef Berling, a Swedish footballer being courted by the best clubs on the planet. She went through the list of Sacha's colleagues who could possibly help her. The only one was Clémenti. A C.I.B.

commissaire who was both efficient and discreet. And had been a friend of Mars. But could she trust him?

11

The phone rang just as she was leaving. She hesitated about going back. It had taken all her diplomatic skills to convince the police headquarters secretary to tell Clémenti. *Come early, he might agree to see you before he leaves on a case.*

She picked up. Armand Bianco.

"Is your computer on, Lola?"

"No."

"Look at your emails. Right now."

He had sent her a video. Two journalists who had been celebrities in the '90s were interviewing President Borel. Smiling, looking relaxed but switched on, Borel was explaining that he liked Johann Sebastian Bach as much as the new French singers.

"What about it?"

"Look in the first row of the audience. The little tousled-haired fellow decked out in a scarf the size of a flag. His round glasses make him look like an owl."

"Who is he?"

"Gildas Sénéchal. He might look like a floor-mop, but he's a genius."

"An unknown genius."

"Sénéchal has only ever displayed his talents in the shadows of the corridors of power. Borel's re-election was thanks to him."

"I thought it was thanks to Gratien's notebooks."

"Yes, Gratien fired the final bullet that finished Candichard off. But even without it, Borel would have crushed him. Watch the film to the end."

She listened to the president charming the two media stars and several million voters.

"Can you see what's happening, Lola?"

"No."

"Isn't Borel wonderful? Isn't his performance remarkable?"

"Bianco, I adore you, but I've got to see someone . . ."

"Sénéchal was the facelift king. Throughout his first term, Paul Borel looked old-fashioned, fossilised, too prudent, not to say lifeless. Sénéchal turned him into a wily old sage, methodical and lofty, but ready to listen to his country's youth. Borel secretly loved the French: Sénéchal made him tell them so. Borel was seen as lacking in culture: Sénéchal made him drop his natural reserve and flaunt his impressive knowledge of music and the theatre. I must admit I've always admired the little fellow. Before he came on the scene, the journalists would demand interviews with the head of state. He changed the equation. The president summoned them, chose not only where but who he would speak to, even the setting that would most suit his message. Sénéchal employed a leading lighting expert to sculpt the presidential head and make it look majestic. He thought – quite rightly for those days – that television was all that mattered; he'd even created an ultra-modern studio in the presidential palace. Nothing was left to chance . . ."

Bianco added that the great spin doctor had spent a fortune on opinion polls. And personally watched focus groups on a control screen while they were being scientifically questioned.

"He took France's pulse continuously. And only advised the president when he had well-founded arguments. Meticulous, our Sénéchal."

Lola wished Bianco would get to the point. Clémenti wouldn't wait forever.

"All of which means what?"

"Sénéchal was a friend of Mars."

"A friend or a professional acquaintance?"

"A friend. I remember I used to see them in the politicians' favourite watering-holes. Good food, excellent wines, conversations they both seemed enchanted with. Which was no small thing, because Gildas Sénéchal is not the sort to waste his time. I don't know if this is any use to you."

"Mmm, nor do I."

"I'm sorry, that's all I have for the moment."

She thanked him, put on a pair of loafers that did nothing for her silhouette but allowed her to get a move on. The metro platform was crowded, and the carriage smelled of stressful mornings. She thought about the relationship between the president's media expert and the divisionnaire. Part of Mars' career had been in embassies, so he had a natural link to the world of politics. He was reputed to have had an incredible contacts book.

The train was stuck for several minutes "due to an incident with a passenger". She cursed herself for having answered Bianco's call.

Ten minutes late. She tried a quick sprint, but felt her heart and legs protest.

The turbulent Seine was crashing against the quai des Orfèvres. The security screening. An off-hand attendant. She presented her credentials, desperate to be let through, rushed along the corridor, climbed the imposing staircase with its worn-out linoleum, and burst into the C.I.B. unit pouring with sweat. A youngster informed her that the commissaire and his team had just gone out to the car park. Stifling a curse, Lola leapt back down the staircase, and out into the car park. Her lungs were like two arthritic elephant seals.

Clémenti was poring over a route map spread out on the bonnet of a police Renault. He raised his head and gave her a warm smile, then took her a few metres to one side. He plainly did not want his men to overhear their conversation.

"Serge, I need info. To help Sacha. So tell me straightaway if I'm making a mistake talking to you."

A look of irritation in his grey eyes. Angry at the suggestion.

"Can you see me tipping off the G.I.P.?"

"I wouldn't have thought so."

"He might have killed Mars. It's his revolver. But his position is as clear as the Civil Code. A man is considered innocent until proven guilty."

"Good for you!"

She explained what Sacha had told her.

"He claims he left his gun in Paris. Somebody used it in his place."

Clémenti looked as if he wasn't swallowing this for a second, but Lola didn't give up.

"Sacha swears he didn't kill Mars. I believe him. I'd like to know where he kept his gun when he didn't have it on him. In his office?"

"He often used to leave his revolver in a drawer, until one day a suspect broke into it. There was almost a massacre. After that, he either wore it in a shoulder holster or kept it at home when he didn't need to be armed."

"So before he went off to Africa, he left his revolver in his apartment on rue du Petit-Musc."

"In theory. But it was definitely his gun that killed Mars."

"Someone could have smuggled his Smith & Wesson to Africa."

"Possibly, but I never heard any mention of a break-in at Sacha's. And the G.I.P. found his revolver there in the search after his arrest."

Lola found it hard to conceal her frustration. She had imagined the service revolver being left in Sacha's office at police headquarters, where it could be easily "borrowed" by someone determined enough. Clémenti had just scrubbed that possibility.

"Do you know how he travelled to Africa?"

"The most discreet way would have been by boat, but he took a plane."

"Did he tell you that?"

"No, I overheard a rather heated discussion he had with the new divisionnaire. Our superiors weren't exactly happy that Sacha dropped everything to rush off to Africa, even for his summer vacation. I remembered afterwards that I'd seen an e-ticket on his desk. For Kinshasa. I was keeping my eye on him. The Mars affair had got to him. I was afraid he might do something he would regret."

She could hear him thinking: *Something like he in fact did.*

"Did you mention the e-ticket to Hardy?"

"Yes. There was no reason for me to keep it from him. When Sacha returned, he made no secret of the fact that he'd gone looking for Mars."

She asked about Joseph Berlin.

"He used to be another of Mars' closest associates."

"Used to be?"

"The last time I saw him he had harsh words to say about the divisionnaire."

"A cop?"

"No, retired from the intelligence services. More of a pen-pusher."

The Central Bureau of National Security. That was all they needed: a spook in the works.

"Sacha mentioned Berlin's name. It's important."

"I don't know anything more, Lola."

"Can you put me in contact with him?"

"No, I'm sorry."

"Why?"

"That guy will drive himself mad, if he hasn't already. He's paranoid. I don't want anything to do with him."

He turned towards his team. The two men were showing signs of increasing impatience.

"You ought to put your trust in justice, Lola."

"You know Hardy."

"Hardy is only a link in the chain. Justice itself is impartial. Don't give up hope."

She watched him walk off. He was an experienced, honest officer. And he was wagering that Sacha was guilty.

She left the police headquarters, walked to Châtelet, went into the first café, and ordered a large glass of white. It was a ridiculous time of day, but so what: retirement was more dangerous than wine. Paradoxically, Clémenti's attitude acted as a spur. It was obvious that Sacha really did need her. His supporters at police headquarters were thin on the ground, if not non-existent.

Her mobile. Barthélemy.

"Hello, boss?"

"What's new?"

"Joseph Berlin – C.B.N.S."

"I know, I've just seen Clémenti."

"You're dashing about all over the place. Make sure you don't overdo it."

"My heart's in good shape."

"I've got Berlin's address. And a telephone number."

She jotted them down. Mars' friend lived in the 16th arrondissement.

"He worked for a while under the command of a legend."

"Who's that?"

"A fellow who it seems had brilliant intuition. And who pursued his ideas to the limit. Someone like you . . ."

"You can shine my shoes some other time, my lad. Get to the point, will you?"

"Berlin's boss was called Yann Rainier. Rainier like the old prince of Monaco, the one with Grace Kelly . . . An easy name to remember . . ."

Barthélemy's explanations were always valuable, but you had to have your whole life ahead of you to get through them. Lola choked back her impatience.

". . . this Rainier was a specialist in Islamic terrorism, especially small groups in Africa. So it suddenly occurred to me that this spook could possibly be linked to Mars because Mars had been head of security in various embassies there."

"That's an interesting link. And?"

"No luck. Yann Rainier is no longer active."

"I suppose he's retired as well?"

"No, a massive stroke sidelined him. My contact said he's a vegetable these days. For the past ten years, apparently."

"O.K., thanks, that's enough for now about Berlin and his legendary vegetable. Tell me, do you have any contacts at Roissy?"

"I sort of know a lieutenant who works for the airport commissaire."

"Could you do something for me?"

"You don't even have to ask, boss."

12

Above the Seine, a luminous gap in the clouds lifted her spirits. She called Joseph Berlin, explained that she was a friend of Sacha Duguin and was after information on the Mars affair.

"To what end, madame?"

A steady, calm voice.

"Let's meet to talk about it. I imagine you have the time. You're retired, aren't you? So am I, from the police force."

"My, I see you've done your homework."

Lola was afraid he was going to hang up on her.

"Hello? Monsieur Berlin?"

"Still here. If you have my phone number, you must also have my address."

"That's right."

"My place, in an hour."

He told her the entrance code and abruptly put the phone down on her.

Tetchy, the old coot. Lola smiled as she took another mouthful of white wine. It was like in the good old days, when a case lent colour to humdrum routine. Her mobile interrupted her thoughts; she replied without checking who was calling. A voice she knew well put a broad smile on her face.

"*What the fuck?! Why didn't you tell me?*"

"Yes, that's right, it's good to hear you too, Ingrid. How's the weather in Las Vegas?"

"It's night-time, Lola."

"Oh yes, so it is."

"Sacha's been arrested and that's all you have to talk?"

Ingrid and the French language. A passionate but thwarted love affair.

"Yes, that's all I've got to say. Who did tell you?"

"Barthélemy. He's worried about you. You're on a solo mission attacking the cops' cop. It's totally crazy."

"At the moment I'm not attacking anybody. I'm thinking."

"It's the same. Tell me . . ."

"I thought Barthélemy had spilled the beans."

"Your words are more comprehensive than his."

Oh yes, comprehensible. Lola launched into a detailed account. This was punctuated at regular intervals by foul expletives at the far end of the line. Ah, Ingrid, her energy, her angelic face and her inimitable vocabulary, like a character from Shakespeare.

Music was playing in the background, and there was the sound of voices. Some fellow was talking into a microphone. Was her American friend calling between two numbers of French cancan, Las Vegas style?

"It's a juridical mistake!"

"Judicial, sweetheart."

"Lola, you can't do this all on your own."

"You're not the first to insist on that, but it doesn't change a thing."

"It can't be just you on one side and a pyramid of idiots on the other."

"You've no reason to worry about me."

"Go and see Commissaire Clémenti. He'll carry out a good anti-attack."

"Serge Clémenti isn't going to mount any counter-attack. May I remind you he has a hard enough job as it is. And he's not even convinced that Sacha is innocent."

"Really?"

"Yes, really."

"I see . . ."

Ingrid knew as well as she did how serious Clémenti was about his work, and was beginning to grasp the true scale of the problem.

"Lola, I have to go. The show's about to start. But promise me . . ."

"What?"

"That you won't do anything dangerous by hurrying yourself."

"I've no intention of pushing up the daisies."

"What? What daisies?"

"Nothing, never mind. Forget it."

"You don't have the death penalty in France, do you?"

"Why do you say that?"

"I mean, there's no risk of Sacha being exterminated by the French Republic. You have the time to prove he's irresponsible."

"Innocent, do you mean?"

"You know very well what I mean."

"You don't get it. In a criminal investigation it's a question of rhythm. Just like in your dances."

"Are you sure you're O.K., Lola?"

"Better than when I'm bored out of my skull at home in my dressing gown. And before you interrupt me again, I was talking about rhythm. Something is about to happen, I can feel it. This is no time to take things easy."

"Lola, come on!"

"Each of us does what they like on their own side of the Atlantic. I don't poke my nose into what you're getting up to with your giraffe friends."

"What giraffes?"

"Give Las Vegas a kiss from me."

Time to put an end to Ingrid's protests by hanging up. People changed, and not for the better. There was a time when her American friend would have moved mountains for Sacha.

Lola realised she had forgotten to mention the Saint-Michel video. She would send her an email at some point. She swallowed the last of the wine, then studied her metro map.

13

Joseph Berlin's building on rue du Commerce had a garage on the ground floor, and several levels of parking. Berlin lived on the third floor, apartment 34. The lift wasn't working. Lola did her impression of an asthmatic buffalo as she toiled up a staircase smelling suspiciously of leaking gas.

She pressed the bell repeatedly, but with no luck. She checked the time, tapped his number into her mobile, heard it ring on the far side of the door, then heard the laconic message on the answering machine: "This is Berlin. I'm listening."

The white wine at Châtelet had put her in a good mood, and so she waited happily enough for the ex-spy to arrive. Besides, did the idea of an ex-spy make any sense? She was an ex-commissaire who couldn't get over it. So she was still a cop. She couldn't give a damn about official papers, the office, paper-clips, the photocopier, or welcome or farewell drinks. What remained was the sensation. The enduring power of that sensation. Her thoughts were regularly interrupted by the distant roar of a pneumatic drill. Paris, a city always on the move.

Half an hour later, she faced facts: Joseph Berlin had been held up by some problem or other. Or he was completely shameless. She scribbled a note asking him to call her, and was about to slip it under his door when she noticed it was open. She entered a mustard-coloured studio that was simply but elegantly furnished. And kept meticulously clean. The light was on, the blinds drawn. A stack of newspapers and a switched-on computer on the desk. Four Beethoven C.D.s on the stereo system. She inserted the top one. His "Appassionata", played by Schnabel.

She felt feverish again. She found aspirin in the medicine cabinet, an open bottle of Sauvignon in the fridge. She poured herself a glass and took two pills. After enjoying Beethoven's virile melancholy for a while, she decided to search the place.

Slim pickings. Nothing mentioning Mars, Sacha, or any professional activity – with the C.B.N.S. or anywhere else. What she did learn was that Berlin was an obsessive who not only left people high and dry but ironed his underpants and his socks. And cleaned his fridge with vinegar.

The party was over: she left the apartment, slamming the door behind her.

Her mobile rang as she was going downstairs. Barthélemy, not best pleased. In short, his colleague at the airport had refused to give him any information. He wanted Lola to go there in person.

"Sorry, boss."

Leaving the building, she saw the passers-by looking up to the sky, as thrilled as young kids: it was snowing in Paris. Big snowflakes, coming down thickly.

In the metro she felt too hot. The Sauvignon was playing games with her stomach. She thought of Yann Rainier. He had a prince's name, but had been laid low by a massive stroke. Perhaps it was time to pay her doctor a visit?

The world had changed. The steps at her metro station and the streets all around had a thick covering of white. Behind the snowy veil, the Porte Saint-Denis was a sketchy outline.

The lock on her front door had been smashed.

Panic, a poisonous flower always ready to bloom. She swallowed fear with her saliva. Her apartment had been searched. She thought of her ancient Manurhin pistol in the sideboard drawer, and crept silently into her living room. Empty, freezing cold. The window wide open. She rushed across the room, searched in the drawer.

"Is this what you're looking for?"

An unmistakable voice behind her. She turned round and finally discovered what he looked like. A face with chiselled features, the eyes of a husky, grey-blond hair short enough to reveal a torn right ear. He was wearing a navy-blue loden buttoned up to the neck. And was pointing her Manurhin straight at her.

Joseph Berlin: an elegant name for someone who looked every inch a killer.

They studied each other, two bookends in a freezing room. She turned away to look at something that shouldn't have been there: a portable computer sitting on the unfinished part of the Corcovado.

"My third eye," he explained.

Vapour was coming from his mouth. The wind was rattling the window shutters. Turning the computer towards her, he pressed a few keys. Lola saw herself searching the studio on rue du Commerce.

"So that you know who you're dealing with?"

"You don't behave like an old age pensioner."

"I can return the compliment."

She regretted having slammed his door. She should have left his studio open to attract any passing burglars.

He seated himself in the wing-chair. Crossed his legs. His expression was neutral, his body relaxed, but the gun was still pointed in her direction. Apparently aimed at her skull. *That guy will drive himself mad, if he hasn't already. He's paranoid. I don't want anything to do with him.* Serge Clémenti had been right. Lola's stomach was grumbling. The Sauvignon again, or her guest's manners?

"What would you like to know?"

"First of all, the nature of your relationship with Sacha Duguin."

"There's no reason to train a gun on me for that."

"I want the facts, not your comments."

She told him about her relationship with Sacha, in no particular order, although she included more or less everything. And yet he stared at her as if she was making no sense. He interrupted her when she was describing how Hardy had arrested Sacha. He put his first finger to his lips. She heard the safety catch of the Manurhin being flicked off. *I'm finally going to cop paradise, Barthélemy my old friend.*

"Look, Berlin, I've nothing against you . . ."

"I said: Silence."

An explosion. Lola gave a strangled cry. The bullet smashed into the sideboard. She remembered the motorbike rider who had spared Ingrid at the last moment. Could these two bastards be one and the same?

"IS THIS SOMETHING THE C.B.N.S. HAS DREAMT UP? TELL ME."

"What are you talking about?"

"You're spying on me for them."

"I've never had anything to do with the C.B.N.S. I was a local neighbourhood commissaire."

"Pull the other one. They're past masters at infiltration."

"I'd never work for Hardy. Not if they paid me a fortune."

"You expect me to believe you're kicking off your bedroom slippers for that little asshole Duguin?"

"Yes, and I don't see why that should astonish you."

"He killed my friend."

"That remains to be proved."

"And you thought I was going to help you?"

"Not anymore."

One corner of Berlin's mouth twitched in a smile. He emptied the revolver, and dropped it on the table. He watched the snow falling for a couple of seconds, stowed his computer in his briefcase. She briefly thought of snatching it from him and hitting him over the head with it, but her arms and legs wouldn't respond. She stared after him as he walked out.

"It was either the sideboard or the television. I chose the sideboard, but an exploding telly is always worth seeing. So keep on watching your series, and downing the plonk. And don't come sniffing round my door again."

His footsteps on the stairs. The front door clicking shut. The shutters banging against the wall outside her window. Her teeth were chattering. Snow was whirling round the Corcovado.

Why on earth did you send me to talk to that psycho, Sacha?

A few minutes later, her front doorbell rang.

"I heard an explosion. Are you alright, Madame Jost?" asked her upstairs neighbour.

She announced that she had been burgled, invented some story about a badly closed pressure-cooker, and got a dubious stare in return. She calmed him down by telephoning then and there for a locksmith to come as soon as he could.

The bill would be steep. She felt her forehead. The fever was gaining ground.

14

The days that followed seemed to last for years. The diagnosis: gastro-enteritis.

She ran out of medicine, but didn't have the strength to go out. The apartment had been turned upside down and smelled of rotting bear. No question of asking for help. Attila Berlin had poured kerosene on her old anger and frustration. The flames mixed with her fever and spread like wildfire. Bad dreams interspersed with flashes of lucidity. Sacha tortured by Hardy and Gratien in tandem; Ingrid covered in blood-red feathers dancing and trampling on their friendship and the happy moments they had shared. During her lucid intervals, Lola tried to devise a strategy that might pull her out of her torpor. Her nightmares stood more chance of getting somewhere than reality did.

The snow was still falling joyously. From her bed, Lola watched the immaculate layer piling up on the balustrade outside. She couldn't remember weather like this in Paris, except perhaps in her distant childhood.

Basically, you have no idea what to do, do you, boss?

Barthélemy's piercing voice in the midst of others. The ringing telephone also put in its pennyworth, the old fellow living upstairs vacuumed his floors, and Joseph Berlin smiled out of the corner of his mouth. *Don't come sniffing round my door again.* Paranoid or not, the bastard would get his comeuppance some day.

15 TUESDAY, 22 JANUARY

The snow still lay thickly, but her virus had packed up its circus tent. The telephone was going crazy. Then the bell, and finally someone pounding on her door. Someone who knew the code to get into the building. Barthélemy? A friendly neighbour? She dragged herself to the door.

"LOLA! OPEN THE FUCKING DOOR!"

She couldn't contain her joy. Decked out gloriously as the ace of spades, Ingrid stood outside on the landing. Mademoiselle Diesel, her blonde locks like short lamb's tails, pink-cheeked from the cold or because she was so worked up. A suitcase at her feet. Mademoiselle Diesel alive and kicking, even more splendid than before, in spite of her frown and her Martian disguise. Lola's rancour melted like an ice cube in a microwave.

Her American friend demanded an explanation. She aired the rooms, rushed to the corner shop and the pharmacy, heated some vegetable stock and tidied up. Between two bouts of cleaning, she explained she had managed to force her employer to give her some leave.

"Sacha needs me. And so do you."

"It's possible."

Ingrid embarked on a vigorous massage. One of her irresistible Japanese–Thai–Californian specials that brought life back to your carcass and your brain. It made you croon like a seal, purr like a lioness, plunge under, return to the surface. Lola hadn't felt so good in centuries.

"Goodness gracious, you haven't lost your touch!"

"Nor have you. That incredible talent of yours for getting into trouble."

"Possibly. And I haven't the faintest idea what I should do next."

"Take a shower, to begin with. I've met jackals that smelled better than you do."

Ingrid raised her eyes to the heavens. Lola went off to sing in the shower. When she came back from scraping off the dirt, she found her friend leaning over the Corcovado. She fitted in well. In her shimmering slimline trousers, her green leather fringed jacket and red cowboy boots, the long-legged American looked as if she had just stepped out of the Rio carnival.

"Is it hard?"

"I'm a black belt at jigsaw puzzles. I'll get there."

"I was thinking on the plane."

Lola saw her pull out a key. The key to Sacha's apartment that she had forgotten to give back.

"We'll take your car. I'll drive. Do you have crampons on your tyres?"

"No, no studs. We don't often get avalanches in Paris."

While they were driving to rue du Petit-Musc, Ingrid recalled that some journalists had turned up at Sacha's place. She had been there, waiting for him like a sailor's wife while he was off playing the fool in Africa. One of those so-called reporters could have obtained a fake press card.

"Are you talking about something you definitely remember?" asked Lola.

"No, I saw quite a few people who asked intelligent questions. They often came in pairs: a journalist and a photographer. One of them could have taken the Smith & Wesson while I had my back turned."

"Are you telling me Sacha's revolver was there while he was pursuing Mars in Africa?"

"I searched the place a bit. I wanted to know where he was . . ."

"Don't apologise. I would have done the same. Tell me if you saw his gun."

"Yes. In a wooden box kept in his desk drawer."

"Are you sure it was the Smith & Wesson?"

"Yes, I wouldn't have confused it with any other make. Sacha told me it was his favourite weapon, although most of his colleagues preferred something less bulky."

"What then?"

"Then nothing. I forgot about it. I can testify to a judge, if need be."

"Save your breath. Nobody will believe us: we're known as the Sacha Duguin Fan Club."

Ingrid parked adroitly, and studied Sacha's building. In the nearby square, some kids had made a snowman, and their joy was a pleasure to behold.

"Paris looks like Montreal, Lola."

"Yes, that's possible. By the way, what's Las Vegas like?"

"The sun shines almost all the year round. And the Mojave desert is one of the driest in the States. At the moment it's windy, very windy."

"Fantastic."

"You ought to come."

"I'm scared of planes. And deserts."

"Of the wind as well?"

The apartment had not been broken into, but Hardy and his minions had made a real mess. Ingrid wandered round the apartment, pressed her forehead against the picture window. The view was not the worst in Paris.

"If it's him, I might as well throw myself out, because it would mean I've never understood a thing about people. Ever."

She picked up the remote and switched on the stereo system. A C.D. was still in the player: before he had been hauled off by Hardy, Sacha had been listening to Aretha Franklin. Ingrid launched into a dance step, headed for the bedroom, paused for a moment. The two women exchanged smiles.

Lola listened to the answering machine. The last message was from March 15. Someone from the police union was returning Sacha's call, and was asking him to call back so that they could discuss his problems and find a solution.

"Go and question the neighbours," suggested Lola. "If a bogus journalist came with the key while you were away, someone might have run into him."

Ingrid left at once. Yet again, Lola admired her energy and determination. She herself took a few grams of it just by breathing the same air. Quick, look round the apartment. Two crumpled pillows on the unmade bed. She sniffed one of them. Sacha's cologne. She picked up the other one. A perfume that evoked a stroll through a forest of damp bamboo. Sacha wasn't living the life of a monk.

No computer: the Hardy boys must have taken it. The desk drawers had been forced open. She found ammunition: 9 mm Parabellum bullets. A cardboard box that she opened. Full of photos: Sacha's parents probably. And a strip from a photo booth. Sacha with Ingrid. Beautiful and serious at first, then dissolving into a funny faces competition. Hilarious. But what a waste. Lola sighed and began to tidy up.

By the time Ingrid came back, the apartment had been returned to a civilised state

"The neighbours didn't notice anything, Lola. Except for Sacha being arrested by the G.I.P."

They sat side by side on the couch. Ingrid rested her long, shiny legs with their garish footwear on the glass coffee table. She smiled as she examined the photo-booth pictures, put them in her pocket.

"Somebody could have stolen the keys at Passage du Désir, Lola."

That was plausible. Until the previous summer, Ingrid was living a few metres from Canal Saint-Martin, in a renovated ground-floor workshop. She used it as a massage parlour: Lola's American friend was a massage artist by day and a striptease artiste at the Calypso, in Pigalle by night Her massage clients waited in the living room, which was open to any passer-by.

"Do you remember any client in particular?"

"No. And if the key was 'borrowed', it was cleverly done."

"O.K. Now to the airport."

"Are we off to Africa? I get paid very well in Vegas: I'll buy the tickets."

Lola's eyes widened. Why on earth did the Nevada giraffe want to go to Africa?

"If you've searched Paris, we need to search Abidjan as well," Ingrid insisted. "We might find Mars' wife."

"Two things, Ingrid. Either Karen Mars is dead, or she's holed up somewhere."

"We could find a witness. Someone who can tell us the people Mars saw in Abidjan."

"He saw nobody: he was in hiding."

"He must have had contacts."

"Those contacts are hardly going to reveal that they helped a fugitive being pursued by the French police."

"Perhaps Captain Hardy didn't tell you everything. And it's always better to get information from the source. You were the one who taught me that."

"Frankly, I've no desire to go gadding off to Africa."

"Well, anyway, if we're not going to Africa, why are we going to the airport?"

16

Commissaire Kernec couldn't have been more helpful. Lola noticed he was friendly to the point of unctuousness. Was this due to Ingrid's seductive, exotic presence? It wouldn't be the first time. So far, their trip to Roissy had been worth it. Kernec was adamant that Sacha Duguin could not have taken his weapon with him on the flight to Kinshasa. If he had tried to, it would have been spotted. Even if it had been dismantled and put in the hold.

"Every piece of luggage goes through the X-ray machine, and more often than not twice rather than once, after 9/11. Believe me, the barrel of a revolver shows up very clearly on a security screen."

"Even wrapped in aluminium or some other material?" asked Ingrid.

"Yes indeed, mademoiselle. Impossible to smuggle a weapon through without it being seen. To travel with a gun, you need authorisation from the top brass, and that takes time. And if I've understood correctly, Duguin wasn't on an official mission."

"There's always the diplomatic bag," Lola said.

"That's a different story. It's true, you can get anything through in a diplomatic bag. But Commandant Duguin is a policeman, not a diplomat, is he not?"

"What about private planes?"

"There you're putting your finger on a specific problem. It's obvious that controls aren't as strict at airports like Le Bourget or Nice as they are in big places where the airlines operate."

Lola was barely even surprised when they left Commissaire Kernec's office: there stood Hardy in a dark suit with tie as yellow as a coyote's liver, carrying a black briefcase. His bearded acolyte stood next to him. Too cooperative to be honest, the unctuous Commissaire Kernec had tipped off the G.I.P.

"You don't like taking advice, Madame Jost."

"It's my age. Memories, advice, it all gets lost."

"Mademoiselle Diesel, I presume?"

"Correct presumption."

"Might I know what you are doing in France?"

"Tourism, visiting friends."

Hardy declared he would take them back to Paris.

"Thanks, but I have my own car."

"My young assistant will drive your Twingo. You two come with me: I've planned an interesting detour."

Lola debated whether to send him packing or not. The last time he had shown her something, she had gleaned important information.

He installed Lola in the front passenger seat, put the beacon on the roof, and headed for the city. On the *périphérique*, despite the snow, he slalomed in and out of the traffic. The three of them sat simmering in silence for a while. Hardy caught Ingrid's eye in the rearview mirror.

"After seeing the video, I can't understand why you came back to Paris."

"What video?"

"I thought you took more care, Madame Jost. Especially when it came to your friends' lives."

"I haven't had time to talk to her about that blasted video. And Ingrid isn't the sort who warns you of her arrival."

"Will you stop talking about me in the third person?" Ingrid protested.

Hardy explained. Lola and he agreed on one thing at least: on quai de Montebello, the killer had changed his mind at the very last moment. Conclusion: the contract was quite probably still out. The person behind it had only to find a new hitman. Lola glanced at her friend. She didn't seem bothered in the slightest.

"In short, you're not safe here, mademoiselle. Take the first plane home."

"Message received and understood."

Lola thought that for once this pest Hardy was right. Ingrid ought to go back to the States. But she would have a hard time convincing her.

The snow was coming down even thicker. Hardy took his foot off the accelerator and was overtaken by a motorbike. The rider turned his head in their direction. A stocky figure. A compact but powerful bike. Like the one on Saint-Michel. Panic fluttered in Lola's brain. She took a pill. The biker was already nothing more than a black dot engulfed by the whiteness.

When they reached Paris, Hardy ignored the G.I.P. headquarters and turned onto the Left Bank. He spoke again only when he pulled up outside La Santé prison, telling the two women to follow him. He called the guard at the security screen by his first name.

He was led in, handcuffed, between two guards. Ingrid barely recognised him. She had never met him in person, but his photograph had been on the front pages often enough. In a few months he had lost ten kilos and put on twenty years. Puffy-faced, the air of a hunted animal.

Richard Gratien. The man who had ordered her death. And most likely Mars' as well. She was amazed to find she didn't hate him.

"You have to transfer me, Captain. I've been beaten up again. They want my blood."

"You're always making demands, but you offer nothing in return, Gratien."

Hardy placed his recorder on the table. Ingrid saw that the prisoner had finally become aware of her and Lola.

"Colleagues from the G.I.P.," said Hardy. "Don't worry about them."

"I repeat, I had nothing to do with Mars. Can you see me contracting someone? Everybody's abandoned me, and you know very well why."

"Because you no longer have your notebooks? Is that it? I still find that hard to believe."

"If I had them, I wouldn't be in here, Hardy. Your colleagues or some other agency must have them. Put me in solitary or anywhere else, but do something."

"So you weren't responsible for Mars. Or for Saint-Michel. Do you really stand by what you've said?"

"The war was between Mars and me. No-one else. He ended up biting the dust, but it had nothing to do with me. As for the Saint-Michel thing, why would I want to kill a cop? I'm a lawyer, Hardy, so I know what that means. Somebody has got hold of my notebooks and they're running rings round you at will."

Gratien's face was bathed in sweat. If the former Mister Africa was not in a panic, he deserved the Oscar for best actor. The exchange went on for another ten minutes or so: Gratien would not budge.

Before disappearing with his two guards, he again begged Hardy to change his prison. The whole of France knew what he looked like. Even the France behind bars.

Ingrid had no doubt that small-time thugs would take great pleasure in making life impossible for someone who had associated with the powerful and grown rich by getting rid of his adversaries. An old jackal at the mercy of young lions. His cry for help was genuine.

"I wanted you to see for yourselves, ladies," said Hardy. "He's telling the truth when he says he wasn't responsible. He's out of the loop, isn't he?"

It had been obvious Gratien had no idea who they were. If he had taken out a contract on Ingrid, he would surely have reacted when he saw her alongside Hardy. Ingrid could tell Lola had reached the same conclusion: Gratien wasn't their man. And yet, as a proud woman who stuck to her principles, the ex-commissaire wasn't going to give the smug G.I.P. captain the pleasure of admitting it.

"Face up to reality, Madame Jost. Mars was gunned down in a clumsy, passionate way with Duguin's revolver. And Duguin, thanks to his closeness to Mars, had every chance of tracking him down . . ."

"Sacha would hardly leave the body and a bullet behind, would he?"

"That was what Duguin wanted us to think."

"In that case anything and everything is possible . . ."

"Who's to say he wasn't caught out? He didn't have time to choose the angle of fire for the *coup de grâce,* or to hide the corpse . . ."

"Your dear friend the commissaire at Roissy is convinced Sacha couldn't have got a weapon on board a plane."

"He could have paid someone to take the Smith & Wesson for him, in a private plane or by boat."

"Not exactly discreet."

"Mars knew lots of diplomats, Madame Jost. He could have helped Duguin meet them. What if he took advantage of those contacts to use a diplomatic bag?"

"One of Mars' contacts helping Sacha to kill Mars? You've got a vivid imagination."

"Not as vivid as all that. And I'll tell you something I should keep to myself: Duguin claims he bought a S.I.G. Sauer in Africa."

"Write screenplays. It's better paid than police work."

"Does your sarcasm have a point?"

"Just think for five minutes. If Sacha had really wanted to kill Mars, he would have used a different weapon to his service revolver. A S.I.G. Sauer for example; and he wouldn't have told you about it. It's as simple as that."

"Too simple. And you've fallen for it. Duguin bought it in Africa, and claims to have left it there. But it's possible that the S.I.G. Sauer never existed. I interviewed a former colleague of Duguin's, one Emmanuelle Carle. She worked with him for a long time. He was her boss."

"Emmanuelle Carle detests Sacha. Mars promoted him over her."

"That doesn't prevent her from being clear-sighted. Especially as she has just been appointed commandant and has no reason to be jealous of Duguin. She's a good judge of character. She sees Duguin as both intelligent and manipulative. A sociopath who met his match . . . Let me be clear: don't try anything more. I'm sure it was you who passed a mobile to your friend Duguin. That's the last time you pull a stunt like that. Both of you: go home and get some rest."

Hardy packed his things away in his briefcase, and asked a guard to accompany them out.

No way I'm going back to the States, thought Ingrid.

*

They bent their heads in the swirling white storm. Lola's teeth were chattering.

"I know Sacha. He couldn't kill Mars and then lie to you. He's not one for cover-downs. You mustn't give in."

"We say 'cover-ups' in French, Ingrid."

"Whatever. You understood me."

"And I've no intention of giving in. I know that if Hardy took the trouble to have me meet Gratien, it was to . . . neutralise me."

"What do you mean?"

"He sees me as a potential virus. This case is . . ."

". . . his golden opportunity?"

"That's right."

"Does the virus have a strategy?"

"She soon will."

They plunged into the metro, withstood the icy gales howling along the platform, and boarded a train. They travelled in silence for a while, then Lola said:

"Hardy is right when he says you're not safe here. And by now we're almost certain it wasn't Gratien who took out a contract on you."

"There's nothing to say that you're not on a hitman's list as well. And that being the case, I'm staying."

"I was a cop for centuries, remember."

"I'm staying until we've cleared things up. End of story."

"What about your job at the casino?"

"I get on well with my boss. He'll understand."

"I've seen a hundred and fifty American films where people lose their jobs from one day to the next and leave with their tail between their legs and carrying all their belongings in a cardboard box."

"What tail? I'm not a marsupilami."

"Forget it, and be quiet. I need to think."

"You're fuckin' kidding me! You're not the only one equipped with a brain."

"O.K.! O.K.! Let's be quiet and think."

When they reached Strasbourg Saint-Denis, it was still snowing. They walked quickly to rue de l'Echiquier.

"You'd be better off in Las Vegas," grumbled Lola, shaking off the snow at the foot of the staircase.

"Yes, the weather is warmer. And we even have an Eiffel Tower."

"You see!"

"You're not starting with that again, are you?"

"My intuition keeps telling me this isn't going to get any better . . ."

"A friend of mine is coming from Vegas. He'll help us."

"You talk as if he were Father Christmas. Am I supposed to be reassured?"

"Jake is an athlete. He was in his college football team in New York. One night, some guy tried to rob us. Jake punched his lights out. He has great reflexes, and he keeps calm. Besides, he's a good shot."

"Oh, is he? And can he catch bullets with his teeth?"

"Lola, you haven't changed a Toyota."

"Nor have you. By the way, we say 'changed an iota'. Leave the Japanese out of this, will you?"

When they reached the apartment, Ingrid looked up the word 'iota' in a dictionary, smiled philosophically, and made some tea. Lola watched her, and thought back to her brief conversation with Sacha. He had told her to contact Berlin. She had failed the first time, but that didn't mean she should give up. She called Clémenti and told him of her misadventure with the former spy.

"I did warn you, Lola. Do you want to lodge a complaint?"

"There's no point. But I'd like to understand why Berlin reacted the way he did . . ."

"I'm not sure there's anything to understand. His odd behaviour ruined his career; perhaps he's just got odder with age. It's a vicious circle."

"That fellow knows something."

"I don't know what to say. Or just possibly . . ."

"Yes?"

"I met Berlin and Mars on several occasions with someone called Sénéchal. In fact, Mars presented them to me as his best friends."

Sénéchal? The owl-eyed man in Bianco's video. The spin doctor who had blown the dust off President Borel.

"An expert in his field," said Clémenti. "That's how Mars described him to me. He's a specialist in political communication. A former advertising man."

"Which doesn't prove he'll be willing to 'communicate' with me about Berlin or Mars."

"Give him a try. You'll find out soon enough."

Lola thanked him and hung up. Berlin and Sénéchal, Mars' closest friends. If the latter were as cooperative as the former, there was little hope. She called Armand Bianco all the same. He confirmed that he knew Gildas Sénéchal personally. The old guru was now more than seventy, and lived a quiet life in his beautiful Parisian apartment.

"So in theory at least, he has plenty of free time. I can contact him and try to arrange a rendezvous for you. What do you say?"

Lola hesitated. What use could a political spin doctor be to her? But there wasn't exactly an abundance of leads. She said yes.

"I'll get on to it straightaway, Lola."

"What would I do without you?"

She hung up and turned towards Ingrid, who had an odd look on her face.

"What's wrong?"

"I told you about Jake . . ."

"The man who catches bullets in his teeth. What about him?"

"In fact, he's more than a friend. Jake is a journalist. He was doing a report on showgirls for the *New Yorker*. That's how we met. I like him a lot."

Her eyes were shining. She meant it when she said:

"Jake is someone I can count on."

Lola said nothing, but added a few pieces to the Corcovado.

Ingrid stifled a yawn.

"Well, I need to find a hotel near here."

"Absolutely not. My sofa changes into a bed when I give it the order."

"That's a good idea. I'll sleep here until Jake arrives. That way he can choose the hotel. He's a bit dominating in that way."

"Demanding, you mean?"

"I don't know what I mean any more. Jet lug has got me."

Lola wondered how she had managed to survive so long without French à la mode de *Diesel*.

17 THURSDAY, JANUARY 24

Bianco's efforts were rewarded with success: Lola was given her rendez-vous. The grey skies were melting, and so was the snow. Ingrid had swapped her Brazilian attire for a "sober" ensemble: a pink Tyrolean cap, fake-fur jacket, tight-fitting khaki trousers, tall Doc Martens.

The giant of political communication lived on rue d'Artois. Pale marble and a red carpet on the staircase, one apartment per floor: high-class luxury. A man dressed all in black down to his butler's apron opened the door for them. The scent of a *girolles* stock wafted round his head. A muscular fifty-something, short grey hair and a square jaw. A mouth almost as weary as his washed-out eyes, doubtless haunted by unpleasant memories.

"Mondo."

"I'm sorry?"

"My name is Mondo. I am Gildas Sénéchal's assistant. Please follow me."

They walked in his wake through the apartment. Mondo was broad-shouldered, but apparently suffered from sciatica, because he was dragging one leg slightly and kept rubbing his lower back. The rooms they passed through showed impeccable taste. Plush carpets, slightly strange but perfectly chosen contemporary furniture, abstract paintings. A huge rectangular living room, with logs crackling in a hearth you could roast a calf over. A huge grey Persian cat fast asleep at a prudent distance from the flames.

A small fellow with a slightly crumpled look unfolded himself from a sofa the colour of wet sand. Lola had difficulty recognising him as the man in the video. Sénéchal had lost weight and put on centuries. His big glasses, and the sharp, piercing eyes behind them, made him look like a male version of the writer Marguerite Duras.

His handshake was firm, his language assured and polished. The more one listened, the less one thought of him as small. He asked Ingrid for her opinion of her talented president, listened as if she were a C.I.A. analyst, gave his own nuanced view of Barack Obama. Lola had met many charismatic figures, but he was up there with the best of them. Mondo served them champagne, making sure not to overdo it. His boss proposed a toast to friendship.

"The friendship linking you and Mars, Lola, if I may call you that."

She listened to him recount his own relationship with the division-naire. They had become inseparable at the lycée. A link that "lasted beyond death and the catastrophic choices my deceased friend made."

"Mars was a public servant, like me, but he chose a scorched-earth policy. I've read about all the horrors he committed. Of course I don't condone his crimes, but when it comes down to it, I've always admired his panache. A quality that tipped him into lunacy, I'm afraid. Arnaud would have made an excellent politician, even though he claimed to detest them. I could have seen him as a shining light, whereas I spent my life in the shadows of power . . ."

"Luncheon is served," said Mondo.

"Fine. My dear friends, don't be put off: Mondo may look like a paratrooper, but he's an extraordinary cook."

The para did the cooking, served them, and ate at table with his boss without taking off his long black apron. Over a first course of juicy oysters sauce mornay washed down with a bottle of Sancerre, Sénéchal explained to Lola that political communication was neither an exact science nor a confidence trick, but above all a subliminal art. He told her the story that in order to get Russians to eat potatoes, Peter the Great had reserved a portion of his imperial garden for them, and then had it proclaimed they were a food reserved for the nobility. The men in charge of guarding the plants were instructed to "neglect" their duties in order to make stealing them easier.

"Peasants began to cultivate them, and the people took to eating them."

Then he told Ingrid about how in the United States during the Second World War the government was faced with a surplus of offal that Americans didn't want.

"So they launched an anonymous campaign suggesting that eating offal was excellent for your health. It worked like a charm. It's the same in politics. You have to know how to use other people's desires in your favour. If you want the people to sign up, you have to make them dream. A good slice of what you think of as reality is in fact a well-worked fiction."

"Was it by concentrating on those desires that you helped Paul Borel win a second term?"

"Partly, Lola. Paul Borel had considerable natural talent. I simply helped him display it more effectively. It was an honour to serve him."

By now they had reached the roast veal with the famous *girolles* sauce, accompanied by an admirable Chasse-Spleen. Sénéchal talked more than he ate or drank. Lola finished her food and wine before she spoilt the atmosphere.

"I would have thought it wasn't so much a question of natural talent as those notebooks of Gratien's."

Her remark was followed by forks suspended in mid-air, several seconds' silence and two smiles. A broad one from Mondo, a more discreet, elegant one from Sénéchal.

"Hmm, I suspected I was dealing with someone who had done her homework. I must say, it's a pleasure. Isn't it, Mondo?"

The jack of all trades served another round of wine.

"You often deal with much less interesting people, it's true, Gildas."

"You're right, Lola. The notebooks played their part. Back then, Gratien swore allegiance to Paul Borel. We learned that Candichard was carrying around a lot of unhelpful baggage. If Borel had informed the media about him, there would have been an enormous scandal."

"But he didn't have to, because Candichard preferred to withdraw."

"That's right. And I can even tell you I was the person in charge of the negotiations. Working in the shadows, as I was saying. Come to think of it, I confounded the statistics."

"How's that?"

"Politicians who abort their careers are very rare in France. Even those left out in the cold make their reappearance in the arena at some point. With Candichard, that was it, once and for all."

"Are you two a couple?" Mondo asked Ingrid.

"And you two?" she retorted, without skipping a beat.

"No, Gildas is my employer. For as long as . . . for as long as I can remember."

"Lola is my best friend. Period."

"That's already a lot."

Mondo announced he was going to bring in the cheese. The tall Yank stood up and said she would offer him a hopeful hand.

"A helping hand, you mean?"

"Right."

Lola mentioned Sacha Duguin and her run-in with Joseph Berlin.

"I still see Joseph from time to time, but our links have never been as strong as those I had with Arnaud Mars. I'm sorry he behaved that way towards you. But I think there are extenuating circumstances . . ."

"Meaning?"

"It's complicated."

"I have the time if you do."

"Arnaud and Joseph met in Africa. That was one of Joseph's regions, because he specialised in Islamist terrorism. He's an adventurer at heart, and liked being in the thick of it. His wife hated him going away; she died in a car accident while he was on a mission. Their daughter was a teenager at the time. He blamed himself. He stayed in the C.B.N.S. but asked for a posting in Paris. Since he spoke Arabic, he became part of the team of translators and interpreters. He demoted himself, in fact. From then on he spent his days sitting on a chair spying on people whose communications were tapped. That's both reasonable and courageous, but he became frustrated and his temperament suffered."

"I can vouch for that."

"Having said that, let's suppose that Sacha Duguin contacted Berlin for information. If Joseph agreed to provide him with any, he must be regretting it now. Especially after your friend's arrest. Hardy could charge him as an accessory."

"He couldn't be an accessory, because Sacha didn't kill Mars."

"Duguin came to see me, Lola. Just after Mars' disappearing act. And believe me, he was hopping mad. I thought he was out for revenge. Frankly, I wasn't surprised when he was arrested. Arnaud and I had lunched with him on a couple of occasions. Young Duguin thought that gave him the right to interrogate me. I showed him the door. Even if Arnaud committed dreadful crimes, he was my friend."

"Why did Sacha contact you?"

"He thought I had given the Mars family fake passports. That wasn't such a ridiculous idea: I would have if he had asked me. Of course, I would never have dreamed that it would have been so he could escape after murdering Gratien's nearest and dearest. Which brings us back to Joseph. It's more than likely that he was the one who provided them with the passports. That would explain his panic and his exaggerated reaction."

He was laying his cards on the table.

"Did Mars have a contact in Abidjan?"

"I have no idea. Mars was passionate about Africa; I wasn't. By the way, Hardy asked me the same thing. MONDO!"

"YES, GILDAS?"

"WHAT'S HAPPENING WITH THE CHEESE?"

Lola had drunk too much and eaten too well. Ingrid had resisted the temptations of Sénéchal's excellent wine cellar and was on top form. Once they were out on the street, she announced that she had cured Mondo's sciatica.

"In the kitchen, I massaged him until he thought I was the best thing to happen to him in years. He told me I reminded him of his sister. I should patent my Japanese–Thai–Californian massage."

"Did you bring up Sacha?"

"Of course. Mondo confirms that he came to see Sénéchal. According to him, Sacha was nervous and very angry. I've thought it over, Lola. We have to go to Africa."

True enough, it was by going to the source that they would uncover the truth. Or at least, part of it. And the source was the moment when Sacha had found the person who, after first arousing his admiration, had become the biggest disappointment of his life.

"I agree, Ingrid."

"Great. We're leaving tomorrow."

"What?"

"I've already booked the flights. I knew you'd agree in the end."

"You don't waste time."

"As you yourself say, I've got a job back in Vegas. So it's better not to waste a second."

"Unbelievable. You may look like a peaceful Nevada giraffe, but underneath you're as sly as a fox."

Ingrid started to hum, and twirled around a few times. Despite her digestive problems, Lola felt as light as a feather. If hope were to be found anywhere, it was in Abidjan.

18 FRIDAY, 25 JANUARY

Lola had barely slept. They had just checked in; Ingrid had gone off to buy magazines and was reading them in the departure lounge. Lola's mobile vibrated in her pocket.

"Hello?"

"I'm waiting for you in the airport chapel."

Flabbergasted, she couldn't think what to say.

"I'm off in five minutes. So if you want a lead before you plunge into Africa, get a move on."

He ended the call. Lola struggled for two seconds with a sense of unreality. With the idea that Joseph Berlin was nothing but a product of her imagination. Then she swallowed her pride, studied a map of the airport, and charged off as fast as she could. Four minutes and thirty-five seconds later, she pushed open the chapel door. Two women were praying in the right-hand bay. And there he was, the old scoundrel, in the front row opposite the crucifix, dressed in his buttoned-up overcoat.

"Don't be afraid," he whispered. "I'm a believer. There's no risk of me pulling a gun on you in a holy place."

"You're the one who needs confession."

Berlin was trying to be civil with her. Was that a good sign, or was he planning another dirty trick?

"I've changed my mind."

He must be bipolar. The new century's illness of choice.

"And to what do I owe this change of heart?"

"I've been following you for a while."

"By what right?"

"You search my studio from top to bottom, and you talk of rights?"

"O.K., let's start over."

"You don't spare yourself, Lola. I like that. And I think you really do want to help your friend Sacha. I like that too. Loyalty is all too rare these days."

She stared at him in silence. If he could read her thoughts, he ought be suffering torments.

"When I saw you registering your luggage for Abidjan, I told myself Hardy must have found someone to talk to. And I'll pay to get the sideboard repaired."

"That's impossible. It's an antique."

"They can do marvels these days."

"I'd be amazed."

"Look, put yourself in my shoes. You appear out of nowhere, just when the G.I.P. is investigating Duguin. While I'm searching your place, I find a Manurhin . . ."

"The service revolver I forgot to hand in when I quit the police force. And as far as I know, the G.I.P. doesn't take on pensioners."

"You don't look it. Are we square, Lola?"

"Tell me what you know, then we'll see about your blessing."

"First make me a solemn promise."

"I suppose this is the place for one."

"Don't ever tell the G.I.P. I gave you this information."

"Done deal. So?"

"I was the one who supplied Mars with his fake papers. Without asking what he wanted them for. I never questioned him. A matter of faith."

"How touching. Are you ever going to tell me what you want to say, Berlin?"

"I regret not asking Mars about those passports. The G.I.P. could make me pay."

"Sacha came to see you and you told him about them, is that it?"

"I felt betrayed by Mars. So when Duguin told me he wanted to find him to demand an explanation and possibly rough him up a bit, I decided to help him."

"You told me Sacha had probably killed Mars. Do you still think that?"

"Look, you could have come from the G.I.P. I told you what Hardy wanted to hear so that he would forget about me. In fact, I'm inclined to think Duguin is innocent."

"Tell me more."

"Duguin was convinced Mars had left him clues. That Arnaud wanted to explain it to him man-to-man. He did some really stupid things, but he was always a complex character. He lied to Duguin, and yet there was mutual respect between the two of them. And possibly even friendship, despite the age difference."

"How did you guide Sacha to Mars?"

"'Guide' is a big word. He had quite a lot of information already."

"But apart from that? I've got a plane to catch, Berlin."

"A long time ago, Mars confided to me that he had a blood-brother in Africa. Someone whose life he had saved. It was time to call in the favour."

"Do you know his name?"

"Koumba."

"His first name?"

"Kaspar, I think."

"You think, or you're sure?"

"It was a long time ago. Like you, I'm no longer twenty."

"An address?"

"No, nor his measurements."

Berlin smiled. It was more of a grimace.

"You have a head start over Duguin, Lola. You know there's every possibility that Koumba lives in Abidjan. That's a huge advantage."

"Abidjan is a big place."

"Above all, you have a head start over Hardy."

"What d'you mean?"

"Hardy has come crashing up against the bureaucratic inertia of the Côte d'Ivoire police, whether deliberate or not. He's still trying to find out where Mars stayed in Abidjan." He turned towards the crucifix, crossed himself, and announced that he had prayed for her. "Be very careful. If it's not Gratien behind Mars' killing, that only makes matters worse."

"How do you know about Gratien?"

"I had Hardy on my back as well. He had me listen to the tapes of Gratien's interrogation. It had the ring of truth, through and through."

For Lola, this last touch made the whole thing plausible. It was typical of Hardy to play the recording to Berlin. She watched him leave the chapel. He walked like an old man, behaved like a lunatic, but his leads were gold-plated.

The two women had not moved: it was as if they were carved from the same wood as the effigy. Lola thought about what had just happened. Hardy would not hesitate to arrest Berlin if he found out he had provided the fake passports. That meant Berlin was relying on her. If she succeeded in identifying Mars' murderer, Hardy would look foolish. He might even be taken off the case, thus taking Berlin out of the firing line. So that was it.

I think you really do want to help your friend Sacha. I like that too. Loyalty is all too rare these days. Nice try, but you're only thinking of your own skin, Joseph Berlin.

Her mobile vibrated. Ingrid, anxious. They met up again in the departure lounge. The American spent the rest of their wait on her smartphone. She tried different spellings, all the available directories.

There wasn't a single Kaspar Koumba in the whole of Côte d'Ivoire. At least, not on the web.

19

Fifty minutes after take-off, the flight turned into a nightmare. The stewardesses had served orange juice, babies were screaming their lungs out. Then the plane hit a series of air pockets. And Lola caught sight of a passenger who resembled the evil biker in Hardy's video. Could there be a trail of blood from Saint-Michel to Abidjan? Two rows behind them, a woman complained she was suffocating, and threw up. The cabin was filled with a ghastly stench. Lola could feel anxiety churning her stomach. She disturbed Ingrid, woke up a young man so that she could get out to search frantically in the overhead locker. Impossible to find her pills.

Another air pocket, even bigger this time. Lola gave up on the idea of finding her medication, and decided to breathe through her mouth. Ingrid recommended she use a damp wipe as an air filter.

Two stewards tidied up as best they could. Lola pressed her improvised mask over her nose. She was sweating profusely, and kneading the arm rest with her free hand. Ingrid massaged her shoulders and temples to calm her. Lola remembered: her Lexomil was in the pocket of her smock. She swallowed one of the pills as if her life depended on it, claiming it was a cough sweet.

"In that case, I'd like one too."

"Alright, I lied. It's an anti-anxiety pill."

She had to confess. How she kept having panic attacks after what had happened on boulevard Saint-Michel. Sleepless nights worrying what her life would have been like if Black Helmet had not spared Ingrid's life. Her American friend went to fetch two miniature whiskies, and they used the in-flight magazines to fan themselves.

Jean-Jacques Goldman began singing in the foul air. Lola groaned like a dying animal.

"What's wrong?"

"I can't stand that music. It's a physical thing. It's so bad I wonder if I should consult someone."

"A shrink?"

"Obviously. Not a plumber."

On the tarmac, the heat had all the gentleness of a rugby tackle, but Lola was overjoyed at the change of atmosphere and the relative quiet.

*

They arrived by taxi at the home of someone called Léontin, a friend of Timothy Harlen's, the owner of the Calypso in Pigalle. A fifty-year-old at ease with himself in an elegant, well-informed way, he was listening to loud African music while he watched a football match on T.V. After changing, Lola felt like new when he gave them the address of the development where Mars' body had been found. Did he know a certain Kaspar Koumba?

"Never heard of him, girls," he said, handing them the keys to his Vespa.

That wasn't very encouraging. Léontin ran Kingo, a nightclub in the Treichville district. No-one knew the nocturnal scene in Abidjan better than he did. Kaspar Koumba wasn't a night-owl, then.

"Be very careful. The scars of the war between the supporters of former president Laurent Gbabgo and the new leader Alassane Ouattara are only just beginning to heal. Politics in my country is like nitroglycerine. One misplaced word and it blows your face off. The French have interfered in our domestic affairs a lot, so there are people who don't appreciate—"

"Lola will be quiet," said Ingrid. "No-one will know she's a French coloniser."

"Very funny," Lola said. "But I'm not sure that Yankees are any more popular. Especially big, brightly coloured ones wearing shorts the size of a postage stamp. But the mosquitoes are going to love you."

Ingrid studied the ex-commissaire's clothes: a long-sleeved, high-necked T-shirt and a pair of voluminous elasticated trousers. She went to change her shorts for combat fatigues. She took charge of the Vespa and they plunged into the suffocating heat of the city, stopping off at a store to buy water and aspirin.

They finally reached the building-site. Lola's head was throbbing, her body aching, and she was dripping with sweat. Ingrid was sweating just as much, but her face was as radiant as if she had spent her whole life in the tropics. Some kids playing football in bare feet; workmen in orange helmets; stray dogs; machines covered in thick red mud. The construction work wasn't finished, and only part of the development seemed inhabited. Ingrid found a painter who passed her on to an electrician, and he led the two women to a mason. A man with a sad face and bent back, he looked like the personification of gloom. His colleagues spoke to him respectfully, then moved away as though afraid they might catch something. Lola managed to get him to agree to accompany them to the spot where Mars' body had been found.

Yellow ochre standing out from the vegetation. The cube of the house: Lola recognised it, even though on the crime-scene photographs it had looked much larger. The doom-laden mason climbed the stairs ahead of them. Lola imagined herself in Mars' shoes, being relentlessly hunted down by his murderer.

From the flat roof the view over the forest was magnificent. A thousand birds and as many monkeys, plus an army of crickets, were all busy making a din. The mason showed them the spot where the body had been found.

"Were you the one who discovered it?"

He nodded, looking even gloomier, and began to tell the story at top speed. He had alerted the foreman, who had gone off to fetch the police. He gave them the address of the police station.

"Were you coming to work on the house when you found the body?"

"No, the house was already finished. There was only the rendering to do. I'd had an argument with my father . . ."

"And so . . . ?"

"This is the house closest to the forest. I wanted to be on my own, to think things over and look at the birds. So I climbed up to the roof."

"Had nobody smelled the decomposing body?"

"The monsoon had devoured the flesh. It didn't take long."

Lola thought back to her talk with Franklin at the Forensic Institute. *They had to identify him. No identity papers on him, just an expensive watch. And on top of that, he was in the country clandestinely. A foreigner.*

"Does the name Kaspar Koumba mean anything to you?"

He shook his head. She described Sacha to him, but he said he had never seen him.

"In our country, we think a dead person stays close to the living before finally departing for good. I sometimes see a shadow passing by my window. It will get better. You being here is a sign."

"How do you mean?"

"You're the French police, aren't you?"

"Of course."

"So you're going to kill the mystery, and this dead person will be freed. And the developer will be pleased because he'll be able to sell his houses again."

"Did the discovery of the body slow sales?"

"It certainly did. And we workmen are wondering if we'll ever be paid as we should be. My colleagues are wary of me because I found the body. You're going to arrest the murderer, aren't you?"

"That's our intention," said Ingrid.

"Was anyone guarding the site on the night of the murder?" asked Lola.

"No. It costs too much to pay someone to watch the rain fall. And back then there was nobody living here. The only ones who might have seen something are these stray dogs."

"Before then, did you notice anyone strange?"

"No, nobody noticed anything."

They questioned the few people living in the development. Then went to the local police station.

Lola studied the front of the building and announced they would be running a risk if they went in. Even if the Côte d'Ivoire police knew Koumba, there was no guarantee they would tell them. Especially since Hardy had doubtless made contact with his African colleagues.

"Let's talk to less dangerous people."

"How about the postmen?"

They visited every single post office in Abidjan. No-one recalled having Kaspar Koumba on their round. They decided to try their luck at the markets, but had no success there either.

20 TUESDAY, 29 JANUARY

Their investigation was at a standstill. They had criss-crossed the city for five days and questioned hundreds of people, but Koumba was nowhere to be found. In the evening, they returned to an empty apartment: Léontin was already at work. Lola was groggy with fatigue. Despite her amazing vitality, Ingrid's strength was waning too.

"Let's call Berlin," suggested Lola. "We'll never get anywhere otherwise."

Mars' friend answered on the second ring. She had obviously woken him up.

"I'm trying, but I can't think how I can help you."

"Try harder."

"I need to think it over. I'll call you back."

Her American friend went to have a shower. Lola collapsed onto her bed under the mosquito net and dozed off. She was woken by the sound of her mobile.

"Mars mentioned children."

"Is that all?"

"Koumba could be a paediatrician, a clown, a schoolteacher or a paedophile. How should I know? It's up to you."

At that, the sweet-tempered spook ended the call. Lola clutched the mobile to her bosom, then gradually relaxed her grip. She soon drifted off to sleep once more.

A silver-haired woman with a glistening, wraith-like body was dancing in the rain. The drops became part of her body and were transformed into points of light. And the dancer was weeping . . .

Lola woke up. She couldn't understand where she was. The mosquito net, traffic noise, the sound of the ceiling fan. She was at Léontin's, Timothy Harlen's friend in Côte d'Ivoire. But somebody really was weeping. She switched on her bedside lamp, saw a mosquito zigzagging through the air, called out to Ingrid. No response, but still the sound of sobbing. Fear rising in her throat, Lola realised that the sobs could only be coming from inside the apartment. A piece of furniture was being dragged across floor tiles. She tiptoed towards the bathroom.

Two men, masked and wearing army fatigues, were sitting on the edge of the bath. Ingrid was tied up, naked, at their feet. She was the one weeping. Lola thought of her Manurhin, left behind in Paris.

A movement behind her back. Everything went dark.

21 WEDNESDAY, 30 JANUARY

Lola gulped down air. A smell of burning. The music was too loud. Her head was going to explode. She was tied up on a chair in the kitchen. Three men facing her. Huge, dark eyes behind the slits of their masks. One of them was slumped on a chair, holding a gun and a cigar.

"INGRID!"

"Shut your mouth! Anyway, your friend has no idea what her name is by now."

The man with the cigar had a guttural voice, an African accent and a big gold ring on his left hand.

"HAVE YOU HURT HER, YOU BASTARD?"

He clicked his fingers. One of his subordinates slapped her. A blinding light flashed across her retinas, exploding into a shower of sparks. The leader kneeled down, blew smoke in her face with a smile, ordered the other man to hold her arm. She struggled, enveloped in the smell of stale sweat. The three hooded men were laughing. The one in charge brought the cigar close to her forearm, then declared he wasn't going to "waste a Romeo y Julieta on an old granny". He waved his hand at the man on his right, who immediately crushed out his cigarette on Lola's flesh. She screamed.

"My men are going to have some fun. Then they'll bury you and the beautiful blonde under the building-site where you were poking your noses."

"What do you want?"

"A bit of amusement."

"I have money . . ."

"You don't have anything anymore. Shut it!"

He waved his hand again, and blows began raining down on Lola's body. Panic gripped her. The chair toppled over backwards. Her skull hit the floor tiles. She slipped into unconsciousness once more.

A few seconds or hours later, Lola came round. Her right side was red raw. One of the thugs was whipping her with a big belt. The music drowned out her screams and the man's grunts. Their leader was drinking beer and singing along. *He was having fun.*

The blows intensified. Time stretched out endlessly. Her brain imploded.

A century later, and the violent music had stopped.

Lola opened her eyes to the chirruping of crickets and the scarcely audible sounds of a different music in the distance. She could see the outlines of the kitchen thanks to the light filtering in from the street. The mosquitoes had enjoyed a feast: her body was one big bite and one big wound. The white floor tiles were stained with blood and earth. Footprints: military boots.

She must have slept, overcome by fear, pain, exhaustion. Now she was conscious again, but could feel only anguish. Her heart was racing; her throat was parched. She focused on her breathing, swallowed an invisible pill. An area of calm lay close at hand, if she could only reach it. She told herself she had the strength to drag herself across the floor, even tied to a chair.

Her crawling lasted an eternity; she called to her friend whenever she could. The dawn took its time. When Lola finally reached her destination, it was broad daylight. The bathroom stank of urine. Ingrid was tied, head bowed, to the toilet bowl. Lola dragged herself over to her legs, laid a cheek on her ankle. Ingrid's body was warm. She shouted her name.

"Lola . . . thank God . . . you're alive . . ."

Her voice was weak, but it was definitely her voice.

"What did they do to you?"

"Nothing serious."

Was she lying so as not to make Lola despair? She was capable of it. Lola had heard the blows, and thought she must be more injured than she was letting on. Impossible to find anyone more generous or unselfish on earth than Ingrid . . .

"Two guys wanted to rape me, but their leader stopped them. So they just tied me up, slapped me about and insulted me."

"Do you swear that?"

"I swear. But they did piss on me. Shit! It's fucking disgusting!"

"Nobody knows we're in Africa . . ."

"Nobody but Joseph Berlin."

"Do you think that . . . ?"

"This may sound stupid, Lola, but if we're still alive . . ."

" . . . it's because they wanted to give us the scare of our lives, or to teach us a lesson."

"Or that the message is: 'Get out of here, we won't tell you again . . .'"

Berlin, that bastard spook. Yes, that made sense. She promised herself she would make him pay. The return to Paris would be hotter than hell.

They tried to help each other untie their bonds. No good. In the end, they had to wait until Léontin got back and untied them. It took Lola several minutes before she felt any sensation in her numb arms and legs. Her right side had turned purple. Her face was swollen and streaked with dried blood. She could barely stand. Léontin wanted to take her to hospital; when she protested, Ingrid managed to convince her, just in case there was internal bleeding.

"O.K., but you're to catch the plane back to Paris. Today."

"No way. I'm waiting for you to be seen to, and then we leave together."

22

They took Lola by taxi to the emergency department at the Treichville hospital. Ingrid listened while Léontin made up something about a Vespa accident, and heard the doctor announce that Lola would be kept under observation until the next evening.

Ingrid stayed with her for almost an hour.

She found Léontin back at the apartment. Ingrid could feel an atomic anger boiling up inside her, but she had a plan. Perhaps Kaspar Koumba had been invented by Berlin. She wasn't going to leave this city without checking every last corner. She asked her host if he could lend her a weapon.

"Can you shoot?"

"Yes, my father taught me when I was twelve."

"Oh yes, of course, America."

"You have child soldiers here."

"It's not exactly the same thing."

"We can talk geopolitics some other time. Do you have a gun or not?"

"I've got the one I keep at Kingo . . . but . . ."

"I've no intention of taking out any of your compatriots. I just want it as a detergent."

"You mean a deterrent?"

"Exactly. Before that, though, I need your help. Please come with me; I can pay."

"I'm a friend of your boss . . ."

"My ex-boss."

"Well, I'm not Timothy's ex-friend. So yes, I will help you. And for free."

She gave him a hug and explained her plan. A laborious job: they were going to search for Koumba all over Abidjan. He had a link to children. So it was simple: they had to visit every school, hospital, dispensary, sports club . . .

"O.K., I get the idea. But it could take a lifetime: do I have a few minutes for a siesta?"

"No."

They took his car, a white Chrysler that smelled new and probably was. They would make enquiries street by street. One on the right, the other on the left.

*

It was almost four in the afternoon in the Adjamé district. Léontin had fallen asleep on his feet, leaning against a draper's window not far from the marketplace. Someone was stewing chicken in coconut milk and spices. Ingrid tamed her hunger and shook her companion's shoulder.

"I've found a little girl. She knows something, but she's afraid of me."

"It's only natural, Ingrid: you scare me too with that devilish energy of yours."

His eyes were bloodshot; she pulled him along by the sleeve. The little girl was playing with her friends in a schoolyard. Léontin signalled to her. She came nervously over to the gate.

"So you know Kaspar Koumba, do you?"

"He's not called Kaspar, he's called Grandpa."

"Grandpa Koumba?"

"Yes, that's right."

"Is he your grandfather?"

"He's everybody's grandfather."

"What does he do?"

"He tells stories that make you laugh and frighten you."

"Tell me where I can find him. I've got a nice present for him."

Léontin let Ingrid drive. He was exhausted, but had just enough strength to guide her through the traffic. The journey lasted no more than a few minutes. Under the biggest tree in a small square, sat a skinny old man surrounded by a gaggle of children sitting on the ground. Ingrid parked some distance away. Her guide took a base-ball cap from the glove compartment, pulled it down over his eyes, announced that now he was going to have that siesta and that it was "not negotiable". Ingrid tried to be patient.

*

"The clouds have held her back for far too long, and so she is savouring her revenge. The fields will come to life again, there is the promise of food for the people, the mosquitoes are already dancing in anticipation of their feast. With her brilliant stripes, the spears of peaceful warriors, Queen Rain is taking over the country once more.

"Listen. You can hear her joy. She falls and falls, laughs and laughs.

"The monsoon season. The song of water on old bones.

"Oh yes, Queen Rain is not as interested in the parched earth as before. What interests her far more is the foreigner. This man who has met his end here, on the concrete roof of an empty house in this country that isn't his.

"She would be happy to wash his skin, but his flesh has turned to dust, and so instead she wipes his carcass clean. She is amused, removing the dirt from this abandoned body, drumming on the darkness of his empty eye sockets. It is a good rhythm, which makes the parrots sway and the baboons dance.

"The only riches the poor man possesses are an elegant wristwatch, a gold wedding ring and a few banknotes. Who is he? He no longer has any identity papers. It's said he is a White Man, but who can really tell? He is nothing more than a skeleton with a gaping smile and a pair of big French shoes. His insides have delighted a family of mice, a swarm of flies, an army of earthworms.

"The person who first found him is a mason who builds houses. And this mason went to fetch the policeman. And that policeman wasn't happy. For once he has a big case on his hands, but he's afraid it will be taken from him. If the dead man really is a white foreigner, he tells himself, other foreigners the same colour will come searching for his remains to try to solve the mystery. And he doesn't like that — not one bit.

"This policeman is pretty stupid, but for once he isn't wrong. Men will come from afar. And will leave again without saying a word. The only one who might know more is Queen Rain. Because she will travel, on a cloud-car. She will tell us who the foreigner was. She will tell us who shot a bullet into his skull.

"But the wind is getting up. The rain sings louder. Listen. Listen carefully. Her song will spare no-one . . ."

"Is that all, Grandpa?"

"For the moment, yes."

"Tell us what comes next!"

"Yes, please, carry on!"

"I will tell you, children. Be patient."

"When?"

"Tomorrow, and a little more each evening."

Léontin was still asleep, but the storyteller had concluded his tale and the children had dispersed. The old man disappeared inside a bar. Ingrid found him sitting near the till. She slid onto the bench beside him. He gave a start.

"I've come about Mars."

"I don't know anyone of that name, mademoiselle."

"You are Koumba. I'm familiar with the story you told the children."

"I'm sorry, but you're mistaken."

He took a visiting card out of his wallet. THÉODORE MOBA. An address in Abidjan and a mobile number.

The waitress, a jolly young girl, brought over a beer.

"How are you this evening, Grandpa Koumba? You're looking well, as ever, my friend!"

Ingrid allowed herself a smile of triumph and ordered a beer. She showed him her American passport, her work I.D. from the Las Vegas casino, and the photos from the booth where she was holding her funny-face competition with Sacha.

"Back in France, Sacha is the ideal suspect. But I know he didn't kill Mars."

She explained that she had found him thanks to Joseph Berlin. The former spy would be discreet, and so would she.

"I have nothing to do with the French or Côte d'Ivoire police, the secret services, or Gratien's henchmen, but I'm not going to let go of you. Help me get Sacha out."

"I would have loved being loved like that," said Koumba, swallowing a mouthful of beer.

"Is your real name Moba or Koumba?"

"Moba. Koumba is for storytelling. Mars is one of my characters now. I tell of his death and the survival of his immortal soul. I know he wouldn't hold it against me."

"So tell me what you know."

"You appear to be who you claim you are, but you could have been followed."

Koumba was right. After the attack in Léontin's apartment, anything was possible. She was putting the old storyteller's life in danger, but then Sacha's too was hanging in the balance. She had no choice but to lie.

"Nothing has happened since I arrived in Abidjan. And while you were entertaining the kids, I checked all round. Nothing unusual. The people who killed Mars have got what they wanted: the notebooks. If Mars was alive, he would want you to help me prove Sacha's innocence."

"It's true he liked that young man a lot. He said he would go far."

"Did you see Sacha in Abidjan?"

"No, but Mars told me he was on his trail. He always knew he would come after him. I even think he left some clues for him."

"What kind of clues?"

"I've no idea."

"Was it you who provided Mars and his family with somewhere to stay?"

"Yes. My sister's house. She died last year."

"Where is it in relation to the new development where Mars was killed?"

"About two kilometres away."

So the murderer would have had little difficulty enticing Mars to the deserted site. Or perhaps he had first attacked him at his house, and his victim had managed to reach as far as the building-site, hoping to hide there.

"Were there any signs of a struggle at your sister's house?"

"I don't think so, but I didn't stay long. Anyway, I found Mars' fake passport. That was when I grew worried. Arnaud would never have gone out without it."

"Where is his wife now?"

"She's safe. Free, but with her daughter. It's so sad . . . He was meant to meet up with them. He thought that by travelling separately they would attract less attention. That was a mistake, fate took a hand in the intervening days . . ."

So Karen Mars was still alive. Ingrid had to speak to her.

"Do you have any way of contacting her, Koumba?"

He chewed his lips, and studied her in silence.

"If Karen can prove in any way that Sacha didn't kill her husband, I need to speak to her," Ingrid insisted. "Let me talk to her. I won't try to discover where's she's hiding, I promise."

Koumba studied her for a moment longer, then walked off towards the bar. Ingrid saw him use his mobile. After a fairly lengthy conversation, he returned and handed her the phone. Ingrid seized it, heard background music. Aretha Franklin? The same as at Sacha's place?

"Hello, Karen?"

"Koumba has just told me about Sacha. I'm really sorry, Ingrid."

"Did you see him when he found your husband?"

"Yes, it was tough but they ended up making peace. Sacha did not stay long. He flew back to France before I left Abidjan with my daughter."

"So before your husband was killed?"

"Yes."

"Could you testify that Sacha didn't do it?"

"I'd never run that risk, because of my daughter. We've made new lives for ourselves . . ."

"Sacha is the victim of a conspiracy. Help him, Karen."

"Impossible. Arnaud kept his plans for revenge from me. All that violence . . . He presented me with a fait accompli. I didn't have any choice. We had to leave France. Arnaud explained that the people who were after the notebooks would come for me and Aurélie."

"Who are they?"

"I know they're dangerous, but I don't know who they are. You have my word on that. I think very highly of Sacha, but I can't afford the luxury of helping him. Forgive me."

From the tone of Karen's voice, Ingrid knew she had no chance. She looked for another line of attack.

"Your husband wanted to use Gratien's notebooks against someone . . ."

"Arnaud told me as little as possible about that. What you don't know, you can't tell. But he was very concerned by what he found."

"And you've no idea . . ."

"Arnaud carried a copy of the notebooks around with him the whole time."

"What do you mean?"

"On a U.S.B. stick."

Ingrid remembered what Lola had told her about the crime scene. An expensive watch, a gold wedding ring, some money. If Arnaud always had the U.S.B. on him, it ought to have been found. So the killer knew what was on it.

"Apart from Sacha, have you been in touch with anyone else?"

"We left France with a friend of Arnaud's: Doris Nungesser. The police were after her because she shot her child's murderer. Arnaud had promised to get her out of France. It was because of her that Sacha found us. He knew her face, and was the only one aware she was a friend of my husband's. Koumba used to bring us food, but Doris couldn't bear being cooped up all the time. Sacha spotted her at a market, and followed her to the house Koumba was letting us use."

"Are you trying to tell me she was the one who killed Mars?"

"No. Doris left for South Africa before the murder took place. She has nothing to do with it."

Ingrid felt frustrated. Karen's memories weren't proving very helpful.

"Oh, and there was that man . . ."

"Tell me about him."

"I was ill. A bad fever. Arnaud got worried, so Koumba sent a doctor."

"An African?"

"Yes."

"Can you describe him?"

"Impossible, I was almost comatose. But two days later I was better, thanks to his treatment. He was a proper doctor, not a killer."

It was obvious from her voice that Karen was growing impatient.

"If things got really bad for Sacha, is there any chance you'd change your mind?"

"I can understand you insisting, Ingrid, but . . . Listen, I know Arnaud was intending to contact a young judge. Someone cleaner . . ."

"Cleaner than who?"

"I don't know. Arnaud was considering giving him the notebooks. He might have done so. In that case, justice may take its time, but the truth will eventually emerge . . ."

"Karen, wait!"

"Good luck."

She had hung up. Ingrid dropped the mobile and thumped the table with her fist.

"FUCK! FUCK! FUCK!"

Karen thought highly of Sacha, but just when he most needed her, she didn't want to know. With a little imagination she could surely have both helped him and protected her daughter at the same time.

Koumba had carefully picked up the mobile and deleted the number from the memory. He was as calm as a giant tree. Ingrid forced herself to concentrate.

"Mars contacted a young French judge. Do you know anything about that?"

"No."

"Really?"

"Mars didn't discuss his problems. The only thing I know is that the last day I saw him, he seemed calmer."

"Do you remember when Karen was ill?"

"Arnaud asked me for help. I went to the nearest N.G.O. to ask them to send someone. I paid up front. We agreed to give a false name."

"Did you see their doctor?"

"There was no need to: Karen was better. She left with her daughter. Mars stayed behind. He never mentioned the doctor again."

"What happened then?"

"One morning I went there with provisions, and the house was empty. No message, nothing. It wasn't like him just to disappear like that. I thought he must have had a problem. I looked everywhere for him. And then . . . after the rains, a mason found his . . . abandoned body."

Léontin was still asleep in the car. Ingrid shook him and introduced Koumba. They were going to talk to people at an N.G.O. To see a doctor.

"I was dreaming that Beyoncé was performing in my club," said Léontin, stretching. "Are you ill, Ingrid?"

"No, never better."

"That's what I reckoned."

23

Koumba recognised the receptionist and questioned him. The man stared at him and then glanced down at his register. Ingrid felt the hairs on the back of her neck bristle, and signalled to Léontin. He yawned. The receptionist phoned for a certain Dr N'Diop to come at once, then waved to a guard and a male nurse. The three visitors were seized immediately. The old storyteller protested: all he wanted to do was to talk to the white doctor who had treated his friend Karen.

"You're joking. Koumba. N'Diop is blacker than you are; he's an African born in Dakar. And he was mugged."

Dr N'Diop appeared, as angry as anyone in his position would be.

"My bag with all my instruments was stolen. Now I've got hold of you, you're going to pay me back, you old jackal."

Ingrid calmed things down by giving him five hundred dollars, and asked him what had happened.

"When I got where I was told to go, it was dark. Somebody mugged me. When I came round, I had been robbed and left in the middle of the countryside."

"Did you see your attacker?"

"No. He knew what he was doing – drugged me. He only had to use what he found in my bag."

"Did you tell the police?"

The doctor burst out laughing.

"I'm from Senegal, and the Côte d'Ivoire police like to make foreigners pay. So I've got into the habit of sorting out my problems without their help. Later, I went back to the house with some N.G.O. colleagues. No-one came to the door. I concluded I'd been taken there because it's an isolated, almost abandoned house – an ideal place to rob a medic. Do you swear to me you had nothing to do with it, Koumba?"

"You have my word . . ."

"Your name means something to me . . ."

"I'm a storyteller. The children know me."

"Oh yes, I remember: my son has told me about you. He loves your stories. I hope what you've just promised isn't another one."

"It could turn into one. You would make a good character. The doctor who gets everything stolen and fights back."

"And meanwhile, can I know a bit more about this mess?"

"Once it's sorted out I'll come back and tell you all about it, N'Diop, I promise. Anyway, you know who I am and where to find me."

"Alright, but leave now, because I have patients waiting. Real ones."

Léontin had to go back to work as well. The Kingo restaurant was already open.

When they reached Treichville, Ingrid asked Koumba to wait for her in the Chrysler.

Your hands feeling everywhere for me
In the morning when I'm still asleep . . .

Salif Keita, "I'm Going to Miss You". She loved that song. Inside Kingo, three couples were already intertwined on the dance floor. Ingrid made a few dance steps behind Léontin's back, and reminded him of his promise to lend her his gun. He rubbed his face with both hands.

"Timothy dreams of taking you back at the Calypso, Ingrid. Your place is on stage, dazzling your audience, not poking your nose in all over a dangerous city. Those guys who attacked you are real mercenaries, not the Village People."

"I know . . ."

"And if you're counting on old man Koumba to protect you, you're making a big mistake. Besides, where are you going tonight?"

"To the house where Mars was hiding."

"How will that help?"

"I'm one step ahead of the French police – I want to take advantage of that."

"What if your friend did it? Have you thought of that?"

"Sacha is innocent."

"Whoever said love is blind knew what he was talking about."

"This is nothing to do with love. We're not together anymore."

"If you did use my gun, it would be easy to trace it back to me, and I'd lose my business. It's taken me twenty years to get where I am. I'm not going to sacrifice all that for—"

". . . for a girl like me?"

Ingrid considered calling Timothy Harlen. Perhaps he'd be able to convince his friend? No, definitely not. A false hope. Léontin wasn't the sort who could be persuaded. *It's taken me twenty years to get where I am.* Léontin, Karen: they only thought of themselves . . .

"You're a fine woman, but you're in far too deep. Go back to France with your friend. Believe me, that's best."

By looking for yourself everywhere
You risk losing yourself despite everything . . .

Choking back a curse, Ingrid left the restaurant. Koumba was leaning against the car, looking up at the stars. Only this old fellow was left to help her.

"Where is the place they hid in?"

"At Attécoubé, near the Banco forest."

He guided her through the northern neighbourhoods and beyond the building-site to the outskirts of the city, where the national park began.

The house was on the crest of a hill. It must once have had a garden, but nature had already reclaimed it. Ingrid launched the Chrysler along a bumpy track. When this disappeared into the vegetation, they left the car and walked on for about thirty metres. They were surrounded by the noisy chatter of crickets.

Ingrid's torch lit up a pick, some rusted shovels and a lawnmower. Koumba had the key on his belt, and so he opened up the house and switched on the electricity. On the first floor, the beds were made, and everything was neat and tidy. In Mars' room, there was a canvas hold-all containing men's clothes and a Lonely Planet guide to Quebec.

"No passport?"

"I burned it so the police wouldn't find it."

"Did he have a visa?"

Koumba hesitated, then admitted the passport did contain a Canadian visa.

So the former divisionnaire had decided to make a new life in Quebec with his family, using a false identity. It had only been a matter of days. Karen had probably found refuge there, but that wasn't important now. She had been unequivocal – she wasn't going to help Sacha Duguin. Ingrid searched the rooms without finding anything of interest. She returned to the ground floor, saw a bottle of whisky on the worktop, and two clean glasses on the sink.

"Mars and you?"

"No, I never drink spirits."

She got her torch out again to examine the kitchen. The tiled floor was too clean. Mars had died during the monsoon season. His visitor must have had to come down the same track as they had. She eventually found a brownish stain at the foot of the refrigerator and a few more under the door.

"Is it blood?"

"Probably," said Koumba.

"Your friend was ready to leave. His bag was packed, the house was clean and tidy. No doubt he was going to say goodbye to you the next morning. But that evening, somebody turned up. Somebody he opened his door to and drank whisky with. Someone he trusted.

A strong man, because Mars was strong enough, and it turned ugly."

"The bogus doctor?"

"Why not?"

"Yet that man treated Karen."

"Mars could have opened the door for him. Of course you'd trust the man who saved your wife."

The floor had been cleaned, but not as thoroughly as it should have been. What if the blood were the murderer's? The D.N.A. could be analysed. She scraped the stains with a penknife and slipped the deposits into an envelope Koumba handed her.

They sat on opposite sides of the table while Ingrid listened to his story.

"During the Mobutu era, I was employed at the Central Bank in Kinshasa. Regime officials often used to embezzle huge sums of money. A colleague and I overheard conversations we shouldn't have. Soon afterwards, my colleague died in strange circumstances. Mars was head of security at the French embassy, where my wife worked. She turned to him for help, and he immediately offered to accompany us, with our four children, to the Côte d'Ivoire, where my sister had married a local."

His brother-in-law had helped him pick up a job as a driver. Koumba had assured the Frenchman of his eternal gratitude, and his help should he ever need it. This promise was only redeemed much later on, when Koumba, now a widower, received a call from Paris. Mars asked him if he could find a safe hideout for an unspecified length of time.

"You're going to find his murderer, mademoiselle. I can sense it."

"I wish I was as optimistic as you are."

"When you do, will you call me?"

"Sure, why not?"

"You have my card with my phone number. I want to know how the story ends. It's very important for me, you understand?"

"You have my word."

"His murderer didn't succeed in killing him, mademoiselle. I welcome Mars into my stories so that he can live forever. After me, another storyteller will take up the baton. And the children of Abidjan will never forget that Arnaud had a courageous, loyal heart."

The sound of footsteps. Koumba froze. With her back to the door, Ingrid turned round. A stranger in military uniform, weapon at the ready. He wasn't wearing a hood, and his expression revealed that he had every intention of killing them. Ingrid saw fear and then resignation in her companion's eyes. She regretted ever having dragged the old man into this nightmare.

The man slapped Koumba, sending him sprawling, before launching into an invective in his African dialect.

"He's done nothing, leave him alone!"

"Any African who helps foreigners is a traitor. And you don't seem to learn too fast."

She recognised the voice of the cigar smoker. The one who had been the first to piss on her. She imagined ripping his nose off with her teeth. He pointed his gun at her. She knew she was going to die.

A volcano of blood. The top of his head exploded.

Ingrid and Koumba threw themselves to the floor. Broken glass all over it. Ingrid yelled for the old man to stay still, and crawled towards the door. It was wide open, the garden a rectangle in the moonlight. The gardener's tools caught the light.

A silhouette. A torch beam hid the figure and blinded Ingrid.

She grabbed the pick, and ran out screaming.

"STOP, INGRID, IT'S ME!"

Sweat was running into her eyes; she was trembling. She leaned back against the wall, slid down it. She blessed her lucky stars and Léontin's bravery. He came up, stuffing his gun into the top of his jeans.

"Damn Yankee! I knew you'd get into trouble. I followed you in a taxi. And hid just in time when that mercenary arrived."

"You certainly grow on people, Léontin."

Koumba was crouched in a corner. The man in uniform was spread-eagled on the tiles, a halo of blood round his head. Léontin searched him, and found his papers.

"Hector Gassa. Do you know him, Koumba?"

"He spoke *bété*."

"What's *bété*?" Ingrid wanted to know.

"The language of the cocoa belt, in the centre-west of the country. What Laurent Gbagbo's people speak."

Léontin pointed to the gold ring on the dead man's right hand.

"It's the insignia of Cecos, the Command Centre for Security Operations. When the former president was in power, they committed atrocities. Rapes, abductions, random heavy-arms fire against pro-Ouattara demonstrators. And they were among the last to surrender. Gassa probably became a mercenary when the whole thing collapsed. You have to live."

"You shot in self-defence, there's no doubt about that," said Ingrid. "And he was a complete bastard. But the time he attacked Lola and me, he was with two subordinates. We mustn't stay here any longer . . ."

"You can forget self-defence, Ingrid," Léontin replied. "I was an Ouattara supporter. I fought with my weapon in my hand. The police are bound to see it as an act of political revenge. If you don't want to go to jail with me, we have to get rid of the body and all traces of us being here. If either of you has a problem with that, say so now."

Ingrid and Koumba shook their heads. Léontin told the old story-teller to clean up the blood, and the American to help him wrap the body in oilcloth. Picking up the casing, he dug the bullet out of the wall, and went for the spades stacked in the corridor. They put the body in the jeep parked a few hundred metres lower down; the ignition key was in one of the dead man's pockets. Ingrid and Koumba took the Chrysler; Léontin drove the jeep. They drove in reverse until they came to a track that plunged into the forest.

Ingrid helped dig the grave while Koumba kept a lookout. Then they set off again towards the south. Léontin went to hide the jeep in a mountain of old cars in a scrapyard.

Koumba lived in the Vidri district. They dropped him off there and headed back to the club.

"You and Lola are going to catch the next plane."

"But Léontin . . ."

"No buts. You can see we're not exactly overrun with tourists. Until recently, people were wreaking revenge here. The army and its supporters against those who had backed Gbagbo. It was very ugly. Worse than you could ever imagine. Before that, despite my age, I had hopes. Not anymore."

"Listen . . ."

"Politics is a deep well of shit I no longer want to hear about. So don't create any more problems – for yourself or for me. Agreed?"

"O.K., Léontin."

"Don't leave the club. And dance. I want witnesses who can say you and I spent the night at Kingo. Any objections?"

"None at all."

"About time."

Ingrid danced. It wasn't hard. With a bit of luck, Gassa's face would fade away, and so would the smell of blood and shit. She saw Léontin forcing himself to laugh with his friends. From time to time he came to put his arms round her for a slow dance. Wrapped in his reassuring embrace, she thought of the choice Mars had made. He had chosen to find refuge in a world in turmoil, a city that still bore the stench of death and war. He did so because he knew that in this chaos there was less risk of being discovered. And yet Sacha had followed his trail here. They had made peace. Sacha had left with relief in his heart, unaware of what was to follow. Like a curse.

She remembered the mason and the building-site. *I sometimes see a shadow passing by my window. The dead stay around for a while before they leave for good.* Did Mars laugh at all that?

I'm so tired.

She forced herself to go on dancing. She drank neat rum. And danced and danced.

So tired.

Towards midnight, she shut herself in the toilets to cry. She had almost died. Twice. First of all in Paris, then in Abidjan. Both times because of Sacha. Lola, Koumba and Léontin had almost lost their lives as well.

You bring me bad luck. I'll do anything to get you your life back, but after that, it's all over.

Taking her mobile out of her mud-stiffened jeans, she punched in the number. Everything would be better once she told him how much she missed him.

"Jake?"

24 THURSDAY, 31 JANUARY

Lola was snoring softly as Ingrid watched the daylight strengthen through the slats of the shutters. She was exhausted from her sleepless night, but her conversation with Jake had reassured her. All the more so because he was going to catch the next plane to Paris.

When her friend woke, Ingrid asked her what the diagnosis was.

"There's no internal bleeding, so they're releasing me tomorrow. What about you? Tell me."

"I finally found him."

"Koumba?"

"Yes."

"You did? Who is he?"

"Someone like Sénéchal. He spends his life spinning stories. Only his are more poetic."

She recounted her misadventures. Lola sat up in bed and clutched at her heart.

"I don't want anyone else dying on me, Lola," protested Ingrid. "Your heart can take it. Both our hearts can. Quick, put your clothes on and we can get out of here right now. Come on!"

They took advantage of a rush of patients to slip out of the hospital unnoticed. Léontin was waiting for them at the wheel of the Chrysler.

He headed for Port-Bouët and the airport. He knew a manager on the airline and had booked them seats on the first flight. Lola appreciated yet again how resourceful he was. Timothy Harlen was friends with lots of people like him. People who knew or had known the military, political or media worlds. She had often wondered whether the owner of the Calypso wasn't in fact a spy: his Pigalle cabaret would be a perfect cover.

An all-singing, all-dancing cover.

She was still wondering.

Pairs of soldiers were parading the check-in hall. Lola avoided catching their eye: anything was possible, even spitting out the appalling Hector Gassa.

"I admire you two, but it's a great relief to see you leave. When it comes to wreaking havoc, you take the biscuit. You ought to be renamed Ebola and Chikungunya. My regards to Timothy," said Léontin.

Ingrid gave him a bear-hug, warning him to be careful. Lola shook his hand and thanked him.

In the departure lounge, the ex-commissaire kept a sharp lookout, half expecting to be seized by thugs in military fatigues and thrown into the deepest of dungeons. She only relaxed when the Airbus finally began to cleave its way through the burning blue of the sky. Soon Abidjan was no larger than a hundred-thousand-piece jigsaw puzzle. She laid her head back on the rest and turned to look at Ingrid, who was listening to music on her headphones, staring into space. It would take her American friend a good while to digest the humiliation and violence. Lola patted her arm, then happily accepted the tray of food that the stewardess slid onto her table, though it didn't look very appetising.

Ingrid had mentioned a "young judge" whom Mars wanted to give the notebooks to. Which one could it be among the thousands of French magistrates? And anyway, youth, especially to someone as ancient as Arnaud Mars, was a relative concept. In other words, they hadn't advanced a Toyota, and yet their bodywork was severely dented.

"What's so funny, Lola?"

"Nothing. Or everything. I've no idea anymore."

25

Paris was shivering beneath torrents of icy rain. Lola almost missed Abidjan.

"I'm going to have a shower," Ingrid announced.

"Fascinating. Why's that so important?"

"You go into the shower with all your worries, and when you come out again they all look smaller. You have to believe in rituals, especially when there's nothing else."

Another wonderful *made in America* concept. Lola tipped the contents of her suitcase into the dirty laundry basket and recovered her faithful Manurhin. To each her own ritual.

They changed into warm clothing, gulped down coffee strong enough to wake the dead, and went out to face the snow. They took a detour via Sacha's apartment to pick up his toothbrush.

The lashing rain was streaking the red bricks of the Forensic Institute. The ex-commissaire called Franklin on her mobile.

His green smock bulged out from beneath a big black umbrella. He slid into the back seat of the Twingo. Lola caught the smell of the rain, of rotting flesh and disinfectant, and wound the window down. Ingrid had put the envelope with the dried blood and the toothbrush into a plastic bag. She handed it to the pathologist.

"Lola, my God! Did you collide with a baobab or something? This is getting out of hand, I'm not sure whether . . ."

"Do you prefer Sacha to be locked up for good, and for the Mars affair to be buried once and for all? Send these to the lab for analysis. And if you can, to someone you really trust. I want a comparison with both Mars' and Sacha's D.N.A. If it's not either of theirs, search all the available records. Can you do that all in one?"

"Apart from sexual delinquents, there aren't that many D.N.A. records."

"I may be retired, Franklin, but I know that in recent years the D.N.A. database has grown a lot. It includes everyone who's ever been arrested, doesn't it?"

"In theory, yes. In reality, it's not so clear-cut. The files are still mostly filled with sexual deviants. And if you want my opinion, this case doesn't have much *bunga-bunga* about it . . . In short, the best you can hope for is an unknown person's D.N.A. And what's the point of that?"

"We can start by ruling people out. Once that's done, we'll see . . ."

"Shit, shit and more shit! As if I didn't have enough work. If one day somebody invents a black hole to travel back in time, I'll buy the first ticket. The day I met you has to be marked with a red cross."

"Thomas, I adore you!"

"A flashing red cross!"

He climbed out of the car, still grumbling to himself. Lola remarked that Thomas Franklin's affections often took complicated detours.

"Speaking of affection, let's go to the 15th arrondissement, Ingrid."

"What is *bunga-bunga*, Lola?"

"An Italian fairy tale; don't bother about it."

"I'll look it up in the dictionary," sighed Ingrid.

"Yes, good idea."

They found somewhere to park on rue du Commerce. Several passers-by turned to stare at them. Ingrid was wearing her airman's jacket, a skirt the size of a handkerchief, white leggings with black horizontal stripes, and her faithful Doc Martens. Her friend's bruises had turned a caramel colour, and her expression was somewhere between utter concentration and the determination of a big game hunter.

They didn't switch the staircase light on, but sat on either side of Berlin's door. Their stay in Africa had taught them patience. Lola had time to mull over some troubling thoughts. Had Berlin really retired from the C.B.N.S. or was he still with them, working behind a smokescreen?

He listened to Beethoven for quite a while before deciding to leave his den. The lock turned. Bounding to her feet, Ingrid kicked the door hard. They heard a muffled cry. They went in, slammed the door behind them. Berlin was holding his bloody nose. Lola covered him with her Manurhin. Ingrid tied him up with the plastic straps she used to secure her suitcase, then found a bottle of milk in the fridge and poured it over his head.

"You're crazy!" he cursed under his breath.

"It's organic milk. Good for the skin. Much better than urine."

"And what do you think of my new look?" growled Lola.

"What are you talking about?"

"The treatment your friends dished out to us in Abidjan. And now we want an explanation."

"I have absolutely no idea what you're talking about."

"Somebody wanted to kill us. You were the only one who knew we were in Abidjan."

He swore he had nothing to do with their misadventures. They weren't exactly inconspicuous – anyone could have followed them. Once they were in Africa, all you needed were good connections.

"That's right," Lola said. "The good connections a good spook would have. Particularly one who was a specialist in Africa. It was there that you met Mars. Sénéchal told me so."

"Yes, Arnaud and I met in Africa. What of it?"

Lola had had time to think since Abidjan. About the N.G.O. doctor whose equipment and identity had been stolen. The guy who treated Karen, but in fact was scouting out the place. Who discovered that Mars, his wife and the little girl were all alone in that isolated house. He could tell how worried Mars was by Karen's fever. Did Mars tell him his wife had to get better within a few days because she had a plane to catch? Why not? What don't you tell a doctor?

"After his family left, Mars opened his door to someone he knew," Lola went on. "A friend, for example. He had a drink with him; they talked about the good old days. Days they had spent together in Africa."

"Can you see me tracking Mars down to Abidjan and killing him? It's been years since I left France."

"Prove it."

Berlin swore he had spent the summer and part of the autumn with his daughter. She and her husband had bought a cottage in a Breton village, and he had helped them do it up. Ingrid found the daughter's number on the internet. Lola called it. Following some confusion and the son-in-law's demand to speak to his father-in-law, the matter was settled. Berlin really was staying in Brittany when Mars was gunned down in Africa.

"I told you about Koumba. Did you find him?"

In order to get at the truth, Lola revealed some of what they had learned. She told him about their torturers from Cecos, and the possibility that Mars had tried to contact a young French judge while in Africa. She didn't mention the exchange between Ingrid and Karen Mars or the D.N.A. sample. All this seemed to be news to the former spook. Lola had to admit he appeared sincere. She asked Ingrid to untie him, but kept hold of her Manurhin.

Berlin wiped his face with the towel Ingrid handed him.

"So you're a G.I. trained at Guantanamo, are you?"

"Just going with the flow."

"It's obvious somebody wants you off the case, and hired mercenaries to pass on the message."

"Well done, Sherlock, and then what?" Lola said.

"That somebody can't be Gratien. How could he organise all that from jail? If you say they were from Cecos, the person behind it must be well connected with international political circles."

"That's exactly what I was thinking on the plane."

"Sorry to disappoint you, but yet again I can't help. What does occur to me is . . ."

"Tell me."

"The person behind this didn't simply hire attack dogs. He wanted a precision strike. Those paramilitaries rape, kill and think afterwards. But you two are still alive."

"Yes, I noticed that. Any suggestions?"

"The Candichard clan. But that's only one possibility. The notebooks are stuffed with names and addresses."

"Louis Candichard committed suicide. Too late there."

"Mathilde Candichard has never accepted her husband's death. The same goes for their son, Guillaume. Their name has been dragged through the mud. In the circles they move in, that's even harder to accept."

"What do you mean by 'has never accepted'?"

"Candichard killed himself at home with his shotgun. Soon afterwards, Mathilde Candichard did the rounds of all the officials. Police, judges. And a fair few journalists."

"She didn't believe it was suicide?"

"Everyone knows it was. But I'm not inside that woman's head. All I know is that in the end she calmed down. But that doesn't mean she accepted it . . ."

"Wait a minute. Can you imagine the family paying someone to murder Arnaud Mars because he pushed Louis Candichard to commit suicide?"

"Candichard was once foreign minister. His family inherited a healthy address book."

"So according to you, the Candichard family might know someone who knows someone who knows a gang of mercenaries ready and willing to put the fear of God into two busybodies who might just bring the contract on Mars to light?"

"It's no more ridiculous than any other supposition."

"Where do the Candichards live?" asked Ingrid.

He gave them an address close to Les Invalides.

"It's an ivory tower where you'll need to do more than ring the bell to gain entrance, Lola."

"Do you know the magic formula, Ali Baba?"

"I don't know anything. I don't even know Mathilde Candichard personally."

"But you know someone who knows someone who . . ."

Berlin thought it over for a moment.

"Gildas Sénéchal," he said. "The political aristocracy is his milieu."

"That's good, I've already met him."

"I know, I followed you and your G.I. friend here. And above all, I know that with him you're running no risks. You can cross him off your list of those keen to get their hands on . . ."

"On Gratien's notebooks?"

"Sénéchal devoted most of his career to Paul Borel. He even set up office in the Elysée Palace. And President Borel died at least twelve years ago."

Cancer. Lola remembered it clearly: it was the same year as the Al-Qaeda attack on the Twin Towers.

"Sénéchal lives in his memories?"

"That's right. And the iniquities of the current crop of politicians do no more than amuse him. He's always been a cynical gambler. At his age, he might still want to have some fun before the last act. So yes, I guess he'll help you."

Ingrid had finished mopping up the rest of the milk and was wondering whether there was a recycling bin. Berlin confirmed there was. Ingrid tossed the empty bottle away. The ex-spook studied the young American woman.

"I really don't understand what two girls like you are doing mixed up in such a dangerous business. Two tiny Davids against a huge Goliath. A Goliath whose face no-one has ever seen."

"I thought your bet was the Candichards," Lola said.

"I repeat: that's just one possibility among many. And while you're trying to untangle this mess, you two could very well get yourselves shot."

Ingrid received a text that left her beaming. She replied as rapidly as possible. Lola used the remote to start Beethoven again. Berlin gave her a crooked smile. The two women left.

As they walked towards the Twingo, Ingrid was humming a song Lola did not recognise. Lola revealed her doubts. Gratien had spent a lifetime filling his notebooks. There were as many people named there as in the Chinese army. Among them, the person who had ordered Mars' murder and implicated Sacha. And he had already identified them. They on the other hand could only guess at his identity. The Candichard clan, for example. But it was hard to imagine a former minister's family adopting a drug cartel's methods.

"Candichard or not, somebody has us in their sights. The tragic end of an American tourist and a retired commissaire aren't exactly up there with the death of Paris Hilton or our minister of justice, are they? Who would give a damn?"

"Jake would."

"And you think that's a joke?"

Ingrid announced that her fiancé had just landed in Paris and "was jumping into a taxi". She started the Twingo's engine, set a course for rue de l'Echiquier, and launched into an enthusiastic description of all Jake Carnegie's qualities. Youthful recklessness, thought Lola. How could she limit the damage? She would have to convince this Jake to put his intended on a flight back to Uncle Sam's fair land as soon as possible. And ask her friend Bianco to create a stir in the press. So that she would no longer be so anonymous. After all, there was a story to tell. The story of a retired commissaire who refused to accept the arrest of a young cop and the death of an old one. Once she was visible in the media, she would no longer be an impersonal target.

Some hope. Bianco had been out of the loop for ages. And who would be interested in the portrait of an old busybody like her? There was a simpler, more reliable and much less glorious solution. She could place her trust in Captain Hardy, tell him about the information they had stumbled on in Abidjan, including the D.N.A. samples, and call for the French police to protect them.

She could hear the chatter of monkeys and crickets. She imagined the face Mars would have pulled as he poured himself another whisky and split his sides laughing on the flat roof under the baking sun. "The French police's protection! That's a good one, Lola!"

Brown hair combed back, high forehead, hazel-coloured eyes in a well-defined face that was slightly weather-beaten, an ample, serious mouth: Jake Carnegie looked more like a playboy than a journalist, but Lola liked him on the spot. His whole being seemed as firm as his handshake, and he didn't beat about the bush.

"I should never have let you leave. What happened in Africa is atrocious."

"We came out of Africa brilliantly," said Ingrid.

"You have a very strange idea of what's brilliant."

"It helped us make progress, and now that you're here you can lend a hand."

Visibly overjoyed to see him, Ingrid felt no shame contradicting him with that astonishing effrontery she pulled out of her hat from time to time.

"That's absurd. I don't see why you'd make a better job of it than the French police. Besides, if I've understood correctly, your friend Lola is still one of them to some extent. She'll be able to find useful support. Anyway, I'm not letting go of you again."

"O.K., we can talk about all that at the hotel, baby."

"You won't get your way, Ingrid."

Lola watched them walk off. Jake was carrying the two suitcases: from the back, his physique was even more impressive. If anyone was able to make Ingrid see reason, it could well be this providential young man.

26   FRIDAY, 1 FEBRUARY

On the pavement outside her building, Lola saw a scooter and a motorbike, their saddles dusted with snow. For once, the lift cage was plunged into silence. She arrived at the second floor breathing heavily.

Joseph Berlin was squatting on her doormat, a black helmet at his feet. He smiled at her, but somehow that didn't seem very encouraging.

"Ah, Lola, at last . . ."

"You have a motorbike?"

"A scooter. Traffic jams have never been my thing. You don't answer your mobile."

"I had a meeting."

In fact, she had gone to the cinema to clear her mind. She switched her phone back on, saw she had a text message. The ex-spook was staring at her in an odd way. His ice-cold eyes must have perturbed quite a few people in the days when he had been active. She read the message: he was asking her to call him urgently.

"What's wrong?"

"Gratien is dead."

She froze. Berlin had heard the news from a contact at the C.B.N.S.: Mister Africa's throat slit with an improvised weapon by a fellow inmate.

Lola recalled her meeting with Gratien. His terror. The way he had begged Captain Hardy to get him transferred. He swore he no longer had the notebooks, but the names, events, dates were all in his memory. Was that why he had been killed?

"Now's the time to get your Manurhin out of its drawer, Lola, and to keep it with you."

What was it she could read in his eyes? Concern, or something more complicated?

He had already picked up his helmet and was heading down the stairs. The timer on the light came to an end, and everything went dark. The sound of the front door, Berlin's footsteps, the scooter starting up. Lola opened the door to her apartment.

Jake was paying the driver. As Ingrid got out of the taxi, she felt a lump in her throat. She had thought she would never set foot in Pigalle again.

"So this is where Gabriella Tiger, the Queen of the Parisian demi-monde, used to hold court?"

"Yes. Are you sure you want to go in, Jake?"

"I'm interested in everything about you, Ingrid."

She loved his generosity, his open mind. How many men would have accepted her past as a striptease artiste so elegantly? She had never hidden anything from him, and she had been right.

Enrique the doorman rejoiced to see her. She took a deep breath and crossed the threshold of the Calypso. They went to the bar.

Jake ordered two gin and tonics. The light from the spots dimmed a little.

"*AND NOW, LADIES AND GENTLEMEN*, ET MAINTENANT MESDAMES ET MESSIEURS, *OUR WEAPON OF MASS DESTRUCTION, OUR NUKE STRAIGHT OUT OF THE RUSSIAN ARSENAL, THE SUBLIME, THE WONDERFUL, THE ATOMIC BUT VULNERABLE ANOUCHKA!*"

Fade to black. The sound of boots. A regiment was invading the Calypso to the sound of a Status Quo hit record. In a circle of light, a cornered soldier. Floodlights showed a line of paras wearing red berets. The soldier fell to his knees. A para raised his machine gun, struck him with the butt. The two enemies began a choreographed combat.

The para tore off the soldier's helmet, unleashing a mane of blonde hair. The para tore off the soldier's uniform. Not a man but a woman: a tank-top moulded the warheads of her breasts and a wasp waist. "ANOUCHKAAA," shouted a fan. She kicked out at the para's muscular torso.

She grasped the knife strapped to her ankle. The para stepped in and she lost both knife and trousers. The audience could appreciate her long, lithe legs despite the stern lace-up boots, a G-string and a khaki suspender belt.

The para sent the tank-top flying; now the satiny upper body of his adversary was protected only by a see-through bra. A desperate hand-to-hand struggle; the divine Anouchka's clenched teeth and staring eyes stood out dramatically beneath her camouflage paint. The bra capitulated. Anouchka squeezed her formidable breasts in both hands. The para tore off her G-string to reveal a bush matching her mane of hair. An about-turn, provocative buttocks, Anouchka's head dropped. Surrender.

The defeated woman soldier launched into a pleading whirl that produced an enthusiastic "GO FOR IT, ANOUCHKA!" from the audience. The pair mimed a realistic sexual embrace, then the Russian enemy appeared to strangle the para in the vice of her thighs, before finally sparing his life.

Whistles, applause; Anouchka left the stage carried shoulder high by the line of paratroopers.

Jake whispered into Ingrid's ear.

"Not bad, but I'm sure your show was better."

She gave him a hug, but pulled back when she felt a hand on her shoulder.

Timothy Harlen in a white tuxedo. He took her in his arms, shook Jake's hand.

"Aren't you surprised to see me, Timothy?"

"Jake had arranged to meet, sweetheart."

"Do you two know each other?"

In response, she caught a glimpse of two complicit smiles.

They followed the Calypso owner into his office. A waiter brought the best champagne in the house.

"Anouchka performs well," said Timothy, "but she's lacking some soul."

"If you're trying to get Ingrid back, that's not exactly a subtle approach," said Jake.

"You're a reporter, aren't you? All you need to be happy is a computer. Especially in Paris."

"You think Ingrid would be happy in Paris? Possibly. But safe — that's another matter."

"Do I have to remind you I have a wonderful job in Vegas?" Ingrid interrupted them. "What I want to know is what you two are cooking up together."

"Jake told me about your problems in Abidjan with Lola. It's true I dream of having you back here, but he's right. You'd do better to return to the States as quickly as possible."

"No chance. Lola needs me. And sweeping problems under the carpet is never the solution."

Timothy opened his safe and took out a sensational-looking pistol. He found a magazine and gave them both to Jake. It was a Strike One, a stylish recent model. Semi-automatic, seventeen bullets in the magazine, a pistol designed for the Russian police and army. Ingrid protested.

"Timothy, you've been living in Europe for ages now. You ought to know nobody goes around armed like they do in the States."

"Let's just say it's a pretty dissuasive deterrent," said Jake, "and leave it at that. Thanks, Timothy."

"Don't mention it."

Ingrid's mobile rang. She had a short conversation, rang off, took a few seconds to absorb what she had heard.

"That was Lola. Richard Gratien has been murdered by someone in jail."

Jake tested the safety catch on the Strike One, then stuck it in his waistband.

"You may have inherited your enemy's enemy, Ingrid. Let's go back to Vegas."

"If that's true and these are their methods, there's no difference between Vegas and Paris."

In the taxi back to their hotel, he looked grim. She cuddled up to him and broke the silence.

"Jake, admit it. You're jealous."

Just as she had not hidden her Pigalle nights from him, she had also told him about her romance with Sacha.

"You've no reason to be," she went on. "It's over between him and me."

"Are you really running all these risks just for Lola? Be honest."

"I'm being faithful. To a man I no longer love but once did. I bet you would do the same."

"Jake the knight in shining armour? Thanks but no thanks."

"You're a good guy, Jake Carnegie. Whether you like it or not. I know it. And you're the only one I want to be with."

"Well, that's the only piece of good news I've heard all evening."

Through the windscreen, the neon light of the hotel was magnified by the rain. Ingrid slipped her hand under his shirt and felt him quiver.

"And I'm going to prove it to you."

27 SATURDAY, 2 FEBRUARY

Gildas Sénéchal switched off his phone, put it on the kitchen table and started to run a bath. Lola Jost really was extraordinarily tenacious. And she had a remarkable sense of loyalty. A shame she wasted it on undeserving people. Be that as it may, he would do as she asked, and put her in touch with Louis Candichard's widow.

He plugged his iPod into the bathroom speakers, chose a Stockhausen concerto and watched the bathtub rapidly fill.

Lyons, 1950. No washing machine. His mother uses the square tub to wash clothes with a brush, a washboard and a big block of Marseilles soap. She needs a lot of elbow grease to clean his father's overalls. They have to soak for hours for the oil stains to dissolve. To have a bath, Gildas has to move the washboard and put the overalls in a basin.

Grandfather has been living with them since the death of Grandma. He is passionate about dominoes and the life of ants. His father smokes unfiltered Gauloises, doesn't talk much, but, like all the Sénéchal family, listens to the radio a lot. His mother's best friend is Big Luce, a fortune-teller and the local bonesetter. "You get to understand people, my little Gildas, if you study them closely and let them say their piece. It tires the brain, but it's worth it."

Tilting his head back, Sénéchal's thoughts turned to his wife Geneviève. They were seventeen when they had met. Beautiful, funny, full of energy, from a cultured, well-off family, she should never have given him a second glance. And yet they had stayed together all their lives. She had loved him when he was nothing more than a small-time insurance salesman. Had supported him when he had started at the bottom in a big advertising agency hired by someone without prejudices. Had not once protested when he began to work exclusively for Paul Borel and spent more time with the person she called "your great man" than with their family.

Following her death, Paul had got an artist friend to paint Geneviève's portrait from a photograph. Gildas had struggled to contain his emotions when he had been given the painting. Paul Borel was unique in the world of politics. Of course, he was capable of turning against his closest allies if they had witnessed his own failings, or to wait for years for the opportunity to crush an enemy, but he was never insensitive to real suffering. He had a heart. And a sincere love of his country, which he criss-crossed to exhaustion on his election campaigns.

Gildas still remembered every detail of their battle against Candichard, a man of intrigues and opportunistic alliances. For his part, Paul had earned the confidence of the French voters by winning it from them day after day, with an energy and simplicity that did him proud. He had never cut such an impressive figure as when it was a matter of conquering the country.

And women. *What a contrast with me*, thought Sénéchal with a smile. Paul had a frenetic need to pursue them. All those nights when he slipped away, driven by Mondo, his smiling companion, always discreet and understanding. When things got out of hand, the situation had to be sorted out with the journalists and Gildas had employed all his powers of imagination.

Gildas, I've got a bit of a problem.

I'll sort it out, Mister President.

Those were happy and rather amusing days, trying to mop up the Rabelaisian misadventures of a man who was occasionally stifled by his official garb and needed to kick over the traces.

The sound of footsteps on the wooden floor. Mondo was back from doing the shopping.

"I've bought some calf sweetbreads for lunch, Gildas. In a Madeira sauce, perhaps?"

"Yes, I couldn't care less."

"Are you in a bad mood?"

"No, I have to phone Mathilde Candichard. To ask her to receive Lola Jost. And that's such a bore. I've always found Mathilde so dull. You call her."

"It will be more persuasive if you do it."

"That wasn't a suggestion, Mondo. And close the door. I can't bear kitchen smells when I'm taking my bath."

28 MONDAY, 4 FEBRUARY

Morning. A pale sun. A small, happy crowd.

Mondo glided off, hands behind his back, turned a wide curve, spun round, accelerated, became a spinning top. He slowed to a halt, took a bow. Ingrid impressed him with a few figures, then joined him by the barrier. Behind them, the Paris city hall was like a cinematic castle. He told her he was born in the Alps. His sister, a champion in her youth, had taught him to skate.

His black woollen hat was pulled down over his eyes. With his hair invisible, his features looked harsher, but Ingrid liked his lively eyes, the way he could switch between being serious and funny. It had been his idea to fit in this skating session before the meeting.

They handed in their skates and climbed into his car, a comfortable metallic-grey Volvo. Mondo blew on his hands before he turned the key in the ignition, then pulled away gently along rue de Rivoli. Ingrid also liked the way he drove: extremely careful, but smooth. On the way he explained that Valérie had suffered from the stress that ruined the lives of many sports champions. After the competitions, the medals, the fifteen minutes of fame, when it was all over and her partner and lover had dropped her for a younger member of the team, his little sister had gone into a decline.

"She was strong and ambitious. It was the same in reverse when she went off the rails: she hit rock bottom."

"What does she do now?"

"She's dead. An overdose."

"I'm sorry."

"Don't be. There's nothing to be done. I miss her. I go back home twice a year to visit her grave. I tell her of my joys, my troubles. Recently I haven't had much to say: I'm growing old. But you make me feel young again. You're like a burst of energy, Ingrid. It flows all round you. Do you have someone in your life?"

"Yes."

"Lucky man."

They chatted easily throughout the rest of the journey. Mondo confessed he could have become a chef. A profession that would have satisfied him for quite a few years.

"But you met Sénéchal . . ."

"Yes, it was a turning point in my life. He's a real brain, and on top of that he's trustworthy. I've never had to fear he would change his mind and sack me. In fact, he saved me."

"Tell me about it."

"He took me on to be President Paul Borel's driver. I used to be a racing driver, I have good reflexes."

"So I've noticed. Was it interesting working for him?"

"Fascinating. He never spared himself."

Borel's right hand was damaged because the cartilages had been stretched from shaking hands so many thousands of times. His fans didn't know their strength and couldn't control their enthusiasm.

"I was in charge of the ice-bucket," said Mondo with a smile. "The president dipped his aching hand into it between meetings. He worked like a dog. And at night he would see his mistresses."

"Did that involve you too?"

"Twenty-four hours a day. That was the flipside of the coin, but we both had some great times. He was the opposite of a snob. He really loved people, whatever their origin, and in return the French loved him. That happy episode came to an end. After his death, the hangers-on were waiting for me."

"Why?"

"The survivors from the Borel era made me pay for being so close to their great man. We had had too much fun, and I had witnessed certain aspects of his personality that some people were keen to forget. They wanted to turn him into a statue. In short, I was thrown out. Gildas was the only one who gave me a helping hand. But there's no such thing as a free lunch . . ."

Ingrid could read between the lines. Mondo lived a life of luxury, but he was still a servant. For all his intelligence and glorious past, Sénéchal was a demanding old man who must have his little ways.

"Were you ever married, Mondo?"

"Only once, and for a short time. I have the soul of a loner."

He made a detour via a florist's. The scent of lilies soon filled the car.

A freezing Lola was waiting patiently for them outside Mathilde Candichard's apartment block.

"Lola, what have you . . . ?"

"I tripped getting out of my wing-chair when I was doing a puzzle, Mondo. It's nothing."

He gave them some advice. Madame Candichard was probably depressed: she had never recovered from her husband's suicide. It was only with great difficulty that Sénéchal had persuaded her to see them. As usual, he had made up a story.

"As far as Mathilde is concerned, you're writing a long article on Mars."

Ingrid watched him drive off. He raised a hand level with the rearview mirror and waved a brief goodbye without turning round. Ingrid did the same.

"You two have become the best of friends," Lola remarked.

"I remind him of his sister."

"Yes, so you told me. Shall we go in?"

"I would have liked Jake to be here."

"I can't really charge into the home of Candichard's widow with an army in tow."

Jake's parting look that morning flashed through Ingrid's mind. He had slipped the Strike One into her bag, and made her promise to call him at the slightest problem.

A small red-haired woman who looked weary and sad, Mathilde Candichard was wearing an elegant dress, but had sock-mittens on her feet, wore flip-flops and plastic gloves she seemed reluctant to take off. She did not react when she saw Lola's swollen features or Ingrid's baroque outfit. The apartment was huge, with too much furniture in it. It smelled of polish. A collection of antique kimonos was hanging on the walls from wooden poles. A black iron teapot with a delicate design stood waiting for them on a low table in the living room.

"Japan is my favourite country. I've made several trips there. If I had the money, I'd go and spend my last days there."

"In spite of the nuclear problem, the tsunamis, the earthquakes and the recession?" asked Lola.

"It's a dream, not market research."

She poured the tea. In the next room Lola could make out a piano, a vacuum cleaner and a bowl full of cleaning products. No cleaning woman was apparent. She imagined Mathilde scrubbing her big apartment from morning to night to fill the void, calm her nerves, or forget that this was where her husband had committed suicide. According to Sénéchal, after withdrawing from the election campaign against Borel, Candichard had spent his time in the political wilderness, surviving thanks to second-rate jobs. A rich friend had lent them this apartment so that the ex-minister could keep up appearances. Candichard had never left the wilderness. *Politicians who abort their career are very rare in France.*

Lola introduced Ingrid as her researcher, and asked if they could record the conversation. Mathilde accepted, provided she could see the text before it appeared. The ex-commissaire switched on the recorder. Did Louis Candichard know Arnaud Mars personally?

"No, that man destroyed us without even knowing us. After the article in *Le Canard Enchaîné*, Louis seemed calm, but I was wrong. I didn't understand what he was going through . . ."

"Did you hate Mars for it?"

"No. . . . What good does it do to hate anyone?"

"Really?"

"The notebooks were a sword of Damocles. I thought Louis had learned to live with it."

"Mars was killed as well. And Gratien has just been murdered in jail."

Mathilde Candichard placed the tea infuser in a porcelain cup. Her hands were trembling. Her eyes blinked rapidly.

"I don't know what more I can add. In fact, I don't think I can be of any use to you. I live in my memories and my dreams."

"There are several reasons why Mars could have been killed. Revenge. Gratien's notebooks. I learned from a reliable source that he had the notebooks with him. On a U.S.B. stick that wasn't found on his body."

"It's possible."

"In his final moments, Gratien swore he no longer had the notebooks, but he must have had names and facts in his head. Perhaps that's why he was killed."

The widow raised her head.

"We went to Abidjan to investigate Mars' death. We almost met the same fate."

"You've chosen a fascinating but dangerous career."

"That's what I tell myself every day. I'm here because I met somebody who thinks you may be the person behind Mars' murder. An act of revenge. How would you respond to such an accusation?"

"I'm going to have to ask you to leave."

An expressionless voice. The face unchanged. She leapt up and headed for the door, her flip-flops clacking on the wooden floor. Lola apologised: she provoked people to get information. It was a journalist's technique, not exactly polite but it got results. Could they start again more calmly?

"Out."

She and Ingrid left. The widow slammed the door behind them with astonishing force. While they were waiting for the lift, she reappeared to fling Mondo's lilies after them. Ingrid picked up a stem and followed her friend into the contraption, an old-fashioned model with wrought iron and frosted glass. Through it they saw a shadow racing down the stairs.

When they reached the ground floor, their way was barred by a blond forty-something, out of breath and extremely angry.

"Guillaume Candichard. My mother is distraught. What is it you want exactly?"

"We're writing a book on the Mars affair. From first-hand information."

"I overheard your conversation. Do you think you can simply waltz into people's homes and insult them?"

Lola declared that she was counting on leaving the lift and the building without hindrance. The Candichard son let them pass.

"Whether you're writers of crappy biographies or journalists from the gutter press, you're all vultures. You don't have enough readers to buy your books or your rags anymore, so you turn to sensationalism."

"Think what you like, young man."

"If you drag my father's name through the mud, you'll have my lawyer to reckon with."

29

To their surprise, Mondo was waiting for them in his Volvo. Ingrid slid in beside him, Lola got in the back.

"How did it go?"

"Badly," Lola said. "She threw us out. And the offspring added his pennyworth. His face was a picture: a mixture of humiliation and anger. Possibly fear as well."

Mondo simply nodded, then dropped her at rue de l'Echiquier before driving on with Ingrid. Through the windscreen, Lola could see her sniffing the lily.

In her apartment, the puzzle was gathering dust. Rain was beating at the windowpanes. She called Berlin and told him about her meeting with the Candichard widow and her son. What did he do for a living?

"He's a surgeon."

"You don't say."

"A dead end, Lola. I've already checked. When Mars was killed in Africa, he was attending a medical conference in Germany."

"You can pretty much come and go as you please in those conferences."

"You think the Candichards hired someone?"

"The mother lives on her friends' charity. If the son paid somebody to follow Sacha, steal his gun, smuggle it to Africa, execute Mars and then put the Smith & Wesson back where it belonged, that's much more expensive than simply hiring a hitman."

"A surgeon would have the means . . ."

"I suppose so."

She opened her refrigerator. Almost empty apart from a curled-up slice of ham and three yoghurts. She suddenly felt like inviting Berlin to meet at the Belles restaurant. A kind of complicity seemed to be establishing itself between her and the old spook.

She thought better of it. Gratien been murdered, taking with him secrets that were vital if they were to prove Sacha's innocence. He meanwhile was rotting in his cell. No, she didn't feel like celebrating with Maxime and her friends in passage Brady.

"Gildas gave you a hand. I thought he would; he's friendly enough when he likes people. He has lived a full life and wants to enjoy every last drop of it. But watch out for the flunkey."

"Mondo?"

"Yes, he's an ex-drug addict. I've always been suspicious of his kind."

Mondo parked outside the Hotel Renaissance. Ingrid opened the car door. He brushed her shoulder.

"Come and have something to eat. Wherever you like."

"My fiancé is waiting for me . . ."

"You're going to spend the rest of your life with him. That means around . . . sixty thousand meals. You can spare one for me."

"That's true."

"Perfect. Where shall we go?"

"To the Belles, near Canal Saint-Martin. It used to be my canteen when I lived in Paris."

They went there on foot. The restaurant was full, but Maxime found a table and two folding chairs for them, and placed them near the kitchen. Sigmund, the Dalmatian belonging to their shrink friend Antoine Léger, came dancing between Ingrid's legs and went wild with joy when she scratched him behind the ears.

"You don't know how happy it makes me to see you again," Antoine declared poetically.

"The same goes for you, doc."

"If you run into Lola, tell her we can't wait to see her."

They were served a carafe of Maxime's house wine, and she asked him to choose their menu for them.

"You're not exactly a stranger here, are you?" Mondo remarked.

"They're my friends, and I missed them a lot in Vegas."

*

They were installed in the bar at the Hotel Renaissance. Mondo's back was hurting, and he was squirming on the bar stool.

"It's odd, Ingrid. Who would have thought I'd find someone I felt as good with as Valérie? When she retired from competition, my sister was offered several opportunities. A Canadian company wanted to hire her for an artistic ice-skating show. An extremely well-paid international tour."

"She didn't accept?"

"No. She lived from day to day. In fact, she was already hooked on drugs."

"What a waste."

"Yes, she would have been perfect in the show. I was younger than her; I admired everything she did. I took drugs like her, and with her. When she died, I went on doing so. Her death didn't stop me. I think I wanted to be with her in the eternal snows. Then one day I realised I had hit rock bottom."

"Why?"

"I snorted her ashes."

Ingrid stared at him without a word.

"I had the urn at my place, so I made a line. That same week, I met Gildas during a political rally Paul Borel was giving in Annecy. Shortly afterwards he paid for me to go into rehab in a private clinic. Because he could 'see my potential'."

"You sound bitter when you say that."

"I've learned a lot thanks to him. Especially about cookery, on a very fashionable course he insisted on paying for. But his intelligence is scathing, cold as ice."

"For example?"

"*If there are forests, it's because squirrels are stupid.*"

"Meaning?"

"That they have a poor memory and forget where they've hidden two-thirds of their store of walnuts, acorns and hazelnuts. Thanks to that, trees can spread and grow. Similarly, according to Gildas, stupidity is indispensable to democracy. Voters are stupid in the main, but it's thanks to them that there are politicians. In other words, people get themselves elected on the basis of promises that are either lies or fantasies. If that weren't the case, we'd be governed by grey but efficient technocrats, or worse still by computers that would oblige us to lead lives as virtuous as they were irritating."

"And there'd be no room for spin doctors."

"Exactly."

"What about you – do you think that voters are stupid?"

"My father was employed by a firm that made ski-lifts; my mother was a café waitress. I've rarely met anybody as full of life and free as those two were. They didn't want success, they wanted to live surrounded by the beauty of the mountains. No, people aren't stupid. Possibly just a bit too romantic."

"If that's a failing."

"I often wonder if all that noise and effort to get us where we are now isn't simply a waste of time."

"What do you mean?"

"Gildas helped Borel win his first election. At the end of his first term, he stuck to it and helped him win again. But when his 'great man' died, the country was in the same state as it had been when he came to power. Borel allowed the deficit to increase. Just like his predecessors. He wasn't one to take unpopular measures."

"He wanted the French to love him."

"Yes. The worst of it was that he didn't have any precise plan before the elections. Gildas' mantra has always been: *Let's win first, then decide*. In other words, Gildas and Borel were masters at winning elections, but their record in office is catastrophic."

The pianist was playing "Human Nature" by Michael Jackson. Ingrid started humming the tune, and Mondo smiled at her.

"Dancer or singer?"

"Definitely a dancer."

"Me too. I love this song. Gildas only listens to contemporary music. It's hellish. Some days I wish I was deaf."

He grimaced. Ingrid went to talk to the hotel concierge. She won the right to use the beautician's room.

Mondo undressed, stretched out, and surrendered to Ingrid's expert hands. She massaged him until she felt all his nervous tension dissolve.

"You could just be the third important person I've met in my life. And in spite of yourself, Ingrid."

"Why 'in spite of myself'?"

"You're a sign from the heavens."

"What do the heavens tell you?"

"I'm not sure. Possibly that my time with Gildas is coming to an end. That I should pack my bags. That I should devote the last part of my life to something more than being the factotum of the spin doctor genius."

"Spin doctors are all the rage back in the States."

"They're all the rage the world over."

She ran to pick up, slipped, recovered her balance, grabbed the phone naked, her teeth chattering.

"You kept me waiting, Lola."

"I was in the shower. Have you got the results?"

"It's not Mars' blood."

"Fantastic! And it's not . . ."

"At your age, it's sad to get in such a state over a good-looking kid who could be your son," sniggered Thomas Franklin.

Lola couldn't help thinking she had more in common with Sacha than her own son.

"Cut it short, for God's sake."

"You can rest assured that the D.N.A. is not Sacha Duguin's either."

She could not contain a whoop of joy.

"Thanks for deafening me. Well anyway, it's as I suspected: the D.N.A. didn't match any of our records."

"Thomas, keep those results under your hat."

"Of course I will, princess. Always at your service for the slightest whim."

The pathologist hung up. Lola stared at the phone as if it were a friendly orangutan, then dialled Ingrid's number.

"Yesterday I had my watch stolen, Lola. Jake gave it to me, and it had my name engraved on it. Now I couldn't care less. In fact, I'd give all my jewels and my Calypso costumes to set Sacha free. We all need a cause that bypasses us, don't we?"

A cause that hoots and overtakes us" you mean, Lola thought after she had hung up. In the meantime, how could she get that D.N.A. to talk?

30 TUESDAY, 5 FEBRUARY

A fellow who never stopped talking. He went on and on, and was starting to make her head spin. Lola was chatting to an elegant fellow in a white suit. A tag on his left breast pocket named him as "The Big Boss". He was explaining that Ingrid had cheated death twice, but now her number was up. The next time would be for real, there was no extra credit. The times were ruthless, even for the employees of the Bank of Heaven. He rang a little glass bell, not once taking his eyes off Lola.

She woke up with a start. Who was that white-robed old creep? Her digital alarm clock showed 1.43 a.m.

"Hello? I wanted to warn you right away, boss. It's Sacha . . ."

The Barthélemy of her worst nightmares.

"What about Sacha?"

She flapped her hand across her chest. Her heart had just done a double backwards somersault. *Had Sacha been killed, like Gratien?*

"He's confessed to killing Mars."

"What are you talking about . . . ?"

"I don't know the details, but apparently Sacha has admitted that the purchase of the S.I.G. Sauer and the botched crime scene were a fake. All his idea. To make people believe it wasn't an experienced cop who had done it."

"That's impossible . . ."

She knew it wasn't Sacha's D.N.A. in Koumba's house.

She had got up and paced around, but now she collapsed into her wing-chair. Flashes of light behind her eyelids.

"He's been formally charged with murder by the prosecutor," Barthélemy continued.

He tried to comfort her. She let him.

When she had hung up, she concentrated on her breathing. She had to stay in one piece.

Her world was a sandcastle. A few walls were left standing, but the howling wind would soon put paid to her poor ramparts. Philippe Hardy's voice resonated in her mind. *Duguin is both intelligent and manipulative. A sociopath who met his match.* Had Sacha been taking them for a ride? All of them, apart from Hardy? Had she been blinded by her affection for him? By all the time she had spent waiting for Ingrid to come back, for life to have some passion, for her son to send her a puzzle for her birthday? She struggled to avoid confronting the booze-sodden face of reality.

Could it all really have been nothing more than a story of revenge? Revenge for Gratien, who despite his protests had ordered the attack on Ingrid? And revenge for Sacha, who had cunningly organised the pursuit and death of his former chief? Had he used her, her stupid faithfulness? He knew she would never accept his arrest, and would do all she could to prove his innocence. To the extent of perjuring herself, if Hardy had let her.

Hardy has been crafty and patient. Sacha realised that without my false statement backing him up, he was done for.

She remade Christ's body with the tip of her first finger. A real brain-teaser: ten thousand pieces, hours of fun.

At eight in the morning, she called Ingrid. Her American friend sounded very happy. Lola regretted having to spoil the atmosphere. Ingrid gave a stifled cry, and fell silent.

"Ingrid?"

"I have to think. I can't take it in for now. I'll call you back."

A short time later, Lola tore up the Corcovado with both hands and threw the pieces back in their box.

Game over.

Ingrid rang back two hours later.

"I've never been mistaken about my lovers. Other people, perhaps, but not the men I've slept with. It's not Sacha. He doesn't have it in him. I just know. That's all there is to it."

Lola's only reply was an exhausted sigh.

"Someone's putting pressure on him, Lola. His confession is a fake, like all the rest. Bullshit. But we can't leave it at that. You can't, and I can't."

Lola waited for her to go on.

"I've had an idea."

"I'm listening."

"It came by chance, thanks to a conversation I had yesterday with Jake. He's a novelist as well as a journalist. When he's stuck on a scene in a novel or screenplay, he turns things upside down."

"Ah."

Lola wondered what she was getting at.

"For example, he changes a character's sex, which makes the scene stronger. Or he reverses the setting. Instead of a lowlife dive at night, it becomes a slice of life in a sunny spot."

"O.K."

"In fact, this idea brought back a feeling I always had without realising it, Lola."

"It did?"

"Those motorbike riders on Saint-Michel. What if they'd been paid to kill Ménard rather than me?"

Lola's mouth dropped open, but she couldn't produce any intelligible sound.

"They were meant to kill me as well while they were at it," Ingrid went on, "because they had to get across their message, that it was Gratien who was behind it. But what if I was the bait, and Ménard the target?"

"I admit there's something to that."

"I think they tailed Ménard for several days to discover his routine. That day it was he who insisted we went to Saint-Michel for a drink."

"Did he often go to that café?"

"I don't know, but it was close to midday."

"Had you already been there with him?"

"It was the second time . . ."

Ménard's routine checked by the killer. It made sense. The young lieutenant arranges to meet Ingrid somewhere he knows. No sooner are they installed on the café terrace than he is shot. So it wasn't a stray bullet, but one that hit the mark. Black Helmet is a good shot then. He has to deliver a message to direct suspicion onto Gratien, who is the ideal suspect, the perfect fit. *For Antonia Gratien!* But the terrace is too crowded, the message risks getting lost amongst all the chatter and traffic noise. To make sure, they'll kill Ingrid as well. No quarter given, a spectacular show. Who will pass on the message? A bystander, one of the second-hand book browsers. At that time of day there are always people about, but not too many of them, the warning will be heard . . .

Oh yes, it made a great deal of sense.

31   THURSDAY, 7 FEBRUARY

They had spent several days questioning Sébastien Ménard's colleagues. They all knew Lola and had been willing to talk. All except Emmanuelle Carle, who said she was far too busy. She had been the one closest to the lieutenant in the Duguin team. They simply had to interview her. Clémenti told them that Carle and her people had been given a homicide case early that evening, apparently drugs-related: a guy with his throat slit.

Jake parked the Twingo in the Cité de la Musique car park and said he'd keep a lookout. Night had fallen, and searchlights lit the crime scene. The corpse was covered in a fluorescent yellow sheet. There was quite a crowd, with the forensic team, the *Brigade Criminelle*, the local uniforms, people from the public prosecutor's office and curious onlookers. The different groups seemed to be milling around in confusion, but in fact were working quickly and efficiently.

I loved that job, thought Lola.

Commandant Carle was chatting to a tall, brown-haired man who was elegantly dressed and was probably the deputy public prosecutor. A lost seagull squawked overhead; the wind brought with it an unpleasant smell from the canal. Carle turned her head in their direction. Ingrid and Lola took a few steps forward. She came to meet them.

"Have you had an accident, Madame Jost?"

"No, it's nothing serious."

"Listen, I'm very busy . . ."

Emmanuelle and Sacha had never hit it off, but Lola had a card up her sleeve: her reputation. She had been one of the first women commissaires, and Carle admired her for it. She had quite rightly suffered when Mars had given leadership of the team to Sacha; she had more seniority, her service record was impeccable and she had a much greater sense of team spirit and hierarchy than her detested rival.

"I heard about your promotion. You're a team leader now. Bravo, Emmanuelle, you deserve it."

"Thank you."

"Your evidence is vital. I need to know what cases Sébastien Ménard was involved in."

"Far too many, like all of us. Duguin waltzed off to Africa leaving us all the hard work. And Sébastien was something of a lone wolf."

"Hardy has taken all Ménard's documents. The statements he had collected, his notebooks. I haven't been able to look at anything . . ."

"Nor have I. Even with the best will in the world I can't help you, Madame Jost."

"I've drawn up a list of names. Just in case one of them suggested any kind of link to Ménard . . ."

Carle turned to survey the crime scene. The deputy prosecutor was staring in her direction.

"It won't take long, Emmanuelle. Please."

"Only because it's you."

"Thanks. O.K.: *Joseph Berlin.*"

"Berlin was an old friend of Mars. Ménard had a drink with him from time to time . . ."

Lola hid her feelings. If the ex-spook was hiding something about the death of the young lieutenant, he would have her to deal with. She continued with her list:

"*Grandpa Koumba, Théodore Moba, Hector Gassa . . .*"

"Never heard of them."

Carle gestured to the prosecutor that she hadn't forgotten him. Lola went on:

"*Gildas Sénéchal, Mondo . . .*"

"Sénéchal was Mars' best friend. They often had lunch together."

"Did Ménard know him?"

"Sénéchal is a snob who has been close to power. He doesn't have anything to do with little people. And yet Sébastien studied politics at the best university in Paris, and read a lot."

She gave a smile tinged with sadness. Lola knew the feeling. It was hard to lose a partner. Especially a young one, who had his whole life ahead of him.

"*Mathilde Candichard, Guillaume Candichard . . .*"

No flicker of recognition. Lola had no more names on her list. She made one last effort.

"What sort of state was Ménard in towards the end?"

"He was more nervous following Duguin's departure. And I remember he put in for a transfer. Duguin had abandoned us, and Sébastien couldn't understand why. Neither could I."

"What d'you mean, a transfer?"

"I've no idea. Don't count your chickens . . ."

They may get shot in the head . . . Carle was sad. And still angry. It would take a long time for her to forgive Sacha.

"You're taking too many risks for someone who isn't worth it, Madame Jost."

The deputy prosecutor was growing impatient; Carle declared firmly that she had to get back to him.

This time they decided to ring the doorbell and wait for him to appear. He had a book in his left hand. Lola restrained herself from slapping him.

"Now I'm getting to know you, Lola, I can tell you're in a bad mood."

He showed the three of them in.

"And you are?"

"Jake Carnegie, Ingrid's friend."

"Wonderful, we could play a game of poker or Monopoly."

Berlin opened the refrigerator door and offered Ingrid a bottle of milk.

"If you're fond of running gags, G.I. girl – help yourself."

"And is the fact that you knew Lieutenant Sébastien Ménard a gag as well?" asked Lola.

"What's the problem? Yes, I knew young Ménard. Mars introduced us."

"For what reason?"

"Why not? He had studied politics. The reminiscences of an old dog from the C.B.N.S. interested him."

"What's strange is that you saw him again after Mars had jumped ship."

Berlin scratched his head and laughed heartily.

"You're getting even more paranoid than me, sweetheart. Duguin had cleared off to Africa. Ménard was fed up with the criminal investigation lot, the Mars scandal, Duguin's recklessness. He asked if I could recommend him to the C.B.N.S."

Berlin's version coincided with what they had heard from Carle. Lola felt a sense of relief. Ingrid drank the remains of the milk and threw the bottle into the recycling.

"Did he meet anyone at the C.B.N.S.?"

"Not that I know of. The poor kid died too soon. Listen, girls . . ."

The two women looked at him inquisitively.

"I reckon someone is aware of everything you say and do. The same goes for me. In other words, we're in the same boat. Conclusion, let's join forces rather than quarrelling with one another."

A phone call from Carle broke the ensuing silence.

"I've just remembered something, Madame Jost. I've checked with the secretary at headquarters. You mentioned the Candichards on your list . . ."

Jake parked illegally outside the building and waited in the car.

They were packed into the old-fashioned lift like sardines, but Lola found Berlin's aftershave rather pleasant.

The two women hung back. Berlin stood in front of the spyhole, rang the bell, gave his name. The widow opened the door and immediately regretted it. They pushed their way in. Ingrid made a quick tour of the apartment. Mathilde Candichard was all alone.

"You have no right . . ."

"We have proof that you contacted Lieutenant Ménard," Lola snapped.

"Who are you talking about?"

"Don't play games with me. Sébastien Ménard was part of Commandant Duguin's team in the *Brigade Criminelle.* He was shot and killed by a motorcyclist in Saint-Michel last summer."

"I wasn't aware of that."

"You're lying."

"I had forgotten his name. In fact, it was Commandant Duguin I wanted to see. The lieutenant received me instead because his boss wasn't available."

And with good reason: he was in Africa.

"Why did you want to see Sacha Duguin?"

"He was Mars' associate . . . I wanted explanations."

"What explanations?"

"So that I could understand. Who the divisionnaire was. And why he had done so much harm to my husband . . ."

Another dead end. The Candichard widow had not told them anything new. Back in the Twingo, they exchanged impressions. Lola had already noticed the fear lurking beneath the anger during their first visit. This time, it had surfaced. The kind of anguished fear you feel for your nearest and dearest.

"Mathilde Candichard won't say a thing. She's terrified of the idea that someone might go after her son."

"Yes, I agree with you," Berlin admitted.

"Contrary to what she'd have us believe, we weren't the first to inform her of Ménard's death. She already knew."

"What shall we do?" asked Ingrid.

"I for one know what we need to do," said Berlin. "But you're not going to like it."

32 FRIDAY, 8 FEBRUARY

He should have been driving a car in keeping with his position, but he didn't own one, and instead was cycling home on a free bike. Lola and Berlin thought this was odd, although Ingrid couldn't see anything wrong with it. In her country, web billionaires dressed like penniless adolescents, so why shouldn't a French surgeon go around on a bike?

Meanwhile, it wasn't easy to tail Candichard junior in the Twingo. They crossed Paris at a snail's pace, trying to avoid being spotted, and discovered that the surgeon from the prestigious American hospital in Neuilly lived in a far from glamorous corner of the 19th arrondissement. Ingrid was delighted by the silhouette of the dragon at the Cité de l'Industrie shrouded in mist.

Guillaume Candichard parked his bike, walked back up quai de la Gironde, went inside a faded yellow porch.

"We can still turn round and go back," Berlin said again. "We're exposing him to risk by coming here."

"We understood you the first time."

"If he's being watched, his mother's fears could turn out to be justified, Lola."

"We've weighed up the pros and cons. We're not going through all that again."

"Don't come complaining to me then," said Berlin, as he got out of the car.

"I'll carry on keeping a lookout," Jake told Ingrid.

The building was dilapidated, with tufts of grass growing round the foot of the walls. There was no lift, so they clambered up the stairs through a smell of urine and the sounds of a tango that grew louder as they climbed.

"It's so beautiful," said Ingrid, closing her eyes.

Lola had a flashback of a dance by Ingrid at the Calypso to music by Carlos Gardel. If only they could teleport themselves into a brighter future . . .

The door opened. Guillaume Candichard might be surrounded by the languorous strains of a tango, but his mood was far more hostile.

"I recognise you two shit-stirrers. And who's this guy?"

Berlin replied that he had a certain number of questions to ask him, and would only accept short, to-the-point answers.

"Who on earth do you think you are?"

"Someone who knows the basics of how to make you talk. You choose: you can find yourself back in general practice, or continue to do operations."

"What?"

"Do as you're told or I'll break your fingers one by one."

He had put Guillaume into an armlock and was twisting his right hand. The surgeon cried out in pain and promised to cooperate. Lola explained her links to Sacha Duguin and Arnaud Mars.

"During our brief meeting at your mother's, I got the impression there was something you weren't telling us," she went on. "Now's the time."

"I find it hard to believe you're doing all this for your friend Duguin."

"Strange but true."

"O.K., let's get started," said Berlin. "Did you pay someone to kill Mars?"

"You're off your head!"

"What about Gratien?"

"My God, never in this world! You're the one who seems to be in the habit of killing people all the time. We don't live on the same planet."

"The name Gratien means only one thing: notebooks. They were used to destroy your father's career. You know something I don't. So does your mother. It's as simple as that."

"You've got it wrong."

"Explain."

"The notebooks didn't 'destroy' his career. When Sénéchal explained to him that if he didn't withdraw from the presidential race extracts from Gratien's notebooks would be sent to the press, he believed him. He knew he'd lost the election against Borel, and yet in the stinking world of politics, you can always bounce back. And that's what my father intended to do. He wanted to win over Richard Gratien. That guy always went to the highest bidder. If my father had won the following election, he would have been the one to keep in with. Gratien knew that. His allegiances always changed according to his interests."

Lola remembered Talleyrand: *In politics, betrayal is only a matter of time.* Could Richard Gratien have turned his coat? If she were to believe Armand Bianco, it wouldn't be the first time.

"Did your father really think he could become president?" she asked Guillaume.

"He had talent and charisma. And the kind of support among party activists that Borel didn't have. My father understood economic realities because he had been the boss of his own firm in the construction industry. He trained as an engineer. He often told me it would be in the public interest to put a bomb under the civil service training college – 'that factory for sociopaths who exist only by stifling other people's talent'. He saw himself as the opposite of a typical French politician. He really wanted to make a difference. At least, when he was starting out. Afterwards, I imagine you learn that compromise is necessary."

"All this sounds like guesswork. Nothing proves that Gratien . . ."

"My father talked to him on several occasions. A link was established between them."

"So what went wrong?"

"I never really found out."

"Make an effort," said Berlin. "You started so well."

"I spent years trying to understand what my father had got himself into. My mother, who was his confidante, never wanted to tell me. But I do know one thing. His confidence collapsed all of a sudden. From one day to the next he was a different man. And it was then that his political career came to an end. Because that was what he wanted, I think. You might say it was out of a sense of disgust."

"When did this belated crisis of conscience take place?" Berlin insisted.

"Following a terrorist attack in Syria. The Aerolix affair. The death of eighteen employees."

"Based at Rennes, specialising in combat 'copters. Yes, I know them," said Berlin. "Go on."

"In Damascus, a vehicle loaded with explosives rammed into the hotel where the French employees were staying. I overheard a conversation between my parents about it. My father was devastated."

"And it was after Damascus that he abandoned politics?"

"Yes. Later on, I looked into it. The French state had a contract to sell combat helicopters to Syria in the nineties, when my father was foreign minister. A contract for something like 730 million euros. My father's election campaign staff received kickbacks. That's a fact."

"Kickbacks from the Aerolix deal?" Berlin pressed him.

"From that and others. It was a complex operation, but the Aerolix contract was the main source of money."

"Do you have a reliable source for this?" asked Lola.

"An old friend of my father's. He was in charge of his campaign. He is dead now."

Berlin and Lola exchanged glances. She guessed he felt the same as her: a feeling that they had finally succeeded in breaking open a locked door. While they were talking, all Ingrid had managed to do was disappear.

Lola and Berlin were back in the Twingo. Jake wanted to go and look for Ingrid, but changed his mind when he saw her walking towards them.

"I gave the place a makeover," she declared.

"In French we say a 'once-over'."

"Whatever. Guillaume seems to be on the level."

His apartment was spacious, but contained nothing more than the essential. Rather than accumulating possessions, the surgeon had apparently invested in humanitarian missions, especially with *Médecins du monde.* For ten years or so, he had been a member of an international association of *Shirurgiens sans frontières,* and had operated without charge on children with congenital disabilities from the world's most destitute families.

"I think he's being sincere when he says politics isn't his scene."

"I agree," Lola admitted.

"A saint?" sniffed Berlin.

"More like a son trying to make up for his father's mistakes."

"*Adiós muchachos, compañeros de mi vida . . .*"

They turned to stare at Ingrid, who was humming the tango with her eyes closed. Jake stroked her cheek with a smile, then switched on the ignition.

33

BLOODY ATTACK IN DAMASCUS AFP, 23 November, 1998
THE ATTACK CLAIMED BY THE ISLAMIST BADA FACTION KILLED 30
PEOPLE IN THE SYRIAN CAPITAL, THE MAJORITY OF THEM FRENCH,
AND LEFT 100 WOUNDED. SEVERAL PEOPLE ARE STILL MISSING.

It was 7.30 p.m. on November 22 in the embassy-and-banking district of the Syrian capital when a suicide bomber driving a Toyota Accord crashed through the security barriers around the Madison Hotel. The vehicle packed with explosives then rammed into the front of the building, producing a violent explosion whose shock waves were felt in a radius of four kilometres.

Employees of the Aerolix company who were in Syria providing technical assistance were holding a meeting in the hotel. Of the 100 people close to the source of the explosion, 30 were killed, including 18 executives and technicians from the French company based in Rennes, which specialises in the construction of combat helicopters.

"I thought at first we had been hit by a missile," said one hotel employee. "The windows suddenly shattered. Fragments of glass hit my head, and I found myself covered in blood. The noise from the explosion was tremendous, people were screaming and trying to find a way out through the smoke and dust. Others were trying to help the victims. As the American embassy is close by, I at first thought the United States was the target and that the missile had hit us by mistake. American soldiers and civilians were quickly on the spot to evacuate us."

Part of the hotel façade was destroyed by the explosion, and the ground-floor meeting rooms were crushed by the collapse of the upper storeys. The local authorities despatched more than 200 firemen, police and rescue workers to clear the rubble and find any possible survivors or more victims. This morning, as Syrian army helicopters are criss-crossing the sky above Damascus, these teams are still hard at work, together with specialist forensic and explosives experts.

Bada, a secretive Islamist group linked to Al-Qaeda, claimed responsibility for the attack a few minutes after it occurred, sending a video to the Associated Press office in Damascus. In it, a masked man asserts the group's intention to "strike a blow at the interests of the Great Satan and its allies". By striking at a time when the foreign executives were holding their meetings and when the Madison's bar and restaurant were full, the terrorists chose a moment when they could apparently cause maximum human casualties . . .

Lola finished reading out the article she had found in the archives of *Politika* online, then asked Berlin and Ingrid if they had any ideas.

Ingrid shrugged and went on drawing invisible spirals on the table top. Berlin dialled a number on his mobile, talked to a certain Gabrielle, took notes and thanked her before ending the call.

"A friend in the C.B.N.S. has just told me that the Aerolix case was handled from 1998 onwards by the investigating judge Pierre-Louis Malbourg, who has now retired. Olivier de Genans, from the same counterterrorism unit, replaced him a few months ago."

"Could he be the young judge Mars was thinking of?" said Ingrid.

Lola beamed at her. Despite her absent look, Ingrid's brain was obviously working overtime.

By that evening they were not so cheerful. Berlin had got through to the counterterrorism unit at rue Saint-Eloi and met with a categorical refusal. He then turned to all the contacts he still had at the C.B.N.S. and elsewhere, but to no effect. Olivier de Genans was far too busy to see them any time soon.

"Or at any time in the future," Berlin admitted. "His clerk has just politely led me to understand that as we are not operating in any official capacity we don't really stand much chance. Nothing surprising there."

"Why's that?" asked Lola.

"A counterterror judge is swimming in an ocean of paperwork because in his area, even more than elsewhere, information is at the heart of the war, and of course deciphering and analysing it. And Islamist terrorists tend to be quite talkative. Al-Qaeda is an ocean all to itself, with thousands of little fish swimming about in it. Added to that, Genans has inherited all his predecessor's files. He must be snowed under. Seeing us will be last on his list."

"We *have* to see him. I'll find a way."

Lola immersed herself once more in reading the press reports about the bombing. She learned that the suicide bomber driving the Toyota had never been identified, despite D.N.A. evidence. However, two suspects who were members of the Bada splinter group had been arrested on suspicion of having provided the car and explosives. The investigators had found part of the engine block serial number and identified the garage that had sold it to the two men. Although they had at first confessed, they had later retracted their confessions. There was therefore no conclusive evidence, but the terrorist angle was still the most likely hypothesis. As the years went by and the investigation appeared to be getting nowhere, the victims' families had come forward to express their dissatisfaction. Their criticisms of the official inquiry were relayed by the press.

Jake meanwhile had gone for refreshments, and reappeared with pizzas and a bottle of red wine. He spent the meal trying to convince the former spy to recount his memories for a profile in the *New Yorker*. Ingrid took a call from Las Vegas. After a brief conversation, she turned to Lola disconsolately.

"My boss. If I'm not back next week, I'll lose my job."

"That was predictable," said Jake evenly.

The two Americans went back to their hotel. Lola was left on her own with Berlin and his Siberian gaze.

The news that Ingrid would soon be leaving had sapped her morale. She looked like a Saint Bernard on its uppers. And for company, all she had was this old husky who couldn't even help her get to see a judge. What use was it having worked for the C.B.N.S. all his life?

"Is the G.I. girl your best friend?"

"Affirmative."

"Sort this affair out and go and live in Las Vegas."

"I don't like gambling."

He shook his head slyly and announced that he would do the washing-up. She continued her searches on the internet. His hands were in the bubbles when he heard her cry of joy.

"What's going on?"

"I think I've found a way."

He listened to her carefully, then rang this intriguing Gabrielle he seemed to be so close to. He obtained a phone number, an address in Rennes, and thanked his former C.B.N.S. colleague warmly before ending the call. He tapped in a code, explaining to Lola that this was to conceal his number. She heard a female voice saying "Hello?" several times. Berlin said nothing, and hung up.

"The target is at home. I suggest we call on her without warning."

"Right now?"

"It's a four-hour drive, Lola, that's all. Even in your clapped-out old banger."

34

The sky was a vast airship whose grey bulk bore down on them. There was a slender plume of light up ahead. Berlin had only stopped once, to fill up the car and check the tyre pressure. Now he was filling the time telling her his life story. Not the bureaucratic part, the rest: the part that was both darker and more exciting. The glory years of tracking down potential or actual terrorists.

"It's a job where you learn once and for all never to trust appearances. The guy who never sleeps with prostitutes is not the most dangerous. Watch out instead for the one who goes clubbing, drinks alcohol, listens to American rap music. That means he's trying to put you off the scent."

He thought the West had been wrong to let the training camps spring up in the Afghan–Pakistani border region.

"They were terrorism's Star Academy. Then when Al-Qaeda began preaching jihad on the internet, their influence went stratospheric. In the end, it's the same logic as in the Middle Ages when they signed people up to go on the crusades. They sold them a good story: their mission in the Holy Land was to liberate Christ's sacred burial ground. And they were promised eternal paradise for their souls."

"The kingdom of heaven is very like the Islamic paradise."

"The science of communication wasn't invented yesterday, but now in the twenty-first century it's found its perfect tool."

Berlin was warming to his theme and kept throwing her sharp glances. A passionate side was showing through this grumpy old man's armour-plating. The professional who had quit an absorbing job out of a sense of family duty. Lola found herself beginning to appreciate his sacrifice.

"All those years sitting there listening to them weren't wasted, Lola. When you're caught up in the heat of the action, especially when the risk of getting bumped off is real, you think only in practical terms. And that obviously limits you. Later on, listening in the darkness to kids boasting of their next coup against the Great Satan, I finally understood what they felt. They're convinced their motives are noble. They've been persuaded they will win whatever happens. In life and in death. Soldiers who survive, or martyrs at the gates of paradise: no difference."

They were not monsters but human beings. Young men often signed up when they were no more than teenagers. Kids who were taught that an eye for an eye was the only answer.

"If you close your eyes and let yourself be inundated by their voices, you end up understanding where they're coming from."

"Have you got a smartphone?"

"No, only a dumb one, like you."

"That's a shame, a G.P.S. wouldn't have been a bad idea, Lola."

Rennes at dusk. Berlin screwed up his eyes to read the road signs. Although she had good eyesight, Lola imitated him to keep him company. First parc du Thabor, then rue de la Palestine.

They observed the apartment block through the car windscreen. The person living there was their only hope of finding a new lead, but would her psychological state permit it?

She opened the door in a lively manner. Brown hair, a firm, frank look, less than thirty years old. Lola had read a portrait of her in the *Ouest-France* newspaper archives. "The Teenager Who Refused Her Father's Medal". At the tender age of fourteen, Géraldine Jolin had become a local celebrity on 27 November, 1998, the day she refused to accept on her father's behalf a posthumous *Légion d'honneur* from President Borel.

She had not accepted the way that Aerolix had treated the families either. Her mother had first heard about the bombing on the radio, because the company had waited several hours before sending a messenger to their home. Géraldine accused them of wanting to control, or even obstruct, the families' quest for justice. She was critical of the military shrinks and counsellors assigned to each family, insisting that "they were supposed to be giving support, but really they were spying on us". She complained that Aerolix had tried to persuade the families not to initiate criminal proceedings. She had been incensed by the suggestion that they took the Social Security to court instead, arguing that this would make it easier for them to receive compensation. She was not interested in money, she only wanted the truth. As a result, Géraldine Jolin had stirred up the eighteen families involved, and managed to convince twelve of them to present a joint criminal charge.

On the doorstep, Lola explained that she was a friend of a criminal investigation bureau officer unjustly accused of murdering a superior officer. And that this murder was somehow linked to the Aerolix affair. Géraldine looked bewildered for a moment, then recovered and invited them in. Lola explained what she had learned so far. Calm and focused, the young woman listened and took notes without interrupting her.

"Just before he died, Arnaud Mars used Gratien's notebooks to show that Louis Candichard had financed his presidential campaign with kickbacks," Lola went on. "It was only today that I learned that the sale of Aerolix helicopters to Syria was one of the sources of that money. Probably the most important."

"Who told you that?"

"Guillaume Candichard, the son of the minister who committed suicide. The contract dates from the beginning of the nineties; the Damascus bombing from November 1998. A small terrorist group claimed responsibility. That's not important: there are lots of shady areas. I want to know who killed Mars and why my friend Sacha was such a convenient suspect. Until now, it made sense that Richard Gratien was the one who gave the order to kill Mars. The same man who was the intermediary for the Aerolix contract . . ."

"Gratien is that lawyer specialising in arms deals who was killed by a fellow detainee in jail? I heard about it on the radio . . ."

"Yes, that's him."

"But I don't have any links with people like that."

"Joseph and I have been gathering information. When I read that you helped unite a group of the families of the dead victims and are their spokeswoman, I thought you must have a close relationship with the examining judge."

"You're quite right, Madame Jost. I am the contact with Judge Genans. Especially now that Pierre-Louis Malbourg has retired."

"*Especially?*"

"I didn't get on with Malbourg. He was always very high-handed towards us, and I felt he was more concerned about protecting the representatives of the state than uncovering the truth. Genans is different. He's energetic, impartial, he calls a spade a spade. Instead of summoning us all to Paris, he's taken the trouble to come to Rennes to keep us informed of progress in the case."

"Has he started again from scratch?"

"Yes, and he's already getting results. He recently managed to speak on the telephone to the lawyers of the alleged terrorists. He would have liked to travel to Damascus to take it further, but what's happening in Syria at the moment has made that impossible."

Lola knew that the two members of the Bada group had been arrested by the Syrian police soon after the attack, thanks to the Toyota's engine-block number. The garage owner who had sold them the vehicle had officially identified them. In addition, the car's papers had been found at one of their homes. After their arrest, both men had confessed before the death sentence was passed on them. Their execution had been postponed several times because the prisoners had retracted their statements, and claimed they had been used. By whom? They had not as yet made this clear, because they didn't want to waste their last ammunition.

"I called Judge Genans, but he won't see us," Lola said.

"Genans is very cautious. He's always being pestered by journalists. Not to mention civil servants troubled by his investigation. And his superiors are just waiting for him to slip up so they can rein him in."

"Could you put in a good word for us? After what you've just told us, I'm more convinced than ever that we should join forces."

Lola caught Géraldine Jolin staring intensely at her. She was sure Géraldine would help them. She saw them as agents provocateurs who would be very useful in her personal battle.

Géraldine dialled a number she knew from memory, asked to speak to Judge Genans, listened to the reply, thanked the other person, and hung up.

"The judge is in a meeting. His clerk promised me he would ring back this evening. Are you going back to Paris?"

It was raining in Rennes. Furiously. Berlin suggested to Lola they spend the night in a hotel and return to Paris early the next morning. She agreed.

"I'll tell him what we've said here," Géraldine said. "That ought to convince him to see you. There's a Don Quixote side to him – he never gives up and isn't afraid of anyone . . ."

"Be careful over the phone," said Berlin.

"He may be quixotic, but he's very careful. He uses a secure line for some of our conversations."

"Good for him."

"I'll try to get an appointment for you as soon as possible."

Lola promised she would keep her informed as to how their investigation was going.

"You don't need to make any promises. I know you'll be in touch. Experience has made me a pretty good judge of character."

*

"That kid's a fighter, Lola. I like her."

"Yes, it's a pleasure to see."

"But if things went wrong, I wouldn't want my daughter fighting like that for me."

"And compromise her own life?"

"That's right. Unfortunately, I can't tell her about our worries. It would only upset her. Do you see my problem?"

"Of course."

"Do you have any children, Lola?"

"A son. The prodigal type. He's lived abroad for years. At the moment, he's in Brazil. You ought to write."

"To your prodigal son?"

"To your daughter. A letter only to be opened after your death. In it, you could demand she live her own life."

"That sounds a bit literary."

"Yes, I was a French teacher before I joined the force."

He looked at her in surprise, wiped the condensation from the windscreen and switched on the ignition.

Wind and rain joined forces against the Twingo. Berlin parked at the first hotel they came across. They were given adjacent rooms. Lola called Ingrid and gave her the details of their meeting with Géraldine Jolin. Her American friend couldn't hide her enthusiasm.

They shared mussels and a bottle of Sancerre. Lola realised this was the first civilised meal she had eaten in weeks. Berlin had insisted they sit at the back of the dining room so that he could keep an eye on the evening's comings and goings. The only other patrons they saw were a Dutch family and a few travelling salesmen.

"I've been gathering info on Olivier de Genans," said Berlin, with his famous lopsided smile. "His superiors take a dim view of him. They stop him going abroad as much as possible, and the number of cases he is responsible for gets fewer and fewer by the year."

"Is that a good sign?"

"It certainly is!"

"You mean that an examining judge can't be dismissed or transferred against his will, but the president of the court has other means to try to tame young rebels like Genans?"

"Of course."

"Was it Gabrielle who gave you the info about Genans?"

Berlin did no more than nod his head. So what was the exact nature of his link to this lady who was so generous with her information?

Géraldine Jolin called soon afterwards. Olivier de Genans would see them at rue Saint-Eloi, in the counterterrorism offices, at two in the afternoon the following day.

"So our judge works weekends as well," said Berlin. "That's a good sign too."

"I'd say so."

"There's a faithful friend you mustn't forget to take with you tonight."

Lola raised an inquisitive eyebrow, waiting for him to go on.

"Your Manurhin, Lola. Keep it within reach."

35 SATURDAY, 9 FEBRUARY

"Seven o'clock. Time to get up. We're off to Paris!"

With that, Berlin had hung up. Lola fell out of bed, grumbling to herself. The previous night, the Sancerre and the unanswered questions had kept her awake a long while. She would have appreciated a bit of a lie-in.

Out in the car park, Berlin examined the streaming-wet Twingo for any possible explosive device.

"We've become two big nuisances."

"I realise that, Joseph."

"So much the better. Lola?"

"Yes?"

"I wrote that letter yesterday evening," he said, tapping his pocket.

"And who is going to give it to your daughter?"

"Gabrielle."

He pulled in at the first service station, filled the car up, and asked the mechanic to check the engine. A short while later, the embarrassed employee came to tell them that the brake system was badly damaged.

"If I hadn't lifted the bonnet, you'd have had an accident. Possibly at top speed on the motorway."

Berlin phoned the hotel. The owner had not seen anyone prowling round the car park the previous night. The garage mechanic tried telling Lola he would return the Twingo as soon as he had replaced the brakes, but got no reaction. He turned to Berlin instead, while Lola sought refuge in the washroom, realised she was shaking, splashed cold water on her face, and sternly addressed her reflection in the mirror.

"For goodness' sake, what have you got yourself into?"

Berlin was calling a taxi. Envying his self-control, she went back to join him. She thanked him for saving her life.

"From the start I knew you were bad luck," he retorted.

"The same goes for me," she replied, copying his twisted smile.

They took the first high-speed train to Paris.

Lola peered out at the countryside, wondering who this mysterious Gabrielle might be. They had left for Rennes on the spur of the moment: who could have known they intended to question Géraldine Jolin?

"You're barking up the wrong tree, Lola. I have complete faith in Gabrielle."

"For someone in the intelligence services, I find you very trusting."

"After my wife's death we were together for a while. Gabrielle is trustworthy: she takes risks on my behalf. She knows if she's caught divulging information from the C.B.N.S. she could face seven years in jail."

"If you say so."

"I can vouch for her. But I wouldn't say the same for the G.I. girl and that Jake Carnegie. Apart from Gabrielle, they were the only ones who knew where we were going."

"You can count Ingrid out. She's my one hundred per cent, like your Gabrielle."

"She's not *my* Gabrielle, I'm not with her anymore."

"I'd understood that."

"Carnegie."

"What about Carnegie?"

"That fellow asks too many questions."

"A journalist who doesn't ask questions is like a butcher without arms."

"Do you really think he wants to write about me for the *New Yorker*?"

A taxi took them to Lola's. Berlin waited while Lola left behind her Manurhin. Then the taxi dropped them at the Palais de Justice.

On the top floor, the Saint-Eloi wing. Marble, dark wooden panels, cathedral-like gloom. This was the first time Lola had set foot in the realm of the counterterrorism unit. They passed through the security check and an armed policeman took them to Olivier de Genans' two personal bodyguards, who searched them a second time. A few minutes later, a softly spoken clerk came to fetch them.

Seated behind stacks of files and a computer, a slender figure with a youthful face, who bore a certain resemblance to the Renaissance writer Montaigne. Instead of a ruff, he was wearing a white shirt and a loosened maroon tie. Above his head, three Balinese puppets were frozen in an immobile dance.

A brief handshake and he motioned them to sit down. Géraldine Jolin had told him the details of their conversation in Rennes, and in the meantime he had briefed himself on "their respective biographies".

"Up to now, Géraldine's instincts have been excellent, but I won't disguise the fact that I find your behaviour extremely irregular."

His tone did not sound very promising. Deciding attack was the best means of defence, Lola asked him straight out whether Mars had ever contacted him.

"No, madame. I have never had any contact with the divisionnaire."

"His wife has confirmed to us that her husband wanted to hand over a copy of Richard Gratien's notebooks to a 'young judge'. The same Gratien who was behind the Aerolix contract and who you will never now be able to question. You've inherited the dossier from your predecessor. Starting again from zero is difficult, especially when it's impossible for you to travel to Syria and so return to the source. But those notebooks are probably another means of getting there."

Genans was no longer on the defensive, but listening attentively.

"Are you telling me you have the notebooks?"

"No, but if anyone is in a position to recover them, it's us," Lola ventured, turning to her companion for confirmation.

Joseph "Husky" Berlin's face remained inscrutable, and he did not even unfold his arms.

"Why would that be, madame?"

"Precisely because we are 'irregular'. Which gives us much greater freedom to act."

The judge stared at her for a moment, then addressed Berlin.

"Who were your superiors at the C.B.N.S.?"

Joseph gave him four names.

"My predecessor worked with Yann Rainier," said Genans. "I tried to question him; it was no use, he's very ill."

"Yes, Yann had a stroke some years ago."

"Did you know he was following the Aerolix affair?"

"Yann followed everything related to Islamic terrorism."

"And so?"

"In 1998 I was no longer part of his team."

"Right, you were monitoring communications. A recent move."

Giving up a responsible job for back-office work? Lola could almost hear Genans thinking how odd that was.

"Don't worry," said Berlin, "I haven't been sent by the C.B.N.S. to trap you or get information out of you."

For a few seconds all that could be heard was the clerk shuffling papers.

"Well then, I suppose I have to trust you."

Genans thought it over for a while, then his face lit up. Lola thought that in this world of old spies and old secrets, his attitude was refreshing.

"Your boss didn't swallow the official version," he said. "When the Ministry of Defence finally declassified some documents, I found a note from Yann Rainier to Malbourg questioning the terrorist hypothesis."

Lola had almost gone cross-eyed looking up on the internet what that official version was. A splinter group from the shadowy Al-Qaeda blows up a hotel full of Westerners, especially Americans, because the Madison Hotel was very close to the U.S. embassy. Thirty people killed, eighteen of them French. A hundred injured. And that was supposed to be that.

Genans told them that Rainier's view was based on his contact with an American official. The proximity of his embassy explained why he had been on the spot in the hotel so soon after the explosion.

"Do you know the name of this American?" asked Lola.

"The note didn't mention it. Either because Rainier was keeping it to himself, or because the documents had been redacted. To make things more difficult still, there were lots of Americans present. Soldiers, embassy staff, C.I.A. agents, who knows?"

"Have you heard anything new from the American side?"

"I came across the note three months ago. Since then, I've been in touch with various American officials. Things with them don't go any quicker than they do here."

"Why is that?" Lola wanted to know.

"The Damascus bombing took place in 1998. In other words, in a different era. After that came 9/11, the Twin Towers attack. The funds the United States spends on counterterrorism have snowballed, and . . ."

". . . and so has their paranoia. Is that what you're trying to tell us?"

"Let's just say you can't ask them questions on the basis of vague possibilities, Madame Jost. You have to present ironclad dossiers. I did though manage to get in direct touch with the man in charge of personnel at the embassy. He wasn't in post in 1998, and can't think who Rainier's contact could have been. Besides, there's nothing to prove he was an official based in Damascus."

Lola finally understood the problem. The contact's name was buried somewhere in the ruined synapses of Yann Rainier, a former legend of the C.B.N.S. who had been laid low by his stroke.

"Yes, it's a long-term project, madame. I hope one day to be able to go to Damascus to talk personally to the convicted men's lawyers and to see the confidential documents kept by the local investigators. Also, there are thousands of pieces of information and documents of all kinds stored on various mobile phones and computers, not to mention Richard Gratien's mythical notebooks. That's why I'm happy to accept your help if there's a possibility it might speed things up. But you must understand that for me you represent just one lead among hundreds. Thank you for whatever you can offer, and keep me informed. Now if you'll excuse me, I have a hearing."

His clerk was already standing beside them, ready to escort them out. Berlin was finding it hard not to show his frustration. He came out of his trance when Lola tapped his arm.

They paused at the top of the grand flight of steps outside the Palais de Justice. It was swept by an icy wind; tiny snowflakes were falling from an ashen sky. Lola imagined Yann Rainier's brain. Was it as cold as the wind? Or were there still a few glowing sparks left up there?

"That's what I call a dead end, Lola."

She suggested they pay a visit to his former boss.

"The poor man is a vegetable."

"Have you been to see him?"

"Yes, twice after his stroke. It was . . . painful to see the state he was in. And it was impossible to communicate with him. Besides, the judge already tried . . ."

"Do you have a better idea?"

They sat at the bar in the nearest café. Lola's mobile broke their awkward silence. She listened, asked a few questions, said to the person at the far end of the line to hang on. She told Berlin that the mechanic in Rennes had found "a strange contraption under the Twingo's body". He questioned the man as well, then ended the call in a fury.

"Somebody tracked us. A G.P.S. linked to a computer."

"Now at least we know how we were followed to Rennes."

Berlin had closed his eyes and was breathing heavily through the nose. When he finally calmed down, he called the ever-helpful Gabrielle. She gave him the address of a care home on the outskirts of Paris, at Le Perreux.

36

"Ingrid. Come in. To what do I owe this honour?"

"I'm going back to the States soon, Mondo. I've come to give you your last massage."

He took her in his arms and whispered that for her and her golden fingers he was even willing to become a tourist to Las Vegas.

"Isn't your boss in?"

"He's gone to a talk at the Collège de France. High-powered stuff. Intellectually, Gildas never gives up."

They installed themselves in his bedroom. Its military sobriety was shattered by a scarlet painting.

"Don't tell me it's a Rothko . . ."

"Yes. Gildas' expertise earned an incredible amount of money."

"I thought he was a mere servant of the state."

"That was what he preferred, but in order to maintain his lifestyle he took on other clients after Borel."

"He did?"

"Have you heard about the top civil servant who kept a bank account abroad?"

"Is that illegal?"

"A little, especially when you're working in the finance ministry and you forget to declare it to the inland revenue. The man was crucified by the media until Gildas came to the rescue. He refused to accept that his career was in ruins. The old man advised him to confess everything. A T.V. studio, a well-known smooth-talking journalist, mystical blue lighting, simple words, a full confession and apology. A man speaking directly to his fellow man. No more cheating, humility instead. The journalist isn't the priest hearing the confession, but the public. They offer absolution or deny it."

"Did it work?"

"It would have worked in the eighties or nineties. Since then the public has wised up and become more suspicious. These confessions don't impress anymore. Gildas and his methods have grown old. He only thinks in terms of T.V., but nowadays it's the internet that counts. Have you heard of the 'Fifty Cents Party'?"

"No."

"A horde of Chinese people who are paid fifty cents for every comment they write on the internet praising their government or the Communist Party, helping to nudge minds in the right direction or to counteract the arguments of political opponents or economic rivals. Political communication changed a good while ago, but Gildas hasn't yet realised it. Anyway, that doesn't stop him pocketing juicy cheques. He's always seen himself as a guru. And expected to be rewarded as such."

Ingrid took a few steps around the room. Space, silence, time held in suspense: the ideal place in which to think. She touched the surface of the Rothko with the tip of her forefinger. If she'd done that in a museum, the alarm would have gone off. Mondo was smiling.

"And you'd be able to leave all this behind?"

"Yes. I know it's immoral, because Gildas is growing weaker and has never needed me as much as he does now. But there's no shortage of private nurses, and I want to go back to my mountains."

"I understand."

She asked him to strip down to his underpants. She found a big white bath towel in the bathroom and laid it on the bed. She got him to lie down on his front. She had brought her jasmine-scented massage oil.

"You haven't even touched me yet, and it's divine, Ingrid."

"I know."

"She speaks. O speak once more, luminous angel, for you shine in the night above my head like the wing of a messenger from paradise when he appears before the startled eyes of mortals, who throw back their heads the better to see him ride the clouds as they drift lazily by, and sail over the calm waves of the sky . . ."

A theatre troupe was performing for the old folk. Berlin and Lola had slipped in among the audience. He pointed to a plump man dozing in a wheelchair. When the performance had finished, they went over to him. His male nurse tapped him on the hand.

"There are people to see you, Yann. Isn't that good?"

The old fellow opened his eyes, stared blankly at Lola, then turned towards Berlin.

"Yann, it's me, Joseph."

Rainier's eyelids began to flutter and his mouth started chewing on some imaginary morsel of food. The nurse moved away. Berlin introduced Lola and explained why they were there.

"Yann, do you remember the bomb attack in Damascus? It was in November 1998."

He repeated the question, louder this time. After several long minutes of an impossible dialogue, they were forced to conclude that Yann Rainier was showing no sign of lucidity.

"You're not family members. Otherwise you'd have known it makes no difference if you shout."

Berlin explained to the nurse who had come back over to them that he had once been Yann Rainier's assistant, and that the old man had some information that could help a police officer unjustly accused of murder. The nurse seemed to weigh this up before responding.

"Yann Rainier suffers from aphasic muteness: he can hear you, but is unable to speak. In addition, his memory has grown worse with age. He has moments of lucidity, but they don't last long."

"Is he able to write?"

"He has motor deficit in his right arm but thanks to physiotherapy he can occasionally write a few words with his left."

He brought over a plastic board, jammed it under Rainier's left arm, and helped him grip a felt-tip in his hand.

"Give it a try. It's up to him to decide whether or not to help you. The last time somebody came to ask him questions, the board stayed blank."

"Who was that?"

"A judge, a few months ago."

"Olivier de Genans?"

"Yes, I think that was his name."

"Yann, do you remember the Aerolix affair?"

Rainier went on blinking. His mouth chewed on inaudible words. His hand was trembling, but continued to hold the felt-tip.

"Yann: Damascus, a Toyota driven into the Madison Hotel. There were a lot of victims. You didn't spare yourself over that case. It really meant a lot to you . . ."

A sudden tempest seemed to distort the old man's features. Lola felt sorry for him, but at last it seemed he was going to react.

"At the time you had your doubts," Berlin insisted. "You wondered if it really had been a terrorist attack. Judge Olivier de Genans came to see you here. Perhaps you didn't want to tell him anything because of his dispute with his predecessor, Malbourg. I can understand that. But you've always trusted me. We always got on . . ."

Several minutes dragged by. Lola could see that the sick man's forehead was beaded with sweat. Berlin took him gently by the shoulders.

"Yann, it's very important. The new judge has found a note. Signed by you, and addressed to Malbourg. That note refers to information about the attack. It was thanks to an American who arrived on the scene very soon after the explosion that you got this information. Tell me who he was."

She went down into the metro and began a complicated rigmarole. When she was sure she wasn't being followed, she took the line she wanted and got off at quai de la Rapée. She entered the nearest café and chose to use the public telephone in the basement rather than her own mobile. The pathologist arrived a few minutes later.

"It's lucky for me that you work on Saturdays, Thomas."

"Speak for yourself, sweetheart."

"Thank you for coming."

"If it's not your terrifying friend, it's you. I'm cursed. And you use the fact that you're built like a goddess to take advantage of your old pal Franklin. That's very sad, Ingrid."

In fact, his smile almost reached his ears. Ingrid handed him the plastic sachet. He put it in his pocket and ordered a ham baguette and a half of beer.

"With gherkins – proper ones!" he told the waiter. "You've laid your make-up on with a trowel, but it suits you, Ingrid. What will you have?"

"The same as you. Gherkins are a good idea."

"I didn't think showgirls ate sandwiches."

"I have a good digestive."

"I beg your pardon?"

"My stomach can take it."

"Oh, you mean 'a good digestion', Ingrid. I'd even say you have a good physique and a good nature."

"Just you try speaking English correctly and you'll see, you block-head."

"There's no point, billions of people already do. But make up some more French, it relaxes me."

"I've got a better idea."

She stood behind him and began to knead his trapezius muscles, staring up at the ceiling. Steel wool meshed finely. A violent promise. The Haussmann façades on the buildings outside took on the sheen of human skin. *We don't have that in Nevada*, thought Ingrid.

They crossed the lobby. As soon as they were outside, they both raised their heads at the same moment.

Grey mush, thought Lola, *just like Rainier's memory*. Their efforts had met with crushing failure. Berlin's former boss would take the name of his contact with him to the grave. La Rochefoucauld once said: "Old age is women's hell." Rubbish. Since the Sun King's day, gender equality had made great strides.

"Taxi or train?"

"Let's take the train. We're not in a hurry anymore."

"Don't give up, Lola. We'll find a way."

"I'm not giving up. I'm going back to my original state. One of lucidity."

They were walking towards the station when someone called out to them. It was the nurse, sprinting towards them, board in hand.

"Did you never hear that patience is often rewarded?"

Five shaky capital letters had been drawn in felt-tip on the board: WOSKY.

Lola looked enquiringly at Berlin.

He shrugged his shoulders, thought about it, dialled a number on his mobile. There was no answer. He ended the call, looking annoyed.

"Gabrielle doesn't answer."

"Can't you ask another of your contacts?"

"She's the only one I trust."

The taxi dropped them at rue de l'Echiquier. Berlin checked there was no-one hiding in the apartment, and gave her his advice. She was not to leave home, and as soon as he had any news, he would be in touch.

Lola stood motionless in the middle of her living room. After all that had happened, here she was, grounded, wearing the leaden boots of a deep-sea diver.

She lay down on her bed. The phone rang. She didn't answer: it wasn't Berlin; they had agreed on a code.

She woke up in darkness. Strange: she thought she had gone to sleep with the light on. A voice was echoing in the room. She sat up in bed and listened. It was only a television. The sound, amplified by the small interior courtyard, was almost loud enough to drown out the violent downpour. She got up, shut the window.

Dark thoughts shrouded her mind. How long would this nightmare last? Perhaps she should never have become involved? Fate would have decided things in her stead. Some nights, when her insomnia fed her consternation, she felt as if free will were nothing more than an illusion. You stirred yourself, tried to make a difference, but in the end nothing you did had any impact. An obscure force directed every one of our gestures.

She went into the living room, pressed her head against the windowpane. These torrents of rain unleashed on Paris. The fury of the elements.

She opened the window on the menacing storm. Saw herself as a child again, on the beach in the last days of summer. The tragic sea beneath a leaden sky. The waves whipped up by the wind. The rain cascading down. Soaked to the skin and excited by this whirling rage, she gave thanks to a pagan god for the fury and energy that joined her body to the universe. She would start to dance and sing in a language of her own.

She stuck her hand out of the window. The rain licked her fingers like a tame wild animal.

She would not be able to get back to sleep, so she might as well read. But when she went to switch the light on, nothing happened. Was she mistaken? Had the storm already broken and caused a power cut in the whole building?

No, no. If her neighbour's television was working, only her own apartment was affected. She groped her way towards the kitchen to replace the fuse.

A shadow. She cried out. A man's body forced her up against the wall, pressed his hand over her mouth. She recognised his smell, brought her knee up as hard as she could into his groin. He gave a moan, but did not relax his grip. He was as heavy as an oak beam.

She struggled, felt herself being pushed out into the cold. Was he going to strangle her? The vertebrae can crack with a single twist, and you're finished. She tried to plead with him, but his huge fingers were blocking her tongue.

She felt herself tipping over into empty space. She shouted as loud as she could. Now he was holding her by the thighs. The rain was whipping her face. The street far below. A white blur: her reflection in the window of the building opposite. She cried out again.

She could feel herself slipping. He had hold of her by the ankles. She stopped twisting and turning. The vice on her right ankle relaxed. Terror gnawed at her brain. She wet herself, upside down. The vice on her left ankle went loose.

He was pulling her back in. She stammered a prayer, and found herself collapsed, gasping for breath, on the wooden floor. But she was not crying; whereas he was sweating, breathing heavily.

"Have you finally got it into your thick skull that you're to stay out of this?"

"Do you make a habit of torturing people, you bastard? You little runt, you're not going to get away with it!"

She heard him sigh, and understood she had made a mistake. He wasn't there to frighten her: he had simply hesitated to carry out the orders he'd been given. It was crazy to have insulted him.

She begged him, swore she would be good. She tried to touch his chest, his face. He lifted her like a straw dummy, tipped her out of the window a second time. She managed to cling on to the balustrade. This time, the man did not show the slightest hesitation: his movements were swift and precise.

He pushed her further out, pressing down on her chest. He jabbed with his left fist at her hand clinging to the balustrade. The tendons in her arm were about to snap.

Her strength gradually ebbed.

She would never see her son again. She called out his name.

With a shriek, she plunged to her end.

37 MONDAY, 11 FEBRUARY

"Hong Kong, Lola? What the fuck?"

"Joseph wants me to go with him. For safety reasons."

"He's not as paranoid as he seems if your Twingo was baby-trapped."

"We say 'booby-trapped' in French, Ingrid."

"That doesn't make sense."

"Perhaps not, but don't count on me to rewrite the French dictionary. When are you returning to the States?"

"I don't know yet. I'm still negotiating with the Bellagio."

"I hope to be back in Paris before you leave."

"That's optimistic."

She wasn't wrong. The inimitable Gabrielle had somehow produced the name Benjamin Wosky from her files. Officially a journalist, he had in fact been a member of the National Security Agency from the start of the nineties. Yet his presence in Damascus in 1998 could not be confirmed. His name reappeared more recently as an Associated Press correspondent in Hong Kong.

Berlin had spoken to him on the phone in his office and asked if he knew Yann Rainier. Wosky had wanted to know what that had to do with him. Berlin had explained he had been his assistant, and wanted information about the Damascus bombing. Wosky had demanded proof. Berlin had sent him a scan of his old C.B.N.S. card. The journalist had replied that he would only pass on any possible information to somebody still working in the bureau. That was the end of their conversation.

This had led Berlin to make a suggestion that Lola had to admit seemed logical.

Let's go to Hong Kong to shake Wosky up a bit. Journalism is the classic cover, Lola. And don't forget that the Damascus terrorists' video was sent to the Associated Press. The National Security Agency monitors and analyses communications. Conclusion: this guy is in the same line of work I used to be in. Paid to listen. We'll find a way to see eye-to-eye . . .

Lola told Ingrid to take care, and hung up. She stood motionless for a moment. She was going to miss that blasted giraffe in cowboy boots. A *ping* announced that she had mail. Berlin had bought their flights. He wanted her to meet him at Roissy at six that evening. He was almost too dynamic for her tastes.

She packed and unpacked her bag several times. She hadn't the faintest idea what she would need for a lightning visit to Hong Kong. A sudden inspiration led her to go out and purchase a pair of flight stockings: she didn't want her legs to swell up to twice their size, as they had done during her apocalyptic voyage to Africa. Once she was more or less satisfied with her wardrobe, she stretched out on her bed and closed her eyes. It soon seemed to her as if the building was a living being, with a heart, lungs and a digestive system. And she was no more than a cell floating in this vast organism. At last she felt reconnected to her city, her neighbourhood, and had not the slightest wish to leave. Her passport was valid for several years, she didn't need a visa for a short stay in Hong Kong. Just her luck: nothing stood in the way of this questionable idea. Flying more than ten thousand kilometres to try to wheedle information out of someone who plainly didn't want to help.

If you move forward, you die; if you move backwards, you die. So why move backwards? Was that a Chinese or an African proverb? At any rate, the phrase served to give herself courage.

Lola thought of her last conversation with Sacha, of Ingrid's farewells, and got up again. She found the bottle of port in the sideboard, and poured herself a large glass. She was forced to admit it once more: flying scared the life out of her.

She was by the window, Berlin was in the middle, and an Asian man was already asleep in the aisle seat. The Airbus' engines were purring, the cabin reeked of fuel, the sky of Paris was nothing more than a black canvas strewn with feeble stars. Her stomach churning, Lola could feel beads of sweat forming between her stomach and the stupid flight stockings she had bought. Why on earth had she stuffed herself into a contraption like that?

The captain announced take-off. Berlin took a pair of the most up-to-date headphones out of his bag, put them on deftly, and folded his hands across his stomach. He had spent a good part of his life wearing headphones, and still enjoyed it. Lola gripped his arm.

"Beethoven?"

"What?"

"Are you listening to Ludwig van Beethoven?"

"No. Lady Gaga."

"Liar."

"It'll be alright, Lola. A night flight is ideal. Sleep, and when you open your eyes again, we'll be in Hong Kong."

He gave her the details of a budget hotel that would suit them fine. In Kowloon, a rather ugly but vibrant district. Nathan Road.

"Have you already been there?"

"A long time ago."

"For work?"

"No, with my wife. We did quite a bit of globetrotting before our daughter was born. Backpacks and light hearts."

She was still clinging to his arm.

"What is it now, Lola?"

"You don't have to pay, Joseph. Especially if your savings suffer. I can buy my own ticket."

"No."

"Yes I can. But tell me the truth: why are you doing this? Who are you doing it for?"

"For myself."

"One last adventure before you retire for real? Properly this time."

"Something like that."

This wasn't exactly convincing, but Lola knew she wouldn't get anything more out of the Husky, at least not that night. She loosened her safety belt, leaned back in her seat, realised you could adjust the headrests, and so fiddled first with one and then the other, shifting around to find the ideal position. No luck. Berlin handed her a pill.

"Just in case you were wondering, it's not ecstasy."

"Ha, ha."

"A mild sleeping pill, Lola. Take it after the meal."

"I'm not hungry."

"Take it now, then."

She had to admit that she liked it when he spoke to her in this more gentle way. She took the pill.

38 TUESDAY, 12 FEBRUARY

She jumped, opened her eyes. The plane was hurtling forward. A squealing sound, as if the world were coming to an end. They had landed.

The Airbus began to taxi beneath a sad sky in a landscape full of hangars. The pilot announced an outside temperature of eighteen degrees centigrade, and said some showers were likely that evening. It was 1.30 p.m. in Hong Kong. Berlin offered her some mineral water, which Lola gratefully accepted. The air inside the cabin had dried out her throat and sinuses.

Half an hour later, they reached the taxi rank, and a uniformed young woman opened the door to a car with red bodywork and a white roof. Berlin handed the driver a bit of paper on which he had written the hotel address.

It was all so simple it seemed too easy. Benjamin Wosky was bound to turn out to be as elusive as a mirage. Berlin was chasing a dream. A very personal dream. Sooner or later, Lola would discover exactly what it meant. Out of the taxi window, densely wooded hills flashed by. To their left, the sea was a grey mass, the horizon blurred.

"Is this winter fog?"

"More like smoke from the factories going flat out behind that mountain range separating Hong Kong from mainland China," said Berlin.

Lola had read somewhere that Hong Kong meant "perfumed port". How ironic. Who would have thought that a city swept by winds from the sea would be just as polluted as one stuck out on a plain?

"Everyone has the right to their industrial revolution, I suppose."

"The West certainly had theirs ages ago, Lola, but since then we've learned to produce more cleanly. The techniques are well-known, it's just a matter of the Chinese adopting them."

"So what's stopping them?"

"An epidemic."

Intrigued, Lola turned to face him.

"It starts with one official who accepts a bribe from an entrepreneur impatient to produce at a lower cost. Then the influence of corrupt officials spreads like wildfire. To the extent that the state can no longer control it."

"You're exaggerating. I read somewhere that the Chinese are tackling the problem head-on."

"So much the better."

The taxi came out of a tunnel and the city lay before them. At least the district of Kowloon did, linked to the continent and opposite the island of Hong Kong itself. The taxi glided between long lines of buildings hazy in the grey mist. Not far from a mosque, Vanessa Paradis was smiling in a flowery dress on a huge advertising hoarding.

The hotel was in a small alley nearby. A dilapidated building squashed between two commercial centres. Berlin paid the driver and carried their bags into reception. He spoke to the receptionist in fluent English, suggested that Lola get some rest while he set out on Wosky's trail. Lola retorted that she had slept quite enough. A quick spruce-up and she would be ready.

Her bedroom was a poorly ventilated cupboard. The walls made no attempt to dampen the traffic noise, the double curtains dated from the first Opium War and stank of grilled prawns. Lola had a rapid shower under a trickle of water in a cabin built for a dwarf. She went down to reception and rejoined Berlin.

"I'm sorry, it's not exactly five-star."

"Palace or not, it doesn't matter. You warned me, and anyway, we're not here on vacation. By the way, I'll pay for my room."

"No way. I'm the one who dragged you here . . ."

"It's no more negotiable than the plane ticket. We're partners in this, Joseph."

A grimy drizzle on Nathan Road, three jeweller's shops dripping with gold in the space of a hundred metres, and to Lola it seemed as if the whole city stank of burnt gas. Berlin had already studied the metro map. Their destination: Central Plaza, opposite the port of Victoria, where the Associated Press had its offices. They got on at Tsim Sha Tsui station, changed at Admiralty, got off at Wan Chai. It was 4.20 p.m., and cars, taxis and double-decker buses formed a solid, choking mass. Dominating the buildings all around it, Central Plaza looked like a giant syringe. In the lift, Lola could feel her ears buzzing all the way up to the forty-eighth floor. Berlin talked to the woman on the desk, refused to give his details, asked to see Benjamin Wosky.

They were made to wait. Finally, a glass door slid open to reveal a fifty-something in a short-sleeved shirt and a broad stripy tie. Shoulders and stomach equally impressive, closely cropped hair, lantern jaw. His half-closed eyelids were like two little shutters over a blue gaze.

"Ben Wosky," he announced, shaking their hands firmly. "Don't tell me you've come all the way from France just to see me."

"It's true nonetheless," said Berlin.

Lola noted how calm and self-assured he sounded. Just occasionally the Husky style had its merits.

"And you are?" Wosky asked Lola.

"Lola, my companion," Berlin replied, before she had time to say anything. "We decided to combine business and pleasure and visit Hong Kong."

"Yeah, why not. Follow me."

They crossed a room with a panoramic view of Victoria harbour and a multitude of boats, fragile wooden vessels, gleaming yachts, enormous container ships. Wosky motioned them to take a good look.

"You need a special permit to sail a boat here. People would give their right arm for one. The regulations are incredibly strict."

Lola followed the progress of a sampan with faded red sails. It crossed in front of a black-and-white container ship. Very close. A combat between mosquito and bear.

"This is the world's busiest port. There are ships coming and going all night long. In the end, believe it or not, you grow attached to . . ."

"This frenzy?" suggested Lola.

"Yes, this crazy atmosphere. In my case, at least."

He showed them into a discreet meeting room with no windows. Offering them two chairs, he sat at a distance from them, took a biro out of his shirt pocket and began tapping himself on the chin with it.

"How is Yann Rainier?"

The smile and his relaxed demeanour had evaporated. The Hong Kong enthusiast had given way to the professional inquisitor. Beneath the drooping eyelids, a hard stare.

"Not good," said Berlin. "But you already know that."

"Yeah, of course. I used to like the guy. We only met three times in Damascus, but that was enough for me to understand he has balls. That's rarer in our professions than people think, isn't it?"

"Why don't you tell me what you have to say, Wosky."

"Alright. In 1998 Yann Rainier was struggling with a big job in Damascus. Thirty dead, a bunch of people injured, and the local authorities either ignoring him or trying to lead him up the garden path. But he persisted: the lone ranger. All the more laudable because he's just been left in the lurch. His best agent couldn't think of anything better to do than to ask for a transfer."

"Listen . . ."

"No, you listen to me, Berlin. I reckon that if your boss had a stroke, it was thanks to you. Or mostly. The last time I saw him in Damascus, he was worried sick."

"Rainier was a big boy, wasn't he?" Lola interjected.

"I only know what he told me, Lola. That he felt betrayed." He turned to Berlin. "You were the only one he could trust. You were more than his assistant. You were his friend. So if you're here looking for redemption, it's a bit fucking late."

Berlin was livid. Lola realised she had finally understood his dream. The Husky wanted to repair the past. To honour his friend. A mute, wheelchair-bound invalid whose memory was still flickering. Did Yann Rainier remember his assistant's defection? Did he still see it as a betrayal?

She explained to Wosky who she really was, and what had led her to poke around in Yann Rainier's past and the ashes of the Aerolix affair. Her friend Sacha Duguin. How vital it was to get information. Damascus was at the root of it all. It's after-effects were tentacles that would strangle Sacha if they didn't help him.

"Your companion, eh, Berlin? Really, deceit comes as second nature to you."

Lola choked back her desire to retort that deceit was the norm in Spookland whether one worked for Uncle Sam or his European cousin. They had to keep on the right side of Wosky.

And finally he gave her what she had been hoping for. Information.

39

She wanted to know why had he tried to push her into the background? Berlin said he had thought there was no point complicating matters with long explanations about friendships.

"You thought Wosky would help us more easily if you didn't say much about our relationship. You were wrong. Just as you were with Rainier."

Berlin had been cut to the quick by the Yank spook's tirade. There was a nasty gleam in his eyes. Lola refused to back down.

"You don't succeed by simply skipping over important topics. We made ourselves look ridiculous. We can just be thankful he shared information with two such obvious amateurs."

She was really angry. The lift mirrors reflected her anger a thousand times. Berlin sucked in his cheeks until they reached the ground floor.

"You treat me like an idiot, Joseph."

"What are you talking about?"

"When we were questioning Guillaume Candichard, you knew more than I did. You already knew that Rainier had worked on the Damascus attack and therefore on the Aerolix affair. But you told me nothing. It would have saved me a lot of time and trouble if you'd just laid your cards on the table."

"I've never tried to manipulate you, Lola."

"Bullshit."

"I think you're the sort of person who needs to reach their own conclusions, in their own time. As for me, there was no longer any urgency. Mars is dead, Rainier is out of the picture."

"Where are you going?"

"I need to think. See you back at the hotel."

He slipped quickly out into the street. Taken aback at first, Lola decided to follow him. It was the first time she had seen him like this. Burning up inside. When it came down to it, she had no idea what someone like him was capable of: a man who shot at sideboards, who sent you into a deathtrap in Africa, lied through his teeth, took a plane to Hong Kong on a whim . . . A man who for more than thirteen years had been eaten away by his shame at having abandoned his friend and boss.

Wosky had not minced his words.

"*Were you monitoring communications, Berlin? You're an Arabic speaker, aren't you? You saw the video Bada released just after the bomb attack like all the rest of us, didn't you? And – especially – listened to it, am I right?*"

"*Yes, you're right.*"

"*Those guys were Syrian. Their accent is unmistakable. And their diatribe was word for word what they usually claim. The video was for real. It was one of the Bada group boasting while his buddy filmed him. The Syrian police have both men's confessions. But if you hadn't been content simply to listen and translate, you'd have realised it was all too easy.*"

"Meaning?"

"*Bada were a bunch of amateurs. They were sincere, but jerks. They weren't the kind of pros who could organise a deadly attack like that so swiftly and efficiently, or to claim responsibility even more quickly. In any case, the message was vague. The Great Satan and his allies. So why not blow up the U.S. embassy? It was only a few yards away. It was Rainier's bad luck that you were no longer paid to think, only to listen . . .*"

Was Berlin ploughing along the streets aimlessly, or did he know where he was going? Lola decided it must be the latter as she tailed him, masked by the crowd. He had left Wan Chai Road and turned into Cross Street. Pedestrians and buildings thinned out. Berlin slowed to call someone on his mobile. Lola kept her distance. They soon came to an area filled with luxurious vegetation, a few villas scattered about, then no more dwellings. The road was enveloped in green and grey, and gradually sloped uphill. Lola was dripping with sweat, and felt as if she were breathing damp cotton wool. At least the smell of burnt gas had given way to that of greenery.

She thought over what Wosky had said. In 1998 he was already working for the Associated Press and was a correspondent in Nairobi. His N.S.A. missions meant he had to hold discreet meetings with American officials based in Africa and the Middle East. He happened to be at the Damascus embassy the day the vehicle loaded with explosives had demolished the Madison Hotel. Very shortly after the bombing, Wosky had taken photographs, made notes and questioned witnesses. And all that material was now sleeping soundly in the N.S.A. archives.

The two Bada terrorists had been arrested shortly afterwards. Tried and condemned to death, they had never been executed. Over the years, their statements had varied with each new lawyer they had.

Before Syria descended into chaos, they claimed they had been manipulated, and called for their convictions to be overturned.

Wosky also thought they had been used. Aged little more than twenty when the attack took place, they thought they had been signed up by some leaders of Al-Qaeda. They had been told to buy a second-hand vehicle and collect explosives. In fact, the people giving the orders were not religious extremists. A Syrian army officer was behind the operation. The proof? The explosives used were of military origin. Wosky had discovered a discrepancy between the explosives found during the police raids on the homes of the apprentice terrorists and the bomb in the Toyota.

A third man was martyred at the wheel of the vehicle. The two jailed men swore they had met him only once, when delivering the Toyota. In short, Wosky was convinced that the Islamist angle was a set-up. The three "terrorists" were poor exploited nonentities. Their role was to be the fall guys for the attack.

Berlin came to a halt several times to take calls. He would crouch down against a tree like an old Chinaman, take notes, then straighten up again, rubbing his back, and set off again. An hour and twenty minutes later, he arrived at his destination. An impressive aquarium: Ocean Park.

By now it was after six. The sun had finished melting into the greenery. Lola bought a ticket and ventured into the first room. Ponds with multicoloured fish swimming in them, but no sign of Berlin. She came out into a sepulchrally lit submarine grotto, its roof pierced by large round glass bays. Head tilted back, Berlin was gazing up rapturously at giant stingrays as pale as shrouds. He moved on. She caught up with him sitting completely still on a bench, hypnotised by a swarm of purple jellyfish dancing in eerily blue water. Lola allowed their gentle swaying to calm her pounding heart, and left the aquarium.

She waited for him seated on a low wall. From there she had an excellent view of the entrance to Ocean Park. She thought of Judge Genans poring over his files, surveyed from on high by his Balinese puppets. In fact, it was the judge who was the puppet. Wosky had been very clear on that score.

"Your government has all the information. The N.S.A. was cooperative. Some day one of your ministers will have to decide to declassify the documents. My superiors have no advice or suggestions regarding that . . . I'm telling you this because you took the trouble to come here, but that's all I have to say . . ."

She and Berlin had travelled to Hong Kong for nothing. Lola couldn't see how all the twists and turns of the Aerolix affair could possibly be of any help to Sacha. Their journey into the Chinese mists had been idiotic. Berlin's fantasy that he could sew up his own past with invisible thread.

Jet lag was starting to affect her. She was yawning endlessly. More and more visitors were leaving the aquarium, but not as many as she would have liked. She went back into the entrance hall to read a panel in English. *Late opening on Thursdays.* Just her luck: today was Thursday.

40

Someone knocking on the door. Could it be Jake already?

She recognised the distorted, smiling face in the spyhole. She hesitated, but then opened the door.

"I was led to believe you liked lilies."

"Jake will be here at any minute . . ."

"I've no ulterior motive."

"They're lovely, thank you."

"It's just that I'm not happy at the idea I won't see you again, Ingrid. When is it you're leaving?"

"Very soon."

"Many years ago, Gildas told me the story of the lonely whale. It's a true story. Just think, somewhere out in an ocean there's a whale that's completely alone. None of the other whales ever relate to her. Why? Because the signals she gives aren't on the right frequency. In other words, the rest of the whales don't realise she is one of them."

"They don't identify her as a whale."

"That's right. But you're like Valérie. You're on my wavelength. And you've opened my eyes. I'm leaving Gildas."

"Really?"

"Yesterday I refused to go to a concert with him. In the middle of the afternoon, a concert of contemporary music. Can you imagine?"

"No."

"That was my first step towards freedom."

"Where will you go?"

"Like I told you, back to my mountains. You look tense."

He had brought a crystal vase "snitched from the old man's Ali Baba cave". She went to fill it with water, thinking of the Strike One taped under the bed, but could sense Mondo staring at her. His big, loose-limbed body filled the doorway. She bit her lip, recognised "Tears in Heaven" sung by Eric Clapton. Mondo had plugged his iPod into the hotel stereo system.

He spread his arms wide.

"Will you dance with me? That'll give me something to remember you by."

He embraced her. When she tried to struggle free, he pulled her closer. She felt a stab of pain between her shoulder blades, and then all of a sudden her body split into two. A pair of clones. Ingrid was dancing with Mondo. And Ingrid was watching Ingrid dancing with Mondo.

"Follow me."

"No."

"I've never wanted to hurt you, Ingrid."

41

A faint bell rang. The aquarium was finally closing. Lola straightened up. She had fallen asleep without realising it, leaning back against the wall. For how long? Down below, Hong Kong was a lake of fireflies. To her relief, Berlin was just emerging from Ocean Park, hands in pockets, back slightly bowed. He hailed a yellow taxi. She did the same, and told the driver to follow him. A few minutes later and they were in the centre. The two taxis were bathed in light before slowing in a crowded tunnel.

10.45 p.m. in Kowloon. The crowds had doubled in size, and an army of neon lights was zapping the night sky. Lola was expecting the yellow taxi to pull up outside their hotel, but it continued on along Nathan Road.

They reached the port. Berlin's taxi turned down an avenue lined with hundreds of metal containers, then branched off down a narrower alley. Lola told her driver to stop, paid her fare and continued on foot, ducking behind a shed when she saw the other yellow taxi coming back towards her. The driver was alone inside.

A row of ten-storey warehouses. Vans and a car parked on the tarmac, where puddles of water shone in the moonlight. The characteristic port stench hung in the air: rotting fish, sea salt, boat diesel, and 5 per cent who knows what. The breeze also brought with it a rank aroma of celery and bananas. Berlin was observing the third building along. A few windows were lit. He went inside.

Lola waited, then walked along a poorly lit corridor reeking of the old-fashioned, repulsive smell of mothballs. The goods lift with its black concertina grille could have admitted an elephant. She could see some inscriptions in Chinese on a dull brass plaque. She guessed they were the names of companies. Berlin's footsteps echoed ahead of her. Lola leaned out in time to see him insulting a closed door.

"*WOSKY, OPEN THE GODDAMNED DOOR!*"

The American obeyed. The door closed behind Berlin. On other floors, men were talking in Cantonese. The goods lift shook several times. Together with the creak of its metalwork, more voices, doors being slammed. Then silence.

A small, unmistakable squeaking sound. A rodent – more likely than not a rat. Lola swallowed hard, pressed her ear to the door. Wosky and Berlin were in the midst of an incomprehensible dialogue. She waited patiently for what seemed an eternity, then heard the noise of a vehicle engine. She went over to a skylight and saw a truck pulling up on the quay. A dozen men in shorts, bare-chested and covered in tattoos, unloaded two white sports cars as quickly as they could. They had the dimensions and grace of the stingrays in Ocean Park.

Night, the ideal time for unloading Ferraris. What was it Wosky had said? You grow attached to Hong Kong and its relentless activity. He hadn't specified *legal* activity. Lola went back to her listening post. For someone who had nothing to say, Wosky was curiously talkative. A little while later, Lola spotted a pair of gleaming eyes. A rat wrinkled its pink snout before disappearing into the darkness.

It was her turn to beat on Wosky's door and call out his name. Berlin with his blasé look opened the door.

"I'm fed up of keeping the rats company. One of them was the size of a Bayonne ham."

"Lola, you must be from the Midi to exaggerate like that," said Berlin, with one of his wry smiles.

"My grandmother was from Gardanne in the Bouches-du-Rhône."

Wosky was leaning back against the hull of a fine-looking yacht. The warehouse must have been eighty square metres in size, with no partitions. On one side there was a rolling metal shutter on which somebody had painted a palm tree and a violet sky. The American explained he was building his own boat. His father had been a naval architect and had taught him a thing or two when he was a boy.

"The boat will take as long as it takes."

"A wooden yacht," Lola said appreciatively. "I didn't think they existed anymore."

"You should never give up on your dreams."

"What is this place?"

"The toilets and shower are broken, but at least I have some space."

"Oh, yes?"

"Enough for me to be able to breathe when I've had it up to here with my tiny cupboard in Wan Chai."

"Lola, you must be tired out," said Berlin.

"I couldn't even tell you, my body clock has stopped ticking. What I do know is that I'm hungry."

42 WEDNESDAY, 13 FEBRUARY

"Come on, tell me," she said.

"Let's eat first, shall we?"

A Cantonese supper. On the top floor of the tallest building in Kowloon. They looked out over Victoria Harbour, their feet at the edge of the void. On the menu, a succession of succulent dishes accompanied by a remarkable New Zealand Cloudy Bay. The fog had been polite enough to withdraw to mainland China. The view of the glittering garland of buildings on the island was superb. The lasers were playing kaleidoscopes with the sky and the mountains. Chinese characters blinked on and off against the black silk of the night.

Berlin was in an excellent mood, and swore he had realised she was following him from the moment they left Wan Chai.

"I've never met such a stubborn woman as you."

"I'll take that as a compliment."

"You can. Did you see that cockatoo in a garden on the way to the aquarium? White with a yellow crest?"

"Yes, and the blond eagles high in the grey sky. It seems you like animals: stingrays, jellyfish, winged creatures."

"I find them soothing. I'd like to see a panda while we're here."

"You don't get many of them in aquariums."

"That's true."

"I'm still waiting for the report on your nocturnal adventures with Wosky."

"Yes, yes, I'll come to that. But first, I need to explain . . ."

"I'm listening."

He took her back to 1998. A fateful year. The year that the "World Islamic Front against Jews and Crusaders" was set up.

"Al-Qaeda became more powerful. Networks, finances, military structures, recruits. The Octopus grew to be XXL. And the training camps were in top gear."

The West had underestimated Al-Qaeda's ambition and determination. They thought that they would eventually be held in check with a bit of time and organisation. The United States reckoned they could quickly overcome them.

"Things were exploding all over the place, Lola. In that same year, American compounds in Tanzania and Kenya were attacked. That meant the Damascus bombing, only a few yards from the U.S. embassy, didn't come as much of a surprise. The Madison Hotel? The wrong target. The Bada group? A bunch of overexcited cretins. All this bloody mess didn't really worry many people because the bombs were going off in countries no-one gave a damn about."

"In other words, not on American soil."

"Exactly. So, Wosky can claim he knows everything, but he wasn't aware of what was really going on either. Today, with hindsight, it's easy to say it was an attack on the French state and Aerolix. Back in 1998, Wosky was in post and so could imagine what he liked. I was on the outside, because that's what I'd chosen."

I believe you, Joseph, Lola told herself. *And I know it wasn't easy. Besides, it's not enough just to take a decision; you then have to stick to it.* Berlin had chosen between his friend Yann and his daughter. But according to what he had told her, he remained a keen observer of the terrorist galaxy. He had simply taken a step back. Into the shadows. A violent, painful choice.

"But I have a question, Lola. Now that you know everything about me and the demons I'm dragging around . . ."

"Fire away . . ."

"I'm not sure I really follow why you're putting yourself through all this for Sacha Duguin's sake. I could understand if he was family . . ."

"I don't see what's so complicated. He asked for my help, and I'll do whatever it takes."

"Have you slept with him?"

"Are you joking? I'm old enough to be his mother."

"In my career, I've seen everything, so nothing would surprise me."

"Sacha is a friend. Full stop."

"Alright."

"In fact, I don't see what business it is of yours."

"I like to know what I'm doing, why, and with whom."

His smile was contagious.

"I'm sorry to have to tell you this, but I'm not sure that life always allows us to control everything."

"Your life, perhaps."

He found that funny. And so did Lola.

Later on, the bottle was head down in the ice-bucket and Lola was feeling good.

"Wosky," she murmured.

Berlin finally told her what the American had said in his rat-infested bolt-hole. It was a terrible story, but Lola enjoyed it as much as if it had been one of the *Thousand and One Nights*. Scheherazade had a mangled right ear and the smile of a centuries-old tortoise, but his words were life-giving. Lola wanted to call Ingrid to share what they had found out, but realised all of a sudden that she had forgotten to take a detour to her phone dealership to get roaming coverage. Berlin handed her his phone with a philosophical air. She dialled her American friend's number. A message replied that the line was no longer in use.

"She must have gone back to the States, Lola."

Bravo, the Husky could hold his wine. Lola thought for a moment, and asked the waiter to find the number of Bellagio in Las Vegas for her. She called it, and someone whose politeness was as cold as a seal's flipper announced that Miss Diesel was no longer part of the dance troupe at the famous casino.

"Why is that?"

"Who are you to her?"

"Her mother."

"Ah, in that case: Miss Diesel was dismissed because she did not turn up for work. Despite our frequent calls to her. None of which she bothered to answer. Has she not said anything to you? What is going on? Is there a problem?"

Lola had ended the call. She turned towards the bay outside, but the view had been stripped of its charm. Like a flayed panda.

43 THURSDAY, 14 FEBRUARY

Lola had not slept all night. When they landed, she shook Berlin so that they could get out of the airport as quickly as possible. During the taxi ride she didn't say a word. It was raining on Paris, the sky was a uniform grey. Berlin was listening to the messages on his voicemail. His face looked grim.

"It's Mathilde Candichard," he said.

The former minister's widow had been pushed out of a window at her Paris residence. The door to her apartment had been forced.

They stared at each other, dumbfounded. Lola remembered: Berlin had warned her.

I know what we need to do, but you're not going to like it . . . If he's being watched, his mother's fears could turn out to be justified . . . Don't come complaining to me, Lola . . .

Berlin had seen the drama coming. But not the face of the victim. Mathilde, not Guillaume. Lola felt nauseous. Berlin asked the driver to pull over to the roadside. Lola just had time to open the taxi door before she vomited.

The taxi dropped them outside the Hotel Renaissance.

A clerk opened the room for them. It was empty, but Ingrid and Jake's clothes were hanging in the wardrobe. A huge bouquet of flowers perfumed the atmosphere. Lola found the remains of one lily in the shower cabin. Could it be a message? *Beware of the surface calm, Lola.*

A muffled ringtone. Berlin dived under the bed and fished out a mobile. Ingrid's. Lola took the call, and recognised Franklin's voice.

"About time somebody answered! You were right, you firebrands! Hats off to you!"

"What are you talking about?"

"The D.N.A. results, for goodness' sake. I spend my life doing them."

The pathologist told her that Ingrid had gone to the Forensic Institute the previous Saturday to give him some hair samples. That must have been six days ago, Lola calculated, two days before she and Berlin left for Hong Kong.

"Bingo!" Franklin went on. "It's the same D.N.A. as in Abidjan."

"Whose hair is it?"

"Your little friend didn't tell me. What's the problem?"

Berlin was holding a gun by the barrel. He said he had found it taped under the mattress. Lola recognised it as a Strike One. A powerful Russian weapon.

They were heading towards an unknown destination. Time was elastic. She was afraid, tremendously afraid, and yet another part of her was very calm, and belonged to Mondo. He was talking to her about Valérie, a sweet, gentle champion skater who was always with him – more than ever since he had snorted her ashes. His big sister, buried in the cemetery of the village where they were born.

She thought of Sacha. Imagined his hand on her cheek. His reassuring hand.

After a short eternity, they were travelling through a world of green. The foliage fell back obediently to let them through, and it was Mondo who, by strength of will, managed to achieve this. Ingrid recalled how he had executed perfect curves on the skating rink in front of the Paris city hall. She was sure he had traced ideal lines in the snow when he skied as a young soldier, rifle strapped to his back. She wondered if they would reach their destination soon. But only children asked questions like that. At any rate, she was unable to speak. She just had to listen to him talking about his love for his sister, his nostalgia, the mistakes he had made. Mondo had come to detest his boss, the political storyteller, the old man who didn't want his stories to die with him . . .

"Hello, Timothy? It's me . . ."

"My dear Lola, what a pleasant surprise . . ."

"Enough small talk."

"Is there a problem? Ingrid?"

He sounded in a panic. Hoping he would finally lay his cards on the table, Lola told him what they had discovered at the Hotel Renaissance.

"I was the one who gave Jake the Strike One."

"Why?"

"Ingrid wanted to gather information and have everything sorted out while you were in Hong Kong. She was afraid for you, Lola."

"You should have warned me, Timothy!"

"Ingrid wasn't alone. Jake was there to help her. She must be with him now."

"Tell me about him. He didn't appear in her life by accident."

"Lola . . ."

"I want the truth. Now."

Timothy confessed that he knew Jake through a friend. When Ingrid went back to the States, he thought she needed some support. The people who had wanted to shoot her in Paris had no reason to be put off by the Atlantic Ocean or any other kind of barrier. Who better as backup than a former American footballer who was still all muscle? It hadn't been difficult to convince Jake to meet Ingrid.

"He liked the idea of doing a story about Las Vegas showgirls. Once he was there, it didn't take long for him to fall head over heels for Ingrid. I have to admit that's what I was hoping for. A long-term guardian angel."

Lola demanded he give her Carnegie's mobile number. Timothy told her instantly.

She called him. Jake was on his way back from Haute-Savoie.

"Is Ingrid with you?"

"No. What's going on?"

She was open with him, told him that they couldn't find Ingrid, and that the Strike One had still been in their room.

Jake cursed. Snowdrifts had blocked the line, and so his high-speed train was stuck in the midst of the countryside. The only solution was to return to Paris by taxi.

"What on earth were you doing in Haute-Savoie?"

He told her he had gone there to carry out a lightning investigation on Mondo. The result: he had been an Alpine chasseur before he was thrown out of the army.

"With that pedigree he's bound to be a good shot, Lola."

"Was it Mondo's hair you wanted the D.N.A. test for?"

"Yes, and the results confirmed it."

"Why did you leave Ingrid on her own in Paris?"

"She was supposed to stay in the hotel. And I was meant to be there and back in one day. We absolutely have to find her. I'll be there as quickly as possible."

He ended the call.

Lola threw her phone onto the bed. She felt like howling with rage.

"You can blow a fuse later on," said Berlin. "Now we need to pay Sénéchal a visit."

A narrow track. Parallel to them in the distance, vehicles on a main road. They were crossing a flat, endlessly sad landscape.

Finally, some light-coloured hangars. Mondo stopped the car, helped her out. Although her legs were like jelly, Ingrid felt better. The other Ingrid, the one Mondo had submitted to his will, had almost vanished.

A terrifying noise. In a reflex action, she pressed herself against him. He took her by the shoulders, stroked her hair. Nothing to be frightened of. A military aircraft had streaked through the sky, leaving a powdery trail in its wake. He opened the Volvo's boot. Took out a large package wrapped in brown paper.

"The Rothko. It's not really stealing, Ingrid. The old man owes me this much. All those years shining his shoes and cleaning up his mess. With this, we'll have enough to get by."

Such a red, red Rothko, thought Ingrid.

44

She pushed Sénéchal out of the way and looked round the apartment. No sign of Mondo. The old man swore he had no idea where he had gone.

She pressed her Manurhin to the side of his head.

"Think hard. He's gone off with Ingrid."

"It seemed to me he was rather keen on her."

"Your flunkey is a former soldier. And an addict."

"Yes, Mondo was a big mistake. I took him on as Borel's driver. He was a good driver, but also big enough to defend the president. After that . . ."

"After that?"

"Mondo lent a hand from time to time. With things . . . that were unacknowledgeable. He performed well for many years. But lately he's been harder to control."

"And is Mathilde Candichard one of those unacknowledgeable things, asshole?" snapped Berlin.

"That has nothing to do with me, Joseph. That poor woman had been suicidal ever since the death of her husband. You know that."

"Mathilde's death was your message to her son Guillaume: 'Go to see Judge Genans and you're a dead man.' Was that the idea, you bastard?"

"You must learn to control yourself, Joseph. It's a very useful skill in life."

Lola let Sénéchal go, and watched as he edged against the wall.

"We know about Borel and Aerolix," said Berlin. "Tell us everything you know."

Sénéchal looked incredulous, but finally smiled. Lola restrained herself from smashing the smile with her fist. She could see Mathilde's frail body hitting the pavement. She could see plumes of flame rising from the Madison and scorching the Damascus sky. She told him that an American agent had talked to them, and they had no reason not to believe him. The Bada group wasn't behind the attack. Neither the Syrian authorities nor their French counterparts had been fooled. The Aerolix affair was a set-up. A farce with Gildas Sénéchal's name written all over it.

The old guru gave her an admiring look.

"The public and journalists are like nature, Lola," he said. "They abhor a vacuum. At that moment, Borel was having problems. Unemployment was rising in France, and so too was the price of oil. The trade gap was widening. It's dreadful to admit, but that attack offered us a great opportunity. An outside threat makes people close ranks round their leader."

Lola remembered the video clips she had seen on the internet. Targeted declarations. Borel assuring his audience that he had the security of his beloved fellow countrymen at heart. *Everything will be done to find the perpetrators of this dreadful attack . . .*

"His approval ratings shot up, if I'm not mistaken."

"You're not mistaken, Lola. That's precisely what happened. In the terrorist world, those fellows from the Bada group were small fry who wanted to look big. They claimed responsibility for the bombing to make a name for themselves. That was logical enough."

"But you never contradicted them."

"Yet again, you're spot on, Lola."

"The true story could not be told?"

"As you say."

"But we came to hear it from you, Gildas," said Berlin. "The man who set it up was a Syrian officer, wasn't he? But who was really behind the bombing?"

"President Borel never had any proof."

"But you've got a good idea," Lola said.

"My dear, you're endowing me with a gift for crystal-ball gazing that I don't possess."

"You're lying. The N.S.A. agent assured us that you knew."

"The National Security Agency! My, you have been hard at work."

"Well then?"

"The truth is that it was one of the intermediaries in the sale of the combat helicopters. To Borel, spiking Louis Candichard's finances also meant refusing to pay people like that. So they could no longer hand out kickbacks."

"Are you telling us that an intermediary took revenge on the French state?"

"Yes, that's what I'm saying."

"You must have proof."

"A conversation. Which wasn't recorded. Between that person and me. He gave me to understand that we hadn't played by the rules, which meant we would have to pay a penalty. He also informed me that in the future we would have to behave properly again . . . I told him that the state doesn't negotiate with blackmailers. I really enjoyed that. And anyway, unfortunately by then the Aerolix employees were already dead."

"Olivier de Genans would love to hear what you have to say."

"Justice is a counterbalance to power, but it doesn't always win out. And the concept of the reason of state is still valid."

"It's not always good to tell the truth?"

"That's right. There was no point seeing our Republic weakened because of an attack that had already taken place. On the other hand, the message had got through to the arms dealers. You don't trample on power. It's the same principle as those states that refuse to negotiate with terrorists. You have to be ready to accept some collateral damage . . ."

Lola applauded. Sénéchal fell silent.

"It's such a wonderful story, Mr Spin Doctor, that one could almost believe it. A shame it's not true."

"But I can assure you that . . ."

"You knew."

"I've already told you as much."

"I'm not talking about that. Stop taking me for a fool."

"How could I ever think that, my dear . . ."

"There was an antecedent."

"I beg your pardon?"

"Before the Madison Hotel bombing. In Damascus. The car of an Aerolix representative based in Syria. A device attached to the chassis was deactivated. And there was an anonymous phone call. That story never came out in the press," Lola said.

"Which could definitely be seen as a warning," said Berlin. "If you don't pay our commission, we'll attack French interests. More precisely, we'll attack Aerolix. And this time for real."

This was what Wosky had tried to keep to himself. Thanks to the efforts of the faithful Gabrielle, Berlin had succeeded in finding the N.S.A. agent's refuge. The place where the American was building his boat, his dream. In that favourable atmosphere, Wosky had opened up to them. And how. Borel and Sénéchal were both aware beforehand that the attack would take place. And in Damascus. They did not know exactly where, but did know it would somehow be connected to Aerolix. That was what Wosky had told Rainier. And that was the truth Berlin's boss had to take on board. An unbearable truth for an honest man. A man who had no-one to turn to. *The last time I saw him in Damascus, he was worried sick.*

"Your concept of democracy leaves much to be desired, Sénéchal," Lola said.

"You know as well as I do that democracy is an illusion. What counts is to manage the country as well as possible, in the supreme interest of the nation and our fellow citizens. That takes quite a bit of hard work."

"Of communication?"

"Exactly."

"You really are a bastard, Gildas."

"Joseph, I hadn't foreseen that cutting off Louis Candichard's finances would have such dramatic consequences."

Borel wanted to undermine his political rival, but at the same time to put a stop to those underhand practices. By refusing to pay the intermediaries, he was also refusing to accept the kickbacks. From 1994 to 1998, when the bombing took place, Borel had not flinched. The threats were explicit: the device deactivated, the warning about Aerolix.

"I never thought the intermediary would carry out his threat. It was a scorched earth policy: if he did that, what government would be willing to work with him in the future?"

"Bad luck, Sénéchal, the intermediary wasn't satisfied with threats."

"Alas, no."

"Gratien was the go-between," said Berlin. "He wrote all the details down in his notebooks, minute by minute. All the names: the inter-mediary's, yours and Borel's. Which makes them worth their weight in gold. So I have another important question for you: did Mars get in touch with you?"

Sénéchal admitted he had called him from his African hideout.

"He really piled it on. The victims' families, their right to the truth. I explained that, on the other side of the scales, there was Paul Borel's reputation and the integrity of the Republic. He could not go down in history as the president who had lied to the nation. Paul Borel was a great statesman. To govern can mean being torn in two."

For once, Lola had the impression that Gildas Sénéchal was saying what he really thought. Paul Borel. His masterpiece. An edifice that had to be preserved for future generations, possibly even for eternity. A reputation for which a price had to be paid. In human lives if necessary.

"I call that dirty work," snapped Berlin.

"It's beyond your understanding, Joseph."

"Of course not. Anyway, leaving that aside, was it you who had Mars killed?"

"When Sacha Duguin came to see me, Mondo decided to keep an eye on him. Duguin could not have been more determined. Without him, we would never have found Mars. But Mondo went beyond my orders. I wanted the copy of those notebooks. I never meant for any blood to be spilled."

"Did Mondo get his hands on that copy?"

"Yes, it was on a U.S.B. stick that Mars always carried with him."

"Where is the U.S.B. now?"

"In my safe. At the bank."

"With the originals?" Berlin asked.

"Pardon?"

"Gratien swore the original notebooks were stolen from him while he was in prison. The C.B.N.S. doesn't have them. Nor do the police. I wager it's you who went through Gratien's apartment to find them."

"You can wager all you like, Joseph."

"Did Mondo shoot Lieutenant Ménard?" Lola wanted to know.

"Yes – that was one of his own crazy initiatives. He was spooked when he realised Mathilde Candichard was trying to get in touch with Sacha Duguin. She couldn't accept her husband's death, and was kicking up a fuss. As Mondo put it, he wanted to calm her down. By killing Duguin's young assistant whom she had shared information with, he was giving her to understand that nobody was safe. Above all, her son Guillaume. I have to admit that, thanks to his methods, Mathilde did pull back."

"Why was she such a danger?"

"Mathilde knew how Paul Borel had ruined Louis Candichard's ambitions. While he was still alive, the Candichards said nothing. After his death, Mathilde went through a volatile period. I explained to her that it wasn't in her interest to wash our dirty linen in public, and gave my word that Mars would be brought to justice."

"You're lying," Berlin interrupted him. "Mathilde Candichard was scared stiff."

"Mondo was the one who scared her. Not me."

"Was it Mondo who killed her? On your orders?"

"I have no idea, Joseph. I repeat: Mondo is out of control."

45

The fear was still there, but the world was slowly becoming less ghostly, and Ingrid had regained the ability to speak. Mondo's breath was dancing on the edge of his lips. In the big, freezing hangar, a red-and-white aeroplane. The Rothko was already installed inside it.

"I've known you longer than you realise, Ingrid."

She looked at him enquiringly.

"I kept watch on Duguin. To find Mars. You didn't see me when I broke into your place."

"It was you who stole Sacha's keys?"

"Borrowed. To make a copy. You often went to his apartment, trying to understand why he had abandoned you. You were waiting for him to come back. When Gildas ordered me to kill Ménard and not to leave any witnesses, I found I couldn't do it. You were too beautiful and too much in love for me to hurt you."

"It was you . . . on the quai de Montebello?"

"Yes, it was me."

"So you killed Mars as well."

He admitting having killed Mars on Sénéchal's instructions. Sacha was meant to take the rap. Sénéchal had planned everything. It had to seem as though there was hatred in the murder. A bullet in the head at point-blank range, looking him in the eye, the proof of the rage Sacha felt towards his former boss. And the bullet was meant to lead the police back to the Smith & Wesson. Oh yes, it had been one of the old spin doctor's best wheezes.

"Was the bogus doctor at the Mars family hideout Sénéchal's idea as well?"

"No, that was mine. I sometimes do have them. Hector Gassa played the part. He managed to get into the house and gather information. I was relieved to learn that Karen Mars and her daughter would no longer be there."

"Would you have killed them?"

"No, that was out of the question. But it would have made life difficult for me. I would have had to lure Mars out of his hiding-place."

Why such meticulous planning? Well, Sénéchal couldn't bear it that his childhood friend wanted to teach him a lesson in morality. Mars was hesitating over whether to hand the copy of those notebooks to Judge Genans. He called Sénéchal to talk about it. He wanted to understand, to hear his justifications. Sénéchal was boiling with rage inside. He had succeeded in getting hold of the original of the notebooks before the police searched Gratien's place, and now found he had to start all over again because of a stupid copy. He couldn't bear having to confess his sins to the great god Mars. Not after all those years he was so proud of, when, instead of serving the king, he had been the power-broker in the shadows, the indispensable strategist.

"Besides, the old man always loved big words: the grandeur of the nation; the inalienable image of the Republic. The giant President Borel. Mars didn't swallow all that guff. At least not at first."

"At first?"

"As I see it, Mars simply wanted to shake up his old friend Gildas before granting him absolution. He had used his copy of the notebooks once already, and it had led to a man's death: Candichard had blown his brains out. I don't think Mars had the mentality of a killer. Not like me."

"You have the mind of a killer?"

"I should think so, otherwise Gildas wouldn't have chosen me. 'You have potential, Mondo, we'll do great things together. We'll work in the shadows. You'll see, it's very satisfying. And thanks to us, nobody's honour will be tarnished.' The sun has several shadows: do you follow me?"

"I think so, yes."

"He paid me very well; I had an exciting life. And then one fine day I remembered my mountains, Valérie, my parents. What we had once been, that freedom. It was when I saw you in broad daylight on the quai de Montebello. You were terrified of me. You thought I was your executioner."

"Yes."

"And I told myself that I really wasn't that kind of person. In some way, you are the one who spared me that summer day. Can you understand that?"

"Yes."

46

Mondo's Volvo wasn't in the garage. They searched his room, and Sénéchal confirmed that some of his clothes and personal papers were missing. A valuable painting as well.

"Did he tell you he was leaving?"

"You can see he didn't."

"Where is his bank?"

Sénéchal smiled smugly. Berlin sat at the laptop and began to tap away.

"You've known for a while that he was going to leave, haven't you?"

"Yes. He was detaching himself from me little by little. In fact, his bank manager, who's an intelligent man, warned me about him ten days ago."

"So you know where he is."

"I put a G.P.S. tracking device under his car the day I learned he had emptied his bank account."

Lola glanced at Berlin. They were both thinking the same thing. The device under the Twingo was the little brother of the Volvo one. And the damaged brakes were the surprise package.

"I'll allow you to use it, but on one condition," said Sénéchal.

"Promise me you'll never reveal the true circumstances of the bomb attack. Paul Borel's image has to remain intact. It was my life's work, Madame Jost. I'm sure you understand . . ."

"Promises are a thing of the past," snapped Berlin.

He had found the Volvo. Sénéchal's tracking device showed its location in real time via the internet.

"His car is near the commune of Fleury-sous-Bois, beyond the Montmorency forest. And there's an airfield close by. I guess that's not a coincidence."

"That's where I keep my private plane," Sénéchal admitted.

"Let's go then," Lola said.

Berlin was still searching on the net. The aerodrome was forty-five minutes away on the A5 motorway. A lot less if they ignored the speed limits. He wrote down the telephone number and gave it to Lola.

"Let's take Sénéchal with us and pick up the notebooks at his bank, Lola."

"No, let's find Ingrid first."

"Sénéchal's bank is very close by."

"It's going to be hard to force someone to empty his own safe in the bank, isn't it?"

Lola's remark amused Sénéchal. She could see herself puncturing his smugness with a couple of slaps.

"Yes, but our friend here has done his calculations, isn't that right, Sénéchal? Either we pick up the U.S.B. stick now and everything is still negotiable if we find Ingrid. Especially the possibility of deleting the parts that refer to the Borel era. Or we inform Judge Genans afterwards, and he has the safe opened so that he can take possession of the notebooks. Your choice, Sénéchal."

The guru's complacency had been well and truly shattered.

Lola needed Berlin to face Mondo. She felt the former spook

wouldn't give in. What he had always wanted was to get his hands on the damned notebooks. To complete Yann Rainier's mission. Trying to argue would mean they wasted more time. She agreed.

"Why did you bring me here with you, Mondo?"

"The wish to have a human being to talk to after a lifetime with the old man, I suppose."

Sénéchal had used him. The recent months had been a nightmare. The old man was making a clean sweep. History had to be rewritten, and quickly. To preserve the myth of Borel.

"Were all those deaths really necessary?" asked Ingrid, unable to conceal her anger.

"Candichard's suicide had unsettled Gildas. It meant that President Borel's mistakes might resurface."

"Are you trying to tell me you were *forced* to kill?"

"Gildas had a fit because I decided there was no point sacrificing you, Ingrid. If I had gone on disobeying his orders, he would have found somebody else. Someone who wouldn't have thought twice about despatching you. The old man wanted a massacre. He wanted everything cleaned up. That's why he had Gratien killed in prison. By a fellow inmate. The notebooks existed not only on paper but in the memory of the person who had written them. Gildas had decided to rub out that memory."

"Was it you who found the inmate?"

"No, but I should have. It was my job. But this time Gildas acted on his own. Proof that he was losing confidence in me. He has never done anything without planning it first. If I wanted to survive, I had to anticipate several moves in advance. I think he intended to sacrifice me so that everything could be pinned on me."

Mondo's aim therefore had been to find the notebooks himself so that he could use them as a bargaining chip. And so, without his employer's knowledge, he had concocted his own plan.

"Why are you telling me all this?"

"So that you'll know who I really am."

"What difference does it make to you?"

"None, sweetheart. Let's just say I admire you. I've seldom met anyone as brave. In Abidjan, Hector Gassa was supposed to give you the fright of your life. But it didn't work."

"He did more than scare us to death. Gassa came back for more. The second time he didn't even bother to cover his face. He was ready to shoot me, and an old man who was with me."

"I organised the surveillance operation in Africa. But like I said, Gildas didn't trust me anymore. I think he got in touch with Gassa directly. And asked him to kill you. Gildas' obsession has rotted his brain. The only thing he believes in is keeping Borel's image intact. I think it all began when he lost Geneviève. His wife was a good woman. She kept him in touch with reality. With simple emotions."

Ingrid could do without a killer's subtle psychological analyses. She wasn't a damned priest in a confessional. She was only sorry she couldn't film him on her iPhone: his testimony would have proved Sacha's innocence.

They took Sénéchal's vehicle: a huge Maserati S.U.V. which had a wheelchair and a defibrillator on board. The guru had prepared for anything for his declining years. Including the worst.

"Comfort, luxury and forethought. How like you," said Berlin. "It's almost beautiful."

He whistled admiringly when he saw the vehicle was equipped with a television and a speed limiter directly linked to the steering wheel.

"So you don't have to keep your foot down on the accelerator all the time on long journeys."

Sénéchal's choice of gadgets interest me about as much as the life and times of lampposts, thought Lola. Why on earth had Mondo taken Ingrid with him?

"Was the Saint-Michel business with Ingrid for show?"

"Mondo wanted a third party to confirm his crime, Madame Jost. Ingrid was his witness when he shouted Gratien's name. It was a cry of revenge. Passionate, theatrical, and it worked."

"There's something in your story that doesn't fit," said Berlin. "Mondo can't have killed Ménard in Paris and at the same time tailed Duguin in Africa."

"Mondo had no problem having him followed from Paris to Abidjan via Kinshasa. He travelled to the Côte d'Ivoire once our contact informed us that Duguin had found Mars."

"What's the name of this contact of yours?" asked Lola.

"Hector Gassa. A former member of the previous regime's special forces."

Lola parked the S.U.V. on boulevard Saint-Germain. The bank was a few yards away.

"There's another detail that's troubling me," said Berlin. "If Mondo was only supposed to recover Gratien's notebooks, how do you explain the fact that it was Duguin's weapon that killed Mars?"

"I learned afterwards that Mondo had planned everything. He took Duguin's revolver from his apartment, replacing it with the same model. He took my private plane to Abidjan, and so had no difficulty getting the Smith & Wesson to Africa. On his return to France, he switched back the two firearms. Duguin didn't notice a thing. Mondo had managed to get a copy of his keys: thanks to your American friend, I believe."

Sénéchal and Berlin went into the bank. Lola saw through the car window how they waited, then stepped forward to the cashier. She was chafing at the bit. Ingrid's fate could be decided in a matter of minutes. She imagined her body thrown into bushes near the landing strip. Dark thoughts filled her mind; her back was covered in sweat.

She saw someone from the bank talking to Berlin. Their discussion became heated. Two men burst onto the scene and immobilised him.

She switched on the ignition and drove off. She stabbed at the G.P.S. buttons: "*Good morning and welcome,*" whispered a female voice. Lola swore: she had no idea how to make the contraption work. What had Berlin said? Fleury-sous-Bois was on the far side of Montmorency forest. That was north-west of Paris. She pulled into the taxi lane and accelerated.

"You have to come with me."

"No way."

"If you stay, Gildas will have you killed. The Cessna has fuel for nine hours. That can take us a long way from here. You can come back when things have settled down. After the old man's death."

"Why are you wasting your time arguing, Mondo? Every minute that goes by increases the danger for you. I imagine Sénéchal knows you're here."

"If I take off outside the authorised time slot, I risk either a collision or being spotted. The old man thinks I'm doing the shopping for lunch. I'm sorry, Ingrid, but you're coming with me. And not just out of kindness: I know you'll raise the alarm."

"I'm staying here. If Sénéchal is as crazy as you say he is, he'll go for Lola. Because she is even worse than me. She never lets go."

"Your friends are fortunate that you love them so much."

47

God of Luck, stir yourself and spare me any speed traps. Lola had never driven so fast in her life. She phoned the aerodrome at Fleury-sous-Bois and asked if Gildas Sénéchal's plane was still in the hangar. The person in charge replied that he wasn't in the mood for pranks.

"A young woman is in danger. Go and see for yourself if you don't believe me."

"I have not noticed any unusual activity, and we do not give out information on the telephone."

With that, he had hung up. By now Lola was on the motorway, level with Franconville. She thought about alerting the local police, then thought better of it. Either they would arrive in force and Mondo would have no choice but to take Ingrid hostage, or they would be impressed by the name of Sénéchal and would waste time going through the hierarchy.

Which left Hardy.

He had authority over the people at the aerodrome. And the ability to act swiftly on his own account. *My only chance is to call him.*

The G.I.P. captain answered at the second ring. Lola rapidly explained the situation.

"You're torpedoing my investigation!"

"We'll settle accounts some other time. Please, please call the aerodrome. Taking Ingrid with him will only slow Mondo down. He's behaving irrationally, and I fear the worst."

"It's a bit late for that."

"I'm begging you, Hardy."

"O.K., I'll call the aerodrome and the local police."

"Ask them to tread carefully. Mondo is a former soldier. And a proven killer."

"Stop teaching me how to do my job, will you? And from now on, stay out of this."

Lola had lifted her foot off the accelerator, but now she pressed it to the floor again. If Mondo hadn't taken off already, Hardy would prevent him doing so. For now, that was all that mattered. But there was no question of her sitting around waiting for Ingrid to be gunned down.

48

Still savouring Berlin's look of astonishment, Sénéchal slipped out of the bank and hurried along the boulevard. The police would soon be on the scene, and keep the cretin busy for a while.

Back at his apartment, he stroked the cat, then put him out on the landing. The beautiful animal mewed at him, offended.

"I know it's a treasonable act, Barnabé, but you'll thank me for it one day."

He double-locked the door, slipped on the security chain, went into his study and took the originals of the notebooks from his safe. The U.S.B. stick that Mars kept with him had been burned in the fireplace; Gratien's biological memory had disappeared along with him, so now there were only these twenty or so grey spiral notebooks, their pages full of cramped but very legible handwriting. They looked ordinary enough, but they were worth more than the finest illuminated manuscripts.

Richard Gratien had worked as hard as any Benedictine monk. The notebooks covered a period starting with the first oil shock in the seventies up to the present day. A sustained, unadorned X-ray examination of the conduct of the arms trade during all that time. Dates, places, declarations and asides, the key players and the small fry, the writer's observations about the weather and about certain personalities. It was all described in minute detail, giving the whole an unparalleled potency.

Sénéchal smiled as he thought of all those who dreamt of possessing them. Editors, journalists, prosecutors, top civil servants. As well as the people mentioned therein. The ones who had grown fat at the Republic's expense. It was a shame he couldn't help carry out the huge cull.

The notebooks established no difference between reasons of state and infamy. And unfortunately, their shock waves could spread far into the past. That meant they were a curse that ought not to survive the man who had compiled them.

He had been forced to pay a price in blood to get them. Now they had to be destroyed. For Paul's sake. So that nothing could stain his memory.

He looked at the photograph he kept of the gardens of the presidential palace. It was from when Borel had won his first presidency; the official photograph. Paul had asked for them to be photographed side by side beneath the huge oak tree. As a memento.

His youthful smile. *We made a great team.*

Stuffing the box of sleeping tablets into his pocket, he opened a bottle of Krug and toasted his doctor. Someone who should have told him not to drink, but had instead suggested occasional indulgence, provided the wine was of good quality. He would miss their conversations: he was a refined, cultured man.

He went over to the window. The rain was pixellating the world outside. Paris was as magnificent as a witch who had discovered the secret of eternal youth.

The Apocalypse can be gentle, doc. Who would have thought it? I wouldn't. And yet I was paid to foresee that kind of thing.

He drew a scalding hot bath; chose a Pierre Boulez C.D.

I'm sorry about Mathilde, Paul. Sincerely. You were fond of her, and found her extremely elegant. But the Candichards had to be silenced. It was tough on Mondo, but he took care of it. He knew that if he disobeyed my orders, I'd find someone to get rid of that young American woman he's so keen on.

The telephone rang. An employee at the aerodrome said he was sorry to bother him, but they had received two strange calls, one from a certain Captain Hardy.

"I thought it best to get my instructions from you directly, Monsieur Sénéchal."

A dizzying choice. Mondo's fate hung by a sentence. Mondo, who had served him for so many years. Mondo, who had abandoned him when he realised there was no going back. What did he stand to gain, the traitor? A few extra years of freedom, provided he didn't make any mistakes. He was one of those people who always ended up paying. A genetic mishap. Oh well, one final gift to the flunkey.

"You were right to consult me. Mondo is indeed doing something for me. Let him use the Cessna."

The jerrycan was stored in the dressing room. He sprinkled petrol throughout the apartment, then placed the electronic detonator on top of the pile of Gratien's notebooks and set the timer. He undressed, stretched out in the hot water and took the first pill with a mouthful of champagne.

He saw himself back in the Salle Pleyel. At the concert he and Paul had been to together. Paul thought it was fascinating that Boulez allowed his musicians to decide whether or not to play certain passages, and to change the order of the score.

You always let me play the music in my own way, Paul; you trusted me. And that trust does me honour. I'll see you soon . . .

49

Flat, boring fields, a dingy, narrow strip of sky, three closed hangars. Mondo's metallic grey Volvo parked diagonally. Between the car park and the hangars, the runway.

Lola jumped out of the Maserati and began to cross the tarmac. The rain was icy, but what she really needed was something far worse: a blizzard, a polar storm that would have made taking off impossible.

She had gone about twenty metres when the iron shutter of the middle hangar began slowly to rise. She broke into a run. And the old white-robed creep from her earlier dream appeared to whisper in her ear that she was out of her mind, that she ought to follow Hardy's orders, let the police do their job. She chased the old fool from her thoughts.

She was dealing with a complex killer, a former addict who had stashed away a fortune before his boss could get rid of him. Mondo had nothing to lose. And he had a fixation for Ingrid. The minute he became aware that he was nothing to her, he would finish her off.

Hardy was no use. That damned Cessna could not be allowed to take off.

She heard the throb of its engine. The metal shutter was halfway up: she could see the plane's wheels, the underside of a red-and-white fuselage. Lola tried to speed up. Her body weighed a ton, and her soaked clothes restricted her movements still further.

The shutter was fully open by now. The propellers were whirling round, and she could see Mondo in the cockpit.

And Ingrid. Alive.

Lola was within firing range. She came to a halt, pointed her Manurhin at the cockpit. Mondo accelerated. *I haven't had shooting practice for decades. I might hit the engine and cause an explosion, wound Ingrid.* Lola fired into the air, leapt to her right, twisted her ankle in a rut, fell to the ground. The plane rolled out onto the tarmac where she had just been standing. She stood up, grimacing with pain. A dirty liquid made it hard for her to see: blood.

Mondo began to wheel the Cessna round to the end of the runway. Lola struggled back to the S.U.V. She clambered on board, dropped the key, picked it up again with a trembling hand, managed to switch on the ignition. She drove at right angles across the tarmac. Mondo throttled the plane's engine. Lola headed straight for it. Mondo accelerated. So did she.

She remembered what Berlin had said about the car. That good old Husky! He would surely bring her luck.

The S.U.V. has a speed limiter. It can control the steering wheel.

She pressed the button, opened the door, yelled to give herself courage, and threw herself out. The tarmac swallowed her cry.

Elsewhere.

Somebody had left the tap full of filthy water full on. It was pouring out. Lola refused to drown in it. She swam to the surface.

Right in front of her face was the tarmac's rough surface. Her mouth was kissing a puddle, she was spitting out gravel. Someone was searching her, thrusting a hand inside her coat. She managed to turn over. It was Ingrid. Who had grabbed hold of the Manurhin. And was asking how she felt.

"Don't . . . worry . . . about me."

She saw her American friend's boots racing away from her, heard her shout. She struggled to raise her head. Two dancing figures in the sheeting rain. Ingrid and Mondo. The first pointing her Manurhin at the second, shouting orders at him in English. The S.U.V. had crashed into the Cessna, and their embrace would have produced sparks were it not for the continuing deluge. The rain and Ingrid had taken charge of everything. Mondo was asking her to let him escape. Ingrid refused.

He edged back towards the car park, his Volvo and an illusory freedom. Ingrid called to him to stop. He continued on his way, head hanging low like someone crushed, exhausted, unable to take all this in, beaten. He thrust his hand inside his jacket. The gunshot made the tarmac shake.

Good God, who had fired?

The rain trickled down inside Lola's ear passage until it reached her brain. She twisted on the ground to see what had happened, but the white-robed old creep hove into view. This time he was running away from her, clutching his cardboard suitcase.

A few centuries later, two policemen lifted her onto a stretcher. Either one of them was wearing the same aftershave as Berlin, or Lola's nose had taken on a life of its own. But she was sure she recognised the high, clear voice: Ingrid wanted to know where the nearest hospital was. Lola smiled. Space swayed around her for a long, pleasurable moment to the rhythm of the policemen's steps.

50 FRIDAY, 15 FEBRUARY

Ingrid had spent ages at the G.I.P. headquarters. Now she was smiling as she sat in a ray of sunshine. Lola thought to herself that her American friend seemed to spend all her time visiting her in hospital. That didn't look promising for the future. Would she come to see her when she was in an old people's home? Would they hold impossible conversations with felt-tips on a board?

"He should have followed Sénéchal's instructions and shot me on Saint-Michel."

"And you think that's funny," moaned Jake.

He had braved the icy motorways in taxis only to find that in his absence Ingrid had almost taken off for the Great Nowhere. Lola could understand why he was annoyed. Even more so because the substances she was being injected with through a kind of small plastic abdomen hanging from a metal shrub were putting her in a strange mood. All this for two cracked ribs and a slight concussion. She came close to feeling extra-lucid, or even to be able to see the white-robed old creep standing in the doorway.

"If Mondo was Sénéchal's big mistake, you were Mondo's, weren't you?" she said.

"Yes. He was wrong to think he could outsmart his boss, the great storyteller. Mondo stole my watch, then brought it back when he came to the hotel. Exactly as he did with Sacha's Smith & Wesson. It could only have been Mondo: I always take my watch off when I'm giving a massage."

"Why on earth did it occur to you to massage a guy like that?" Jake complained.

"I had to get his D.N.A. somehow."

"There are other ways."

"Well, at any rate I got confirmation, thanks to Sacha," Ingrid went on, for Lola's benefit.

"You've seen Sacha?"

"Of course not, Jake. They'll free him, but not for now. Hardy allowed me to talk to him on the phone. Thanks to Gildas Sénéchal's powerful contacts, Mondo managed to get to see Sacha in jail. He laid the watch in front of him."

"Why did he do that? I don't follow," Lola said.

"The watch was recognisable. Jake had had our two first names engraved. Mondo told Sacha that if he didn't confess to killing Mars, he would kill me."

"And this time . . . he would go through with it . . ." Lola breathed.

The silence between them lasted several seconds. Lola could read Jake's mind. He had never met Sacha, but loathed him with all his heart.

Someone came into the room, preceded by a big bouquet of roses. It wasn't the white-robed old creep but Berlin the spook, in his severe-looking navy-blue coat. He told them Sénéchal was dead. A death as proud as the man himself. The whole building had almost been reduced to ashes. An elderly couple had been lucky to escape the blaze, which took the firemen hours to bring under control.

"Sénéchal immolated himself. I would never have thought he had the balls. He used something to get the fire going. Probably petrol. Everything went up in flames, including the originals of Gratien's notebooks and the U.S.B. stick."

"I thought they were at his bank," Lola said.

"The safe there only contains cash, and stocks and shares. Sénéchal fooled us. The bank was a diversionary tactic. Paul Borel's honour is safe. And unfortunately that of a good number of crooks as well. Shit."

"Exactly."

Lola thought of Géraldine Jolin, the young woman demanding justice for her father killed in Damascus. *There's a Don Quixote side to him – he never gives up and isn't afraid of anyone . . . .* Would Judge Genans be able to achieve anything without those blasted notebooks? Don Quixote tilting at the windmills of state?

The situation was sad, but not desperate. The important thing was to realise Ingrid still had many more happy years ahead of her. And that no-one else was likely to pursue her on a quay by the Seine or to force her to board a Cessna. But obviously, the skies were full of much bigger planes, and Ingrid was going to catch one of them. Jake and she had decided to fly back to the nest. And the journalist had made her a precious gift. He had successfully negotiated with the owner of the Bellagio dance troupe: an article in the *New Yorker* in exchange for taking Ingrid back.

"When are you leaving?"

"This evening," said Ingrid, smiling at Jake. "We're getting married next month in Las Vegas, and you are cordially invited, Lola."

The American friend and her fiancé left in search of coffee. Berlin put the flowers in a vase and sat in the chair Ingrid had vacated. He leaned over to Lola and took her hand.

"I was really scared for you."

"Me too. I haven't had much training as a stuntwoman."

"Will you go to Las Vegas?"

"Yes."

"Can I come?"

"As you wish."

Mondo had no intention of making things easy for them. For now he was saying nothing. After the thousands of conversations with the old man, it was relaxing. Now that he was dead, Gildas had succeeded in astonishing him. Not only did he have the gift of the gab and a twisted imagination, but he also had the courage of an old tusker. He had chosen the moment and the time. He had designed himself a Technicolor burial. The paintings he loved so much, the pieces of furniture so jealously chosen, his remarkable library, his collection of old, impossibly boring L.P.s. And his souvenirs. The letters and photographs of his life with Geneviève, whom he had loved so dearly.

The years of good, loyal service to Paul Borel. The life of a dedicated servant of the state. All that reduced to ashes. Because that was what the old man had chosen.

Hardy took off his watch and placed it alongside the tape recorder. He switched it on. Ah, the captain wanted to immortalise his own questions. How droll. Perhaps he liked the sound of his own voice?

"Why are you smiling, Mondo? I'd like to share the joke."

What's making me smile, you little turd? Oh, you're not going to find out just yet, because in fact I haven't decided what the end of the story is to be. There are different possibilities. Above all, to try to negotiate. But for now, I'm tired. And I'm thinking of her. She shot at me, but she was kind; she didn't aim at my vital organs or my arteries. I didn't bleed to death and I'm not in a wheelchair. Thank you, sweetheart, for showing mercy.

I'm going to have a limp, of course, but then I already had one. Of course, she won't be there anymore to help me with my sciatica. I'd never really thought about what femmes fatales were until she crossed my path. If I'd been told that a girl in shorts and a fluorescent top running for her life along a quay by the Seine could be one, I'd never have believed it. I always imagined they were much darker, more calculating. Oh yes, Captain Hardy, I never saw them looking like an angel and with a mind to match.

Yes, my problem is a lack of imagination. Yours too by the way, you little cops' cop. If Gildas were still in this world, he would have explained it to you.

51   MONDAY, 25 FEBRUARY

Berlin was snoring lightly, but it wasn't unpleasant. She dressed quickly and went to buy some croissants from the bakery. The sky was pleased with itself: it wasn't yet the heat of Nevada, but it was a definite improvement.

The countdown had reached "Las Vegas minus ten". She would soon have to find an outfit suitable for Ingrid's wedding. The baker's wife was telling her life story to an old neighbour. Lola waited patiently until they had finished.

"Croissants with butter?"

"Why not?"

When she got back to her building, a motorcyclist was on the intercom. She drew back: old fears were slower to melt than snow.

"Lola Jost?"

"Registered letter for you."

The envelope had the logo of the Calypso on it. An invitation from Timothy Harlen. Ingrid's former boss had even handwritten the message. He was inviting Lola and a guest of her choice to come to a special evening celebrating twenty years of his cabaret. She had "absolutely to come and be one of us".

"What's going on?" asked Berlin, pulling on his pyjama top.

"What's going on is that you are my guest of choice."

"That's good to know."

"For a very special evening."

"With you, every evening is special."

"That's enough of your smooth-talking, you old seducer. Come and eat your croissants."

"Not so good for the cholesterol, but who cares?"

"You can say that again."

"Somebody called while you were out."

"Who was it?"

"Ingrid. She called to tell you Mondo had telephoned her."

"Mondo!"

"He knew the name of the casino where she works."

"Good grief! Mobiles grow like mushrooms in jail. What did he want?"

"I don't know. I'm sure Ingrid will tell you in Las Vegas."

"Did she sound worried?"

"No. Over the moon."

52

Lola had decided on a low-necked purple dress she could wear for both the special evening in Paris and the wedding in the States. Seated at the top table with Berlin, she was sipping a piña colada as she listened to Timothy Harlen explaining his plans for the Calypso. He said he had recruited an exceptional artiste, who had been good enough to offer her first show for the cabaret's twentieth birthday.

She saw him arriving through the club's strobe lights. Grey suit, white shirt, no tie, designer stubble. She stood up to embrace him.

"I can never thank you enough, Lola."

"You'll do the same for me one day, Sacha. It took me a while though to realise why you sent me to see Berlin."

"Because he's a man of honour."

"Yes, that's right. A pain in the ass but a man of honour," she said, whispering in his ear.

Sacha nodded, looking amused. She asked him what he was doing in the club.

"I received an invitation."

They turned towards Timothy Harlen. The owner of the Calypso smiled back at them, his look adding a touch of mystery. A drumroll put a stop to any attempt to say more. The master of ceremonies came on stage:

"AND NOW, LADIES AND GENTLEMEN, *MESDAMES ET MESSIEURS*, the one you've been waiting so impatiently for . . . *Strong and sweet, superb and passionate, I give you now, the one and only, the flaming Queen of Pigalle, the tigress of your wet nights, THE UNFORGETTABLE GABRIELLA TIGER!!!*"

More percussion. Strident guitar riffs. Blue-tinged spotlights.

Lola exchanged looks with Sacha.

"Did you know about this?"

"Yes, she warned me. I wouldn't be here otherwise."

"Have you just dropped in, or are you staying?"

"The latter."

"Good choice."

"What's going on?" asked Berlin.

The curtain rose on an operating table. Masked surgeons in green gowns were busy with an invisible patient. Behind them, a giant screen showed a looped film: an Aston Martin going off the road on a bend and crashing into a line of barrels.

The operating table was enveloped in waves of red mist. The patient vanished, the surgeons formed a perfect line. A wind machine ripped off their gowns to reveal six dancers in glittering G-strings and bras, still wearing their surgical masks and with stethoscopes round their necks. They warmed the audience with a suggestive dance, disappeared into the red-tinged mist. They gave way to a male nurse pushing a wheelchair with a dozing accident victim in it.

Splints on her arms, encased in a metal corset, orthopaedic shoes, and head swathed in bandages, the patient was wearing a neck brace with a thick tube sticking out of the trachea. The nurse massaged his patient's temples. As if given an electric shock, the eyes opened wide – their blue only emphasised by the whiteness of the bandages – and the crash victim took a few clumsy steps. The nurse pushed the wheelchair out of the way, tore off one of the splints, revealing the creamy skin of a delicately muscled arm. A very feminine arm.

"*WE'RE ALL CRAZY FOR GABRIELLA!*" yelled a fan in the audience.

"I must say that Tiger has got talent," Berlin said admiringly.

"You're right there," replied Lola.

"Do you know her?"

"A little."

The wounded woman sent the second splint spinning, and began to move her arms in an undulating dance. On his knees, the nurse freed his partner's long legs from their shackles. The patient pirouetted above him, untied the catches on her orthopaedic shoes. Underneath, she was wearing a pair of buskins with dizzyingly high heels.

"I LOVE YOU, TIGER!!!"

The pair danced together briefly, then the nurse unrolled the bandage hiding his partner's features. Gabriella Tiger's radiant face and improbable cascade of red hair brought fresh cries of joy from her fans. Tiger writhed frantically while the male dancer tugged at the fastenings on her corset. One row gave way, releasing breasts tightly wrapped in gauze.

"TIGER! TIGER! TIGER!"

Putting his arms round her neck, the nurse freed her from the rest of the corset. A slender body, with shapely, opal-coloured hips, an iridescent G-string. Tiger turned her back to give a glimpse of a geisha beside a pond where carp were frolicking. She played with the gauze, taking her time to remove it. A brief glimpse of her glistening breasts. In the audience, a collective groan went up, something close to pleading and ecstasy.

"SET US ON FIRE, BURNING TIGER!!"

Tiger turned to face her public, her transfusion-red lips parting in a provocative smile. Her arms were folded across her chest. The nurse's hands quickly replaced them in a voluptuous caress, then drew back. The generous breasts were hidden beneath red sticking-plaster crosses. The whistling from the audience became deafening. The Queen of Pigalle took her time rippling her lithe body at the edge of the stage, just out of reach of a forest of outstretched arms. At last, she plucked off the G-string to disclose a blonde bush of hair in the warm spotlights. Her companion embraced her, and they left the stage together, still facing the audience. The spotlights faded, there was a last, prolonged guitar riff, and the music was drowned out by a deluge of applause.

The pair returned to take a bow. The bare-chested male nurse was in the wheelchair. Gabriella Tiger, simply dressed apart from her extravagant sandals, was pushing him with gleeful energy. A blizzard of white rose petals fell from the roof flies. A few turns round the stage, kisses thrown to the public, and Tiger pushed her companion towards the wings. They disappeared to loud hurrahs and shouts of "Bravo!"

"Ingrid asked me to keep it a surprise, Lola," Timothy confessed. "I hope you won't hold it against me."

"Of course not. Ingrid always does exactly as she pleases. In the end."

"Something tells me we won't be going to Las Vegas," said Berlin.

"No, we'll stay in Paris. Or we can go wherever you like."

"Paris is fine by me. I don't like games of chance anyway."

Sacha had got up and was heading for the dressing rooms. Lola closed her eyes for a second, allowed herself a sigh of relief.

53 TUESDAY, 19 MARCH

Olivier de Genans put down the telephone and signalled to Marie, his clerk. Before leaving the room, she gave him a knowing smile. They had been fighting for months for a moment such as this. It was an extraordinary feeling, the best in his career as an investigating judge. And surely the best in her time as a legal clerk.

He opened a window. No detainee would be so crazy as to throw themselves out from the top floor of the Palais de Justice. Especially not this one, who had taken the first step towards them. The Seine was a long green ribbon, its peace disturbed only by a ray of sunshine. Paris was waking from the torpor of winter.

He thought of Géraldine Jolin. She was strong, courageous; without her persistence Judge Malbourg would no doubt have buried the Aerolix affair once and for all. He would call her immediately after this interview.

Two knocks on the door. Marie came in first. She was trying hard to control her emotion.

"The man who wanted to see you, your honour."

Genans asked the two policemen to remove the handcuffs and to wait outside. They obeyed at once. An old habit: Genans always avoided measures that were too coercive, to make the dialogue with the people he was questioning easier.

He studied the newcomer for a moment. A man in his fifties, solidly built and dressed in black. Close-shaven. He looked like a trained soldier, but his long hands were more like those of an artist. His eyes had absorbed more ugliness than he would have wished.

Genans went to sit behind his desk.

"Take a seat."

The man seemed determined. And almost free. Mentally at least, because he was facing a long prison sentence.

"Name?"

"Mondo."

"First name?"

"Jean."

"Profession?"

"Servant."

Judge Genans raised his head and met the man's intelligent gaze. Mondo was smiling.

Grandpa Koumba had gathered the kids beneath the big tree. The pest who always thought his stories were too short was in the front row. Koumba clapped his hands several times. The children fell quiet.

"In the small country, the people are happy. The last snow has melted, spring has returned to towns and countryside. Queen Rain has departed.

"At last.

"Everything is calm, reassuring. The sun is friendly towards everyone, and it's time to forget the economic crisis for a while.

"But listen carefully. You there, in the front. And you over here. You back there. You all know that a terrible storm can be brewing in the calmest of skies. Yes, of course it can.

"Nobody sees it, and yet here it comes. There'll be no hailstones, no wind, no broken branches. It will be a storm of words. Burning words that can destroy lives, reputations, dreams. Words as dangerous as poison, strong enough to make the powerful people in the little country quake.

"You already know that the old man burned his house down to destroy those dangerous words. He wanted to take them with him when he died. It could all have turned out as his wished, if someone had not chosen otherwise.

"*Remember. That somebody is the old man's servant. He was the one who was supposed to uncover the poisonous words. They were sleeping in some notebooks. Spiral notebooks, like the ones you use at school. The old man had stolen them and hidden them in a deep chest.*

"*But there was a copy of those notebooks. Oh, yes. And that was kept in a tiny plastic box. A box to be fed into a computer.*

"*At first, the servant obeyed his master. He killed the big White Man on the house's cement terrace and stole that tiny box from him. When he returned to the small country, the servant gave it to his old master. But then the servant thought about all this. He said to himself that his master had spent his whole life telling stories. Perhaps it was time not to trust him so much.*

"*The servant was very crafty. He made a copy of the copy. A long while before the fire.*

"*Now it is sleeping in a locker. The locker you can rent in the big station in the small country. It opens with a code. And the servant knows the code by heart.*

"*Which is just as well, because the servant has been arrested by the police.*

"*He has a lot to feel remorse for. By obeying the old man, he has killed, he has stolen. He is already old himself, and knows that his life will end in the sad prison they have thrown him in. So he has thought and thought, and come to a decision. He wants to do something big, something noble. Why? To impress a beautiful woman he loves. So he has decided to give his copy of the notebooks to an important and honest man.*

"*To a young judge.*

"*It will take the judge time, but in the end he will warn the inhabitants of the small country. Then the clouds will crack open like eggs, and the truth will fall from the sky. It will make a terrible omelette that will be hard to digest. But a lot of people will be hungry for it, especially those who write in newspapers.*

"*And the White Man will not have died in vain in this beautiful Africa of ours. Listen, listen carefully. Queen Rain will no longer be the only one to remember his name.*"

THE END

DOMINIQUE SYLVAIN worked as a journalist in Paris before relocating to Asia, where she lived for spells in Japan and Singapore. She is the author of a distinguished body of crime fiction. She lives again in Paris, where she writes full-time.

NICK CAISTOR has translated more than forty books from Spanish, Portuguese and French, including novels by Paulo Coelho and Eduardo Mendoza. He has thrice been awarded the Premio Valle-Inclán for translation from the Spanish.